Hallmark
PUBLISHING

ONCE UPON A Royal SUMMER

A theme-park princess. A real-life prince

TERI WILSON

For everyone who grew up with princess dreams,
this one's for you. xo

CHAPTER ONE

Not the Kate Middleton Kind

"I DIDN'T REALIZE I'D BE DINING with royalty this evening." Mark Cooper, Lacey Pope's unofficial fiancé, sighed at her when she sat down at the restaurant table.

Uh-oh. She'd done it again.

"I forgot to take off my tiara, didn't I?" she asked, reaching up to check for the massive rhinestone adornment she pinned to her head with no less than thirty-five bobby pins every morning for her day job.

Yep, definitely still there.

"Indeed, you did." Mark nodded and reached for his martini.

Welp, this was awkward. They weren't exactly seated in the sort of establishment where oversized, gaudy tiaras were commonplace. Mark was dressed in one of the crisp, tailored business suits he wore to work every day at his family's investment banking firm. His tie was the same shade of green as his eyes. As usual, his hair was trimmed

1

short with a neat part on the side. Mark always looked like he'd walked off the pages of a Brooks Brothers catalogue. At times, Lacey felt a bit too sparkly and colorful by comparison. Times like now, for instance. This place was fancy. Lacey hadn't even had to put her own napkin in her lap. The maître d' had done it for her, just after she'd dashed to the table to meet Mark, five minutes late for their reservation.

It would've been nice if the maître d' had given her a little heads up about the crown on her head, instead. Lacey could've handled the napkin on her own.

Why, oh why, had she worn her favorite step-in, wraparound polka dot Kate Spade jumpsuit to dinner instead of a dress? One of her cute fit-and-flares never would've made it over her head without snagging on the crown and giving her a clue. Lesson learned.

"Sorry." She pulled a face. "I'll just run to the ladies' room real quick and—"

"Look! It's a princess!"

A little boy and girl, both around six or seven, slowed to a stop beside Lacey's chair.

Yes, technically, Lacey was a princess—only, not the Kate Middleton kind. More like the coach-turns-into-a-pumpkin-after-midnight type who earned a modest hourly wage.

"Here we go," Mark muttered and took another generous gulp of his martini.

"Are you a real princess?" the girl asked, wide-eyed.

The boy glanced around Lacey's periphery. "Do you have a lightsaber?"

"Sort of," Lacey said to the girl, then switched her attention to the boy. "And no." Alas, Lacey didn't have a lightsaber tucked into her handbag, because she wasn't the sci-fi sort of princess, either.

Lacey—known as Princess Sweet Pea at the Once Upon A Time amusement park in Ft. Lauderdale, Florida—was theme park royalty. The very best sort of royalty, as far as

Lacey was concerned.

"Brittany. Benjamin." A flustered woman in a pretty red sheath dress took hold of their two small hands. "Our table is ready. Let's not bother this nice couple." The mom offered Mark a polite smile and glanced at Lacey's ginormous crown with an equal mixture of curiosity and confusion. "So sorry to have bothered you, Your...um...Highness."

Mark snorted.

"Oh, it's no bother. Really." Lacey winked at the children.

Brittany's eyes danced, and little Benjamin's face turned as red as Riding Hood's cape. Lacey smiled as the children moved on toward their table, sneaking Lacey bashful waves behind their mother's back.

Lacey grinned at Mark. "Aren't they cute?"

"Precious," he said, gaze fixed on the menu in front of him.

Contrary to popular belief, being a theme park princess wasn't the easiest gig in the world, and definitely not a fairy tale. For starters, rocking elbow-length white gloves and a ballgown embellished with not one, not three, but *six* billowing layers of tulle could get a tad warm in the stifling Florida heat and humidity. Not quite as stifling as being trapped inside a furry bear costume—as Lacey knew all too well from her stint as Baby Bear from Goldilocks and the Three Bears, her warm-up gig for the coveted role of princess—but still. Glass slippers weren't all that comfortable, either, particularly when the aforementioned ballgown made it impossible to sit down for eight-plus hours a day.

And the glittering tiara responsible for the grimace on Mark's face? It was way heavier than it looked, which Lacey supposed made it all the more baffling to her unofficial fiancé why she sometimes forgot to take it off.

It was simple, really. Lacey always seemed be dashing out of the park thirty or forty-five minutes after her shift was supposed to have ended. She didn't mean for it to happen, but she couldn't seem to tear herself away when there was a line of boys and girls waiting to see her. Lacey always wound up staying until she'd greeted every single one of them.

"We had kids from the Make-A-Wish Foundation out at the park this afternoon," Lacey said.

"That's nice." Mark glanced up from his menu. "I ordered you a glass of champagne. Try it. It's from that region in France where we discussed going for our honeymoon." He flashed her a wink.

Lacey's face went warm as she reached for her champagne flute. It seemed weird talking about a honeymoon when they weren't technically engaged yet. Mark wanted to talk to his parents before he officially popped the question, though. He insisted it was just a formality, but every time they discussed it, Lacey felt a little sick to her stomach.

Mark's parents were lovely people. It wasn't that Lacey didn't like them. She did, and as far as she could tell, they were fond of her too. But the waterfront mansion where Mark had grown up in Ft. Lauderdale's exclusive Las Olas Isles, complete with a yacht docked at the shore, was a world away from the modest Dallas suburb where Lacey grew up. Sunday dinners with Mr. and Mrs. Cooper sometimes seemed almost as fancy as the tea parties Lacey attended every afternoon in the Ever After Castle as Princess Sweet Pea.

"I think I'll have the *coq au vin*." Mark closed his menu. "You?"

Lacey had heard of *coq au vin*, but still wasn't altogether sure what it was. "The chicken sounds good." She took a sip of her champagne and caught herself holding her wrists upturned with her fingertips posed just so—"Cinderella hands," as the theme park princess handbook called them. Sometimes it was hard to turn off the royal thing. She shoved her hands in her lap.

"I had lunch with my mother today," Mark said, leaning forward and smiling at her in a way that told her this dinner might be more than just an ordinary date night.

Lacey's heart thumped hard in her chest. "Oh, really?"

"And she assured me she and Dad would be thrilled if I were to pop the question." He arched an eyebrow. "We might have even set an appointment at the bank to get Grandmother's ring out of the safety deposit box."

Okay, so no engagement *tonight*, but it was definitely on the horizon.

Lacey could hardly believe it. She'd just always sort of imagined that if she ever *did* get married, it would feel a bit more romantic. This was beginning to seem more like a business arrangement than an engagement.

Get over yourself. You love Mark, and he loves you. Fairy tales and castles aren't real, remember?

Maybe she was letting the tiara go to her head.

"Isn't that wonderful, babe?" Mark searched her face.

Lacey forced her lips into a proper smile. "So wonderful."

He signaled for the waiter to bring him another martini. "There are still a few details to work out, obviously."

"Obviously," she echoed. But wait, what was he talking about? Surely they weren't going to start planning the wedding before they were actually engaged.

"Mother asked if you'd given any more thought to what you might want to do once this"—he shot a loaded look at the crown on her head—"princess thing is over. I assured her you have big plans."

"I do?" Lacey's gaze flitted over Mark's shoulder. The two sweet children who'd stopped to talk to her earlier were still watching her, eyes dancing, from across the crowded restaurant.

"Come on, babe. Being Princess Sweetheart isn't exactly a long-term plan. You said so yourself."

"Princess Sweet Pea," Lacey corrected. Honestly, had he

ever cracked open the leather-bound copy of *Classic Fairy Tales* she'd given him for Christmas last year, after he'd insisted he wanted to turn his home office into a library?

"Princess Sweet Pea. Of course." Mark's second cocktail arrived, and he eyed it like Goldilocks eyeing a bowl full of porridge. "The point is you're almost twenty-seven years old. Eventually, and probably in the not-so-distant future, you're going to age out of the princess gig. What are you going to do then? We talked about this, remember?"

They had indeed talked about it. Several times, actually. Lacey knew she was going to have to move on from her job at the theme park, sooner rather than later. She just couldn't figure out what she wanted to do next. Playing the part of Princess Sweet Pea meant the world to her. Giving it up was proving to be more difficult than she'd thought it would.

"I suppose I could transition into wicked stepmother territory." Lacey laughed.

Mark, pointedly, did not. Which was fine, because she wasn't entirely joking. The wicked stepmother role seemed like a total hoot. They were hugely popular with guests at Once Upon A Time.

"Anyway." A muscle in Mark's jaw ticked. "I told Mother you'd mentioned getting your teaching certificate. Or that you might want to work at a nonprofit or something. I know what a heart you have for kids. It's one of the things I love most about you."

He smiled, and Lacey felt a tiny bit better. She knew she was probably being overly sensitive about the job thing. But once upon a time, she'd been a lonely child in a hospital waiting room, and the theme park princesses who came to visit patients and their family members in the oncology ward had gotten her through the worst part of her childhood... the worst part of her *life*, really.

This was her dream job. It always had been. She'd never

wanted to be anything else.

"Mother said she could help get you on the board of one of those charities you love so much. The children's hospital, perhaps?"

Lacey brightened for a moment. Working with kids at the children's hospital was indeed right up her alley.

But board members weren't typically that hands-on with patients and families, were they? She'd want to spend her time in the actual hospital, not in a conference room or office.

"That's a really generous offer." Lacey reached for her champagne flute and then stopped herself. She wasn't feeling particularly bubbly and sparkly at the moment. If he'd expected her to give up anything but her job, she might've considered it. Not this, though...*anything* but this. "But you know how much I love what I do, Mark. I'm not quite ready."

"Lacey, sweetheart." Mark reached for her hand and took it in his. "You can't keep playing dress-up forever."

A painful lump formed in Lacey's throat.

Had she just heard him correctly?

Surely not. If anyone knew why Lacey's job meant so much to her, it was Mark. They'd been dating for almost three months before she'd told him about losing her mom when she was seven years old. She'd opened up to him about it in a way she rarely had before—or since.

"Mark, you know being a theme park princess is more than playing dress-up. *So much* more. I've wanted to do this my entire life."

"I know, sweetheart," he said. Lacey *really* wished he'd stop calling her that. "But you've done it. It's been, what—five years? Isn't it time to start thinking about a proper career? Your schedule is grueling. I barely see you. If we're going to build a life together, shouldn't we see each other more than only on the one or two nights a week you don't have to close down the theme park?"

He had a point. They didn't spend as much time together as either of them wanted to, but Lacey thought being married would solve that problem. She and Mark would be together all the time, morning, noon, and night. Well, except when they were at work. And their schedules didn't exactly overlap much. They'd both been working extra hours the past few months.

Again, Lacey knew this discussion had been coming. She was in full agreement with everything he was saying. She'd thought she was, anyway. Now that the conversation was actually taking place and giving her notice seemed imminent, Lacey wasn't so sure.

She took a deep breath. *One more month. Just give me one more month, and then I'll quit and go back to school to get my teaching certificate.* Why did everything have to happen right this second? "I know the hours aren't the greatest…"

Mark arched an eyebrow. "And by the time you leave work, you're covered in glitter."

"You say *glitter* like it's a bad thing," Lacey said, mustering up a smile. What kind of person didn't like a little sparkle?

The kind you're going to marry, apparently.

And suddenly, Lacey knew she couldn't marry Mark. Not now, and not however many days, months, or years into the future it might be when she couldn't do her dream job anymore.

Clearly, she'd missed some major red flags. Mark had always seemed so sweet and attentive, even though he'd never used any of the free passes she'd given him to Once Upon A Time. Lacey liked how close to his family he seemed. She'd met so many men her age who didn't spend much time at all with their parents.

She'd obviously misread the comments he'd made in the past about her career choice as interest—maybe even pride in how much she loved what she did—when really, they'd meant something else entirely.

Lacey swallowed around the lump in her throat and slid her hand away from his and back to her lap.

They were about to break up, weren't they?

She blinked hard, waiting for the tears to come. The anticipation of the impending heartbreak was excruciating.

But then the strangest thing happened: nothing at all. No wracking sobs, no sniffles, not even a single tear slipping poignantly down her cheek. She simply felt...numb. Which seemed like an even bigger problem than her lackluster career choice.

"Mark, I don't think this is going to work," she said quietly.

Did she actually *love* him?

If there was even a glimmer of doubt in her mind about that, she couldn't go through with an engagement. Doing so wouldn't be fair to either one of them.

Mark shrugged one shoulder. "If you don't want to sit on a board, you don't have to. I'm sure we can come up with something else more suitable."

"Suitable?" What was happening? How had this dinner gone so spectacularly off the rails? "When you put it like that, it makes me wonder if you think there's something wrong with my job. Or worse, with *me*."

Why did there have to be a time limit for her to figure out her future?

Mark sighed. "Lacey, would I want to marry you if I thought there was something wrong with you?"

"I don't know. You tell me. You just said I wasn't suitable. That sounds an awfully lot like you think I'm not good enough to be your wife."

"Lacey..."

"You know what? It doesn't matter. When I said I didn't think this was going to work out, I didn't mean the board job. I meant *us*." She felt her chin start to quiver.

Don't cry. Do not.

Whether she truly loved him or not, breaking up was devastating, and Lacey was now one hundred percent sure that's what was happening.

Mark grew very still. "You can't be serious."

"I am. I'm sorry, Mark." Lacey nudged her chair back, and the maître d' raced over to snatch her napkin out of her lap and help her to her feet. Super. Just what she needed—a witness to this painful moment.

She stood awkwardly at the table, waiting for Mark to acknowledge they were officially over. Lacey's gaze snagged on her reflection in the window beside them. The huge crown on her head glittered like mad beneath the restaurant's elegant mood lighting.

"We could've been good together." He reached for his drink with exaggerated calm, as if she'd just told him she wanted to switch cell phone carriers instead of end their relationship. How on earth had it taken her nearly a year to realize how little they had in common? "Call me after you've given this more thought, sweetheart. We can still make this work. No one's going to come charging in on a white horse to sweep you off your feet. That crown on your head isn't real." He narrowed his gaze at her tiara. "And neither is Prince Charming."

Crown Prince Henry Frederick Augustus Ranier Chevalier stood at the window overlooking the horse stables in the royal palace of Bella-Moritz and peeled back the heavy brocade drapes as subtly as he could manage. He might be next in line to the throne of the most glamorous principality on the French Riviera, but Prince Henry wasn't above skulking around and spying on his six-year-old daughter. And really, what choice did he have?

If he strode outside and joined Rose for her riding lesson, the chances of his precocious little girl actually getting into the saddle would drop to zero percent. Henry was a softie, and his daughter knew it. The riding instructor, not so much, but even in Henry's absence, it was still a fifty-fifty proposition. At best.

Like most royal children, Rose had grown up around horses. She'd started taking riding lessons at the tender age of five, and she'd approached the task in the same way she approached everything else in her life: with fearless determination. But just months into her lessons, the pony she'd been riding had gotten spooked by a rabbit darting into the paddock. He'd reared back, and Rose had tumbled to the ground, breaking her arm. It had healed long ago, but her spirit remained broken.

Rose's fear of horses wouldn't have been much of an issue if she'd been just a regular little girl. But as Henry's mother, Queen Elloise, never failed to remind him, Rose wasn't just a regular little girl. She was a princess—and more importantly, a queen in the making. Queens didn't give up when things got tough. They persevered. They led by example. They got back onto the horse.

Henry was a future monarch as well, obviously, so getting an almost seven-year-old child onto a pony really shouldn't have been so difficult for him, seeing as he was expected to run the country someday. But alas, the greater population of Bella-Moritz proved less formidable, on occasion, as compared to one pint-sized princess.

"You realize the Royal Flower Festival is just two weeks away, don't you?" The clipped voice of Queen Elloise behind him nearly made Henry jump out of his royal skin.

He pinched the bridge of his nose and slowly turned around. The palace contained five hundred twenty-five rooms, and somehow, his mother always knew where to find him. "Yes, Mother, I'm aware."

The queen was dressed in one of her monotone cashmere wool pantsuits with a matching silk blouse. Winter white—which, on an ordinary person, would be the most impractical color choice imaginable. Not so for Henry's mother, who'd been the antithesis of ordinary for as long as he could remember. "Caitriona turns seven years old next week," the queen said, tucking a short, loose curl of her shoulder-length chestnut waves behind one ear and using Rose's full, more formal name. "She's expected to ride in the royal procession, just as every heir to the throne has done for the past fifty years. It's her *royal debut*. All members of this family have ridden in the parade starting at seven years of age. No more watching the festivities from the palace balcony. She's to be a part of things this year. It's tradition."

Henry refrained from reminding his mother he was well acquainted with Bella-Moritz's many traditions and he himself had been riding in the Flower Festival's royal procession for the past twenty-eight years. Doing so wouldn't help matters. "She just needs more time," he said quietly, keeping his gaze trained on his daughter.

Rose wore a black riding helmet and stark-white breeches, the traditional dressage uniform dating as far back as the Chevaliers themselves. She looked like a mini-Olympian as she stood beside her pony on the emerald-green grass of the riding arena—albeit an Olympian who had no intention of actually climbing into the saddle.

The sun shone brightly. Bella-Moritz was famous for its beautiful summer season. Everything seemed more lovely this time of year, from the clear, turquoise-blue sky to the shimmering Mediterranean Sea. June in Henry's kingdom always reminded him of fields of blooming hyacinth, sun-drenched lemons, and perfumed gardenia bushes with glossy dark leaves and the intoxicating fragrance of their blossoms, soft and white like Chantilly cream.

Down on the riding paddock, Rose inched closer to her horse—a pale gray Welsh pony she'd named Daisy. The pony, which had been trained at Buckingham Palace's Royal Mews in London, England, had been a gift from the Duke and Duchess of Cambridge during their most recent royal tour of the region. Rose had been thrilled until she'd learned her grandmother expected her to actually *ride* the pony.

Now, six months later, Rose slipped Daisy a sugar cube while her riding instructor's back was turned. His daughter was perfectly fine, so long as she wasn't sitting astride the animal. The more they pushed, the more terrified Rose seemed to get.

Henry wondered if Will and Kate had this same problem with Princess Charlotte. Somehow he doubted it.

The queen sighed. "Time is the one thing you don't have, I'm afraid."

Right. Two weeks wasn't long. In fact, it seemed almost infinitesimal, which made what Henry was about to say all the more problematic.

He squared his shoulders and met his mother's gaze. "I'm taking Rose on a brief trip for her birthday. I think a break from all the pressure will do her some good."

"A trip? *Now?* Are you mad?"

No, he was a father. Not just a prince, but a dad—Rose's only surviving parent. "It's her birthday," he pointed out. Again.

"I realize that. And if a celebration is what you want, that can easily be arranged." The queen gestured to the opulent surroundings, as if Henry had forgotten that just outside the door, a fleet of footmen and palace staff were waiting to cater to his every whim.

"She doesn't need a royal banquet," Henry said, a bite creeping into his tone. "She needs a chance to be a child for a few days."

His mother arched a brow at his insolence. She might be family, but she was still the queen, after all. "You indulge her too much. You always have."

"Not always." Henry shook his head.

Just the past four years.

Four years of going through the motions, as if losing his wife hadn't changed everything. Four years of preparing for his future role as king, while his young daughter grieved. Four years of unrelenting quiet in the castle.

How long had it been since Henry had heard his little girl laugh—*really* laugh? He couldn't quite remember, and that realization saddened him most of all.

Queen Elloise rested a gentle hand on his forearm. "I know you only want what's best for Rose, but it's been a long time since she lost her mother. You're not doing her any favors by letting her fear get the better of her. Your young princess is stronger than you think she is, and it's time for her to represent the Crown." She pursed her lips. "Maybe if she were educated here at the palace instead of attending public school, she'd have a better appreciation of what's expected of her."

The school thing again. Sometimes it felt like Henry and his mother kept having the same conversations, repeatedly. "The children Rose goes to school with will one day be her subjects. I can't think of a better way to prepare her for her future than befriending them and learning with them, side by side."

"She needs to learn what it means to be a proper member of this family," the queen countered. "She needs to stand up and act like royalty."

"She's *seven.*" No, technically, she was still a six-year-old. Anger seared through Henry. This was precisely the sort of pressure Rose didn't need.

His daughter needed a break. He needed one, too. If they

could just get away for a bit, Henry knew he could figure out a solution to the pony problem.

"We're going." He strode away from the window, toward the door, anxious to get down to the stables and give Rose the happy news. "It's already been arranged."

The queen's mouth dropped open, which in itself was a sort of breakthrough. After decades on the throne, it was nearly impossible to surprise Henry's mother.

"This is non-negotiable. We'll be back in time for the Flower Festival, and I promise Rose will ride her pony in the royal procession. You have my word." Henry lingered in the doorway. Somewhere in the back of his head, warning bells went off. *Don't make promises you can't keep.* "But first I'm taking her to America for her seventh birthday."

"America?" The queen let out a disbelieving laugh. "What could you possibly find in America that you can't find here?"

A year ago...a month ago...heck, even a week ago, Henry might've had the same reaction. But three days earlier, he'd found Rose propped up in bed, watching a movie on her iPad when he'd gone to her room to kiss her goodnight. The film had been set at a theme park, complete with spinning teacups instead of high tea at the palace, sausage-on-a-stick instead of fancy royal dinners, and Rose had been transfixed. She'd been as awestruck by the imitation, garish, fairy-tale world as tourists to Bella-Moritz were by the sight of the very real castle in which she lived. Something had stirred inside Henry then—something he hadn't felt for quite a long time.

Hope.

Henry's heart swooped as if it were on a rollercoaster ride and he felt himself smile. What could America give his little girl that she couldn't find behind the palace walls? The answer was simple.

"Childhood."

CHAPTER TWO

Grumpy Baseball Cap

"**S**o that's it? You *broke* up with him?" Lacey's best friend, Ava Rivera, met her gaze in the mirror that hung in the dressing room at Ever After Castle on Saturday morning. "For good?"

"For good." Lacey nodded and paused to dust her eyelids with another layer of the fine silver glitter that Mark apparently loathed so much.

Now that the initial shock of their breakup had worn off, Lacey felt like she was experiencing every emotion at once—sadness, heartbreak, humiliation...and anger. Oh yes, she was definitely feeling angry, as evidenced by the furious cloud of glitter she stirred up with her slender makeup brush.

Face characters at Once Upon A Time—meaning those who didn't wear a big fur head, like the Big Bad Wolf—were responsible for doing their own hair and makeup. It could be a lengthy process. Lacey's work schedule allotted one hour to get dressed and ready before she made her first appearance for the day as Princess Sweet Pea, and she typically used up every minute.

The castle's dressing room area had a long wall with lighted vanity mirrors stretching from one end to the other. Cast members sat on tall stools, perfecting their fairy-tale makeup and teasing their hair into elaborate princess updos. A row of changing rooms separated by curtains decorated with the Ever After logo—an open storybook with a swirl of fairy dust—stood at the opposite end of the dressing area. In between, costumes hung in neat rows on long silver rolling racks. An ever-present cloud of hairspray hung in the air.

"I still can't believe it." Ava shook her head and went over her lips with velvety crimson lipstick.

Lacey and Ava had already had an abbreviated version of this conversation the night before, when Lacey had shown up at the apartment they shared with tears streaming down her face, a doggie bag full of uneaten fancy chicken in her hand and the tiara Mark had found so offensive still pinned to her head. Lacey had been too mortified to elaborate on the reason for the breakup, so she and Ava had shared the contents of the doggie bag, along with a bottle of rosé, and watched reruns of *Friends* until Lacey had fallen into bed, puffy-eyed and more than a little bit heartbroken.

"I had to do it. He kept asking me about the job thing. I was starting to feel pressured. I just don't want to quit until I know for certain what I want to do next. Even if I decide to get my teaching certificate, the next semester doesn't start until fall." Lacey sighed.

She wasn't sure what was stopping her from going ahead and enrolling in the college classes she'd need to get certified. All she knew was the more Mark had wanted to talk about it, the more confused she'd become.

"When he said something about getting a more proper career, I sort of lost it." Lacey jammed another bobby pin into her blond hair. "Whatever *proper* means."

One of the Three Little Pigs walked behind them, all suited up and ready for work. Lacey glanced at its curly pink tail, then met Ava's amused gaze in the mirror.

She laughed. "Well, maybe I know what proper means, but I disagree vehemently with his assessment of my current job choice."

"I get it. Some of us are just biding our time until we catch a real acting break." Ava pulled her red hood in place and tied it with a red satin bow. "But being Princess Sweet Pea is different for you. I put on this costume and play the part of Red Riding Hood every day, but sometimes I think you truly *are* a fairy-tale princess."

"Don't be silly. I'm quite aware of the fact that I'm not actually royal." How could she not be, after the disastrous dinner the night before?

Nor did she want to be. Besides, Lacey wasn't delusional. She knew none of this was real. But once upon a time, she'd been one of the little girls completely enchanted by the sight of a theme park princess. And that encounter had been one of the most comforting, magical moments of Lacey's life. It'd been what she'd needed most, and what could be more real than that?

All Lacey wanted was to give more people—children, especially—those much-needed moments. It didn't seem fair that she should rush to give that up before she married the love her life.

"He just wasn't the one," she said. "I thought he was, but he wasn't." Disappointment and regret tied themselves up in knots in the pit of her stomach. She stood and smoothed down the front of her blush-colored ball gown—inasmuch as it was possible to smooth down an explosion of tulle.

Her eyes ached. Her entire face hurt from crying, and beneath her theme park princess makeup, her face was a blotchy mess. For once, she might've preferred her former role of Baby Bear, so she could hide beneath a big plush head again.

She really should've seen last night coming. It had been a while since she'd felt as connected to Mark as she had in the beginning. They used to have such a good time together. They'd take walks on the beach or go to their favorite movie theatre in Coconut Creek, where all the seats were deep, plush couches and the popcorn was topped with real melted butter. A few times, they'd even gone up to Boca Raton for tea and a walk through the Japanese Gardens.

It had been months since they'd done anything special like that, though. Right after Christmas, Mark had gotten a promotion at work. He didn't have much time for weekend trips or movie nights anymore. When he wasn't busy working, it always seemed like Lacey was pulling an extra shift at Once Upon A Time. She'd been so ready to chalk up the disconnect to their crazy schedules, but if either of them had truly missed spending time together, wouldn't they both have been willing to make a bigger effort?

Why should she quit her job before she was ready, or before the fall semester even began, if Mark hadn't considered making adjustments to his schedule as well?

Deep down, Lacey had a feeling she knew exactly why. Mark loved his job as much as she loved hers. She'd just never realized they hadn't loved each other quite as much.

"Don't worry," Ava said. "You'll find someone else."

Lacey shook her head. "No, thank you. I'm taking a break from dating. A *long* break. Princess Sweet Pea has far more important things to think about."

Never mind the part of "The Princess and the Pea" about marrying the prince. Hashtag #details. If Lacey had been this wrong about love, she clearly wasn't ready to jump into another relationship.

Ava gave the red bow of her hood a final adjustment. "Like what, exactly?"

Lacey glanced at the clock above the dressing room door. It read three minutes to ten. Almost showtime. "Like hosting a tea party for fifty or so small children."

"Point taken." Ava shrugged. "I'm headed outside for a meet-and-greet by the Ferris wheel. See you later for lunch."

Lacey bid goodbye to her friend and darted out of the dressing room. Ever After Castle held a rotating series of events throughout each day, and Sweet Pea's Royal Tea Party—Lacey's signature event—was one of the hottest tickets at Once Upon A Time. Seating was limited, with park visitors situated at large round tables throughout the castle's ballroom.

Lacey always made stops at every table, greeting each guest and making conversation—totally in character, of course—while children and their parents enjoyed the ultimate high tea experience. Tiered china plates held scones, finger sandwiches, and sugar cookies decorated to look like glass slippers, crowns, royal coaches and, specific to Sweet Pea's particular fairy tale, a canopy bed stacked high with twenty mattresses. Other characters from "The Princess and the Pea" milled about the room too, most notably Prince Charming and his mother, the queen. Tea was served in real china teacups, and near the end of the tea party, Lacey took a few minutes to give her partygoers royal waltzing lessons.

Everything ended when a big grandfather clock struck twelve and Lacey dashed out of the ballroom. Technically, that was mixing fairy tales. The Brothers Grimm were probably rolling over in their graves, but the kids always loved seeing her run away in a flurry of glitter and tulle, so Once Upon A Time bent the rules just a tiny bit.

Lacey's voluminous skirts swished around her legs as she reached the employees-only entrance to the ballroom. Behind the huge walnut double-doors, she heard the footman announcing her arrival.

"Presenting Her Royal Highness, Princess Sweet Pea."

Right on cue, the grand doors swung open. Lacey held her dress up with one hand, posed the other hand in perfect princess position, and swept into the ballroom with a dazzling smile. A chorus of oohs and ahhhs greeted her, as well as dozens of cell phones, recording her every move.

The footman, dressed in a brocade costume and powdered white wig with tall bunny ears, offered Lacey his arm and escorted her to the first table.

"Good morning, boys and girls," she said in a sing-song voice. "Welcome to my tea party. I'm ever so sorry if I'm late. I woke up with a terribly sore back because I tossed and turned all night long. Imagine my surprise when I woke up this morning and discovered a pea under my mattress!"

She held her finger and thumb a fraction of an inch apart, indicating the minuscule size of the pea, and the children collapsed into giggles.

Anxious to show Lacey her sparkly pink manicure, one of the little girls held up her hand for inspection. "Look at my pretty nails, Princess Sweet Pea."

Lacey pressed a gloved hand to her heart. "Oh, so beautiful. Did your fairy godmother do that for you?"

The child gave Lacey a shy smile and shook her head.

"It must've been your mice friends, then," Lacey said.

Everyone seated at the table laughed, and Lacey posed for a picture with the child as she gazed at her young guest's sparkly pink nails, lips curved into her practiced Sweet Pea smile.

At the next table, a toddler dressed in a tiny replica of Lacey's Princess Sweet Pea costume greeted her with a wobbly curtsy. Lacey felt her practiced smile grow even wider. *Adorable.* She dropped into her own deep curtsy in response, and a collective *awww* rose up from the ballroom.

The footman kept Lacey on track, giving her a silent signal when it was time to move from one table to the next.

Servers carrying gleaming silver trays topped with teapots and delicate cups and saucers swished past her. Across the ballroom, Prince Charming visited the tables she'd yet to greet, while the queen moved in Lacey's wake, entertaining the guests who'd already met Princess Sweet Pea.

The entire tea party was like a well-choreographed dance, one Lacey knew by heart. But due to the ever-changing guests, it was never quite the same. In the five years Lacey had been playing Princess Sweet Pea, she'd met children from all over the country. Some even came to Once Upon A Time from other parts of the world.

Case in point: the adorable young girl seated at the second to last table in Lacey's rotation. She and the gentleman sitting beside her—the girl's father, Lacey presumed, although it was hard to tell, since the baseball cap on the man's head was pulled down so low over his eyes—appeared to be the only partygoers at the table. Which meant they'd booked the entire space, since seats at Sweet Pea's Royal Tea Party never went unreserved. It was a rarity for a smaller party to book a table all to themselves, but it happened from time to time.

Although, Lacey wasn't sure she'd ever seen just two guests sitting at a table for ten before.

"How do you do, Your Royal Highness," the girl said in a refined accent Lacey couldn't quite place. She couldn't have been more than six or seven, but she enunciated each word with great care.

"Good morning." Lacey curtsied. "What's your name, princess?"

The man in the baseball cap cleared his throat, but kept his head down. Perhaps he needed to take an etiquette lesson from his unusually poised daughter.

"I'm Her Royal Highness, Princess Rose." The child beamed.

Her father's head snapped up, revealing a pair of piercing

blue eyes. Lacey's stomach did a flutter. She pressed her hand to the satin bodice of her ballgown. There should be a law against brooding men hiding such lovely eyes beneath baseball caps. It was quite...unnerving. All of a sudden, he looked sort of like Prince Charming on his way to the gym. Jogging pants and slim-fit athletic jacket, check. Baseball hat, check. Regal bone structure and dreamy blue eyes—check and double check.

"Just Rose," he corrected, reaching for his cup of tea. "No need for titles."

Rose's cute rosebud mouth turned down into a frown.

"I'm sure you're mistaken, sir. All little girls are princesses, aren't they, Princess Rose?" Lacey winked at the child.

Rose's smile returned at once. Dimples flashed in her round, pink cheeks. She tilted her head, and her pigtails danced as she studied Lacey's tiara. "Your crown is very sparkly. And very, very big. I have a crown at home, but it's much smaller. It's real though, and it's back home in my real castle."

Her grumpy dad choked a bit on his tea.

"I'm sure your crown and your castle are lovely, just like you," Lacey said, tapping the girl on the tip of her nose. *What a precious child! Such a sweet imagination.*

Rose giggled.

"Rose, sweetheart." Her dad aimed the bill of his baseball cap in his daughter's direction. "Perhaps it's not best for princesses to discuss the size of their royal accoutrements?"

"I don't know what that means, Daddy," Rose said.

Her dad sighed.

"Don't worry, Princess Rose. There's nothing in the royal rules that say you can't talk about your sparkly crown." Lacey slid Grumpy Baseball Cap a pointed glance. Honestly, why rain on the child's parade? This was all nothing but make-believe.

"The royal rules?" His blue eyes narrowed. And his

accent—it was even posher than his daughter's. "And what might those be, exactly?"

The fluttering in Lacey's belly intensified. "Surely you're not interested in hearing about how to be a proper princess, my good sir."

"On the contrary, I'm quite interested. Do elaborate." He shot a glance at the footman. "And please tell me these rules somehow explain why your footman has bunny ears."

Ah, a skeptic. Lacey had come across his kind before. The poor man clearly didn't have an appreciation for whimsy. Or royalty, for that matter. No wonder his daughter wanted to live in a castle.

Her father probably wouldn't know a crown if it landed right on his annoyingly handsome head.

"My footman has bunny ears because he's an enchanted bunny rabbit, of course." The woman in the puffy ball-gown—Henry couldn't refer to her as Princess Sweet Pea with a straight face, it just wasn't possible—tilted her head and batted her eyelashes at him.

She was more cartoon character than actual human being, but Henry had to give credit where credit was due. She showed no sign whatsoever of breaking character. He knew firsthand how difficult such a task could be. It reminded him of having to feign interest in whatever the Duke of Spain had been droning on and on about at the most recent state dinner at the palace in Bella-Moritz.

"Of course," he echoed. "Tell me, are all footmen enchanted?"

"Oh, yes." The pretend princess beamed at him as if nothing delighted her more than the thought of a garden animal-turned royal page. She turned toward Rose. "Princess Rose, are the footmen in your royal palace bunnies, squirrels, or frogs?"

Bunnies, squirrels, or frogs?

A bark of laughter escaped Henry. He just couldn't help it. He'd never been party to such a ludicrous conversation in his life.

Then again, that was the whole point of this little adventure, wasn't it? He'd whisked his daughter to America in search of something he'd never be able to give her in the principality where she'd one day sit on the throne. They'd only stepped off the royal jet a few short hours ago and thus far, Once Upon A Time had certainly delivered. Henry just hadn't anticipated the experience would include such colorful commentary on princesses, crowns, and castles. Essentially, his very existence.

"They're frogs!" Rose squealed.

Henry bit back a smile. Rose was correct. The footmen in the royal palace of Bella-Moritz did seem to possess a rather amphibian-like quality.

Still, ought he be encouraging his little princess to think of the respectable men and women in their employ as animals? Definitely not. Their escape had an expiration date. Once all of this was over, he and Rose would be going back to their very normal, very royal lives. And those lives probably shouldn't include Rose offering up flies to the footmen for high tea.

"Rose." He shook his head.

The effervescent Princess Sweet Pea smiled even harder at him. "I'm sure the froggy footmen love working in your castle."

Henry could only hope so. He'd always strived to be a decent prince. A *good* prince—one who understood the duties and responsibilities of the position to which he'd been born.

Despite her giddy exterior, Princess Sweet Pea seemed unconvinced anyone would enjoy working for him, enchanted or otherwise. In her eyes, Henry was probably just a regular dad in a baseball cap and athletic wear who seemed to be trying to quell his daughter's active imagination.

At least he *hoped* that's what she saw when she looked at him. The park planned on assigning a special VIP escort to Henry and Rose for the duration of their visit to Once Upon A Time, but they'd arrived earlier than anticipated. He was determined to fly under the radar for a few cherished hours before word got out that actual royalty had landed in the world of fairy tales. Hence the baseball cap, a purchase from the theme park gift shop. In hopes of blending in, he'd also changed out of his usual tailored suit in favor of an outfit he'd normally wear only to the palace gym. Rose's hair was arranged in two pigtails high on either side of her head, a hairstyle that went against royal protocol every bit as much as the athletic trainers currently on Henry's feet.

Henry had even managed to persuade his personal protection officer to wait outside the castle while he and Rose attended the tea party. Ian had been with Henry for years and was willing to look the other way from time to time as long as Henry wasn't in any kind of obvious danger. Since no one knew they were in America yet, the risk of something untoward happening was minimal.

"Now, about those royal rules." The pretend princess kneeled down so she was eye level with Rose. Her dress puffed around her like dandelion fluff. "Number one: always make friends with birds and butterflies."

Henry felt his lips twitch. *Don't laugh.* It was a sweet thought. Truly, it was. But it had absolutely nothing to do with being royal.

Princess Sweet Pea continued, oozing warmth and sincerity. As crazy as it seemed, Henry was beginning to feel like her personality might not totally be an act. Impossible. No one was this nice. "Number two: reads lots of books. As many as you possibly can."

Beauty and the Beast vibes, obviously, but solid advice, all the same.

"That's a good one," he heard himself say.

The princess's eyes met his for a moment, and warmth spread through Henry's chest.

He blinked. *What was that?*

It couldn't be attraction. Again, impossible. That part of Henry had withered and died years ago.

And in the unlikely event he actually did find himself attracted to a woman, he'd hope that person would be non-fictional. Certainly not a storybook character in a fake castle dripping with so many twinkle lights that it looked like it'd been dipped in sugar.

"What's the next rule, Princess Sweet Pea?" Rose said, as enamored as Henry had ever seen her with anyone or anything.

"The next rule is to always wear white gloves." The princess did a little flourish with her hands, which were sheathed in completely impractical opera-style gloves. "And never take off your crown—not even in a bubble bath."

She winked, and Rose gazed longingly at her heavily embellished rhinestone tiara, as if she'd never set eyes on the Chevalier Crown Jewels.

Henry desperately wanted to laugh. White gloves and bubble baths? This was getting absurd, even for a fairy tale. Rose would be crushed if he so much as snickered, though. This trip was for his daughter, not himself. And by all appearances, Once Upon A Time had already started working its magic on Rose. Henry should be thrilled—this was precisely what he'd wanted. Surely he could put all reason aside for the duration of a single "royal" tea party.

"Pray tell," he said. "Are there more?"

"Just one last rule." Princess Sweet Pea held up a single, gloved finger.

Henry braced himself for whatever hilarity was coming.

"Always, *always* be kind," the princess said, and for reasons Henry couldn't begin to understand, his heart gave an aching tug.

No wonder this place was so popular. Who wouldn't want to live in a kingdom filled with friendly birds and butterflies, snuggly footmen and infinite kindness? Not to mention the kingdom's book-loving, bubble bath-taking princess who seemed to be the living embodiment of joy and happiness.

If only any of it were real.

"I will," Rose promised, and the princess gave her a tender pat on the cheek.

Then, before Henry could thank her for all the personal attention she'd given his daughter, Princess Sweet Pea floated toward the next table in a flurry of pale pink tulle and good wishes.

He glanced at Rose. A spot of glitter shone on her cheek as she shoved an entire sugar cookie into her mouth. Henry's mother would've been appalled on multiple levels. Not Henry, though. For once, his daughter looked like a child—a normal six-year-old on holiday, and the sight of her with crumbs on her lips and glitter on her face filled Henry with warmth.

"Having fun?" he asked.

He'd had his doubts about the tea party. Given a choice, Henry would've opted for a ride through Hansel and Gretel's Haunted Forest or the Little Mermaid water attraction. But again, Rose was calling the shots.

She nodded.

Henry leaned closer and whispered in her ear. "This is a bit different than our palace at home, yes?"

Different, and just what she needed—what they *both* needed. Rose wasn't the only one who needed to find her smile again. Henry did too. Happiness wasn't such a terribly selfish thing to want, was it?

Rose grinned up at him with a mouthful of cookie

crumbs. She'd never looked less like a princess in her life. "It's better."

CHAPTER THREE

Just an Ordinary Dad

L ACEY WAS SWEATING BENEATH THE bodice of her ballgown. She usually didn't get rattled by guests, but the exchange with Grumpy Baseball Cap had left her feeling oddly unsettled.

She blamed it on the brooding man's accent. He sounded like James Bond, minus the charm.

A blatant lie, actually. Charm oozed out of Grumpy Baseball Cap's pores, which made him all the more annoying. Lacey's princess character might be slightly naive, but Lacey herself wasn't stupid. She'd spotted the laughter in those dreamy blue eyes of his, and it hadn't been the usual sort of good humor typical of park attendees. It felt as if he'd been mocking her in his mind.

She smiled so hard that her face hurt as she greeted the guests at the next table. Perhaps she was letting her last conversation with Mark get to her. Why would a random dad have an opinion about her silly princess rules? He was at a *tea party* in the ballroom of a *theme park castle*. What else would he expect?

His daughter had been awfully cute, though. "Princess Rose." How adorable.

Lacey's footman—yes, the one with the bunny ears—nodded at her, indicating it was time for the waltzing portion of the party. She wrapped up her visit at the final table, posed for one last picture, and glided to the front of the room as music began drifting from the overhead speakers.

Prince Charming stood waiting for her and greeted her with a deep bow. "May I have this dance?" He held out his hand.

Lacey placed her gloved hand in his, and then Prince Charming—who was actually a PhD student named Drew—rested his opposite hand on her waist, and they began moving in time with the music, weaving among the tables in a simple box step.

In the five years Lacey had been playing Princess Sweet Pea, she'd gone through almost half a dozen Prince Charmings, and not one of them had stepped into the character's regal shoes by learning how to waltz. Lacey hadn't known how, either, when she'd first started, but after waltzing her way through the ballroom on a daily basis, she'd gotten quite good at it. So good, in fact, that she gave lessons to incoming royalty at the theme park. Having just started at Once Upon A Time a week or so ago, Drew still got slightly panicky every time they danced together. Beads of sweat broke out along his forehead as they crossed from one side of the ballroom to the other.

"You're doing great," Lacey murmured.

Drew shot her a pained smile. She was going to have to lead again. If she didn't, he'd steer her straight into a table full of teacups, scones, and small children wearing plastic tiaras. Their waltz would be all over YouTube within minutes.

She squeezed his hand and tried her best to steer him

toward the narrow spaces between the tables. Thankfully, Drew got the hint and let her take over. He practically sagged in relief as they continued spinning through the ballroom.

Against her better judgment, Lacey snuck a glance at Grumpy Baseball Cap when she danced past his table. Big mistake. His gaze immediately fixed with hers, and she caught a definite hint of amusement in his eyes. Again.

Her face went warm and she nearly stumbled backward into a server carrying a silver platter topped with macarons. She didn't dare breathe until the waltz ended and she was once again safely at the head of the ballroom. Drew kissed the back of her hand and bowed, relinquishing the spotlight to Lacey once more. Time for her to teach a quick waltzing lesson to her party-goers...

Fifteen more minutes.

Why did time seem to be passing so slowly? This felt like the longest tea party in the history of fictitious royal gatherings.

"Would anyone like to learn how to dance a royal waltz?" Lacey pressed a hand to her heart and glanced around the room.

Hands went up, and Lacey called guests forward, one by one. There was a mother-daughter duo, a little boy and his grandma, a brother and sister, plus a group of tween girls who seemed especially eager to dance with Prince Charming. She lined them up in front of the big grandfather clock and counted.

"Let's see, that's nine so far. We still have room for one more dancer," Lacey said. "Doesn't anybody else want to give it a try?"

The room went quiet. The partygoers seated at the table closest to her all stared down at their dessert plates. In fact, most of the guests seemed to be avoiding Lacey's gaze at all costs...save one.

Grumpy Baseball Cap sat watching her with a perfectly

blank, perfectly controlled expression on his face. But as she let her attention linger on him, his lips twitched ever so slightly, as if he were trying not to laugh.

Fine. Lacey squared her shoulders. She was theme park royalty, after all. *If you think it's so easy, mister, let's see you take a turn around the dance floor.* "Why don't you join us, sir?" She beckoned to him with a flourish of her satin-covered fingertips.

Grumpy Baseball Cap's smile immediately died on his lips.

Aha, that's what I thought. Everyone was a critic until it was time to step up and put themselves out there.

Lacey wouldn't force him to dance with her, obviously. She just wanted to prove a point—her job wasn't laughable. And dancing backward while wearing pseudo-glass slippers and a glorified prom dress on steroids was no easy task, thank you very much.

Unnerving or not, she still wanted Grumpy Baseball Cap and his daughter to have a good time, so she was perfectly prepared to let it go and choose someone else. But every head in the ballroom swiveled quickly in Grumpy Baseball Cap's direction, including his sweet daughter's.

"Please, Daddy." The little girl nodded at him, pigtails bobbing. "Please?"

He paused for a beat and then acquiesced. "Of course, sweetheart."

The room burst into applause as he stood and made his way toward Lacey.

Okay, then. She was going to have to dance with him. *No problemo.* It'd been her idea, after all. She'd waltzed with half a dozen Prince Charmings, plus the Big Bad Wolf a few times, when Charming had been sick and the Big Bad Wolf had filled in as his substitute. She could certainly handle dancing with one perfectly ordinary dad.

Except there was nothing ordinary about the way he

carried himself as he crossed to the front of the ballroom. Lacey couldn't quite put her finger on it, but there was something commanding about his straight spine and nice shoulders. Confident.

Dare she think it?

Regal.

But that was just her tiara talking. As Mark had so bluntly put it, her crown wasn't real, and neither was this castle. Grumpy Baseball Cap was just a regular dad—albeit a dad with exceedingly good posture, and a jawline that looked as if it'd been chiseled from fine European marble.

He took his place beside her. Tiny sparks of electricity seemed to dance along Lacey's skin. Nerves, right? It had to be. She could *not* be attracted to this cynical, brooding dad.

He looked down at her with icy blue eyes that seemed to say, *You've got me here. Now what are you going to do with me?*

Lacey's throat went dry. She looked away and went about arranging her students into pairs, designating the leader and the follower for each couple. Then she taught everyone the basic box step, and the dancers practiced on their own a few times as Lacey counted along to the music.

"Leaders, step forward, side, close. Step back, side, close. Followers, step back, side close. Step forward, side close."

She was surprised when Grumpy Baseball Cap picked up the steps almost instantly. Lacey had fully expected him to trip over his feet, but they weren't even in hold position yet. Once he had to do the box step and move Lacey across the floor at the same time, he wouldn't stand a chance—especially not with the added challenge of her enormous princess dress. His feet would be swallowed up by tulle within seconds. She could hardly wait.

Lacey motioned toward her students with a sweeping gesture of her gloved hands. "All right, palace guests, take your partner by the hand, and let's try dancing together!"

She watched as they arranged themselves into stiff pairs, and then turned toward Grumpy Baseball Cap, her princess smile fixed into place. "Now, just put your hand here..."

Before she could get the words out, he took her right hand in his and placed his opposite palm in the center of her back in perfect hold position, as if he'd done it a million times before.

"Oh." She gave a little start. "Yes, exactly like that."

"Very well, Your Royal Highness," he said, eyes glittering in the enchanted lighting of the castle—which Lacey knew was achieved by the use of pale pink bulbs, but she went a little fluttery all the same.

"Here we go, princes and princesses," she called, and as the music swelled, she took her first backward step.

And then, all at once, she forgot about where to put her feet or making sure Grumpy Baseball Cap didn't trip over her dress or plow them into a table surrounded by children sipping tea, because she wasn't doing a simple box step anymore. Instead, she was being led around the floor as if she were dancing on feathers. They spun, they turned, they made a sweeping circle around the perimeter of the ballroom—so fast and in such perfect time to the melody that Lacey felt herself holding her breath. She wasn't even conscious of her foot placement. Her body simply responded to her partner's movement.

Wow.

Her pulse roared in her ears as he pulled her closer to him, his hand firm and warm against her back—so warm that she could feel it through the thick satin bodice of her ballgown.

So this was what it felt like to really waltz? To be led across the dance floor by someone who knew what he was doing? Her feet floated across the floor. After five years of practice, this dance felt like it was what Lacey had been preparing for all this time. The real deal.

The strangest thing of all was that Grumpy Baseball Cap never looked down at his feet or let his gaze wander over her shoulder to see where they were going. Instead, he kept his eyes fixed with hers the entire time. It felt daring and intimate, as if they were the only two people in the room. Lacey couldn't look away. She couldn't even breathe, and just as she started to regain her equilibrium, he lowered her into an elaborate dip.

She gasped as cheers erupted in the ballroom. Lacey had never been dipped in her life, but it felt like the most natural thing in the world, and as she rested in his arms, head spinning, Grumpy Baseball Cap flashed her a quick wink.

"You must watch *a lot* of *Dancing with the Stars*," she blurted.

"Something like that," he said, and then they were off again, waltzing in a long series of spins until the big grandfather clock began to chime.

At last, Lacey broke her gaze and looked away. Both arms of the towering clock pointed straight up, marking twelve o'clock. It was time for the tea party to end and for Lacey to dash away from the ballroom like Cinderella. "Oh my goodness," she said, slowing her footsteps to a halt. "I'm sorry, but I simply must go."

She was supposed to say those words loud and clear so all her guests could hear her, but they came out in a breathy whisper, as if she were fleeing from a real Prince Charming.

Grumpy Baseball Cap frowned. "Wait, where are you going?"

"It's midnight," she said, and right on cue, the lights in the castle dimmed, just as they did every day when Sweet Pea's Royal Tea Party drew to a close.

But Lacey's mad dash from the ballroom felt different this time. Her heart thumped in her chest and her hands shook as she gathered her skirts. She had to concentrate extra hard on remembering to step out of her shoe before she reached the exit.

The ballroom's grand double doors slammed shut behind her, and a backstage assistant promptly locked them to prevent any overeager kids from trying to follow Princess Sweet Pea. Lacey heard another roar of cheers and applause rise from the tea party as she pressed a hand to her chest and tried to catch her breath.

"That waltz was really something." The stagehand looked her up and down and shook his head. "Who was that guy you were dancing with?"

"I have no idea. Just an ordinary dad," Lacey said.

Never mind the fact that ordinary dads didn't typically dance like Fred Astaire...

"Could've fooled me. For a minute there, I thought you might be dancing a real royal waltz."

Lacey's gaze flitted toward the closed doors to the ballroom. *That makes two of us.*

CHAPTER FOUR

The Problem with Fairy Tales

N O SOONER HAD HENRY STEPPED outside the twinkly Ever After Castle, hand-in-hand with Rose, than his personal protection officer appeared at his side.

In truth, Ian Walker was more than just a bodyguard. He had the muscular build of someone whose job required him to wrestle potential kidnappers to the ground if necessary, but Ian's bulky shoulders carried Rose around for piggyback rides as often as they bore the burden of protecting his royal charges. His official job description ranged from personal protection officer to valet to general assistant. Rose had referred to him as "Uncle Ian" since she'd first learned to talk, and he was as much a friend to Henry as he was an employee.

He'd also undergone a recent wardrobe change so as not to resemble a royal bodyguard. A "make-under," if such a thing existed.

As he sidled up next to Henry, Ian smoothed down the

front of his knit polo shirt where his necktie would normally rest. "How was the tea party, Your Royal—"

Henry shook his head. "No titles, remember?" he said under his breath.

"Right. So sorry, Your...er...Henry," Ian said.

Ian had been hired to protect Henry since before Rose had been born, and inside the Bella-Moritz palace walls, they were on a strictly first-name basis. The two men were as close as brothers. Royal protocol, however, dictated Ian should address both Henry and Rose as HRH when out in public. Protocol was apparently so ingrained in Ian that it was a hard habit to break.

Henry could relate. He was having an equally hard time getting used to the sight of Ian wearing cargo shorts.

"How was the tea party, Henry? Rose?" Ian flashed Henry's daughter a wide smile.

"It was *so* fun," Rose gushed. "We had tea and cake and cookies shaped like glass slippers, crowns, and piles of mattresses."

Ian glanced at Henry, brow furrowing. "Piles of mattresses? Am I missing something?"

"Princess and the Pea," Henry said by way of explanation.

"Ahh." Ian nodded. "Of course."

From where they were standing, Henry could spot rides and attractions from every fairy tale he'd ever heard of. Just up ahead, a line snaked its way around a mini-roller coaster that ran through The Three Bears' Woods. The ride tick-tick-ticked up a hill and then whooshed down in a rush of rattling tracks and happy screams. A faux frost-covered mountain loomed to their right, home to The Snow Queen's Mountain Sleigh Ride. Farther down the path, a crowd gathered at the entrance to The Three Billy Goats Gruff Wild Water Crossing. People exited the ride with sloshing sneakers and broad smiles. Booths dotted the park, selling anything and everything from a trio of Little Pig balloons to sparkly ice cream bars shaped like mermaid tails and unicorn horns. All around him, the air smelled of soft pretzels and candy floss. Henry felt as if he'd been dropped into the middle of a storybook.

"Daddy danced with Princess Sweet Pea," Rose announced, dragging him back to the conversation.

Ian and Rose both smirked in his general direction.

Oh boy, here it comes.

Henry's love life, or lack thereof, was a favorite topic among his kingdom and the royal court—his mother, in particular. Not a day passed when she failed to remind him how happy Rose would be if he were to find another "special someone."

In the first year or so after his wife had passed away, no one had breathed a word about Henry remarrying. Everyone had been content to let him grieve in peace. Rose's mother had been a part of Henry's life since childhood. She'd been royal by birth, the daughter of a high-ranking duke who ran in the same noble circles as Henry's family. He and Jolie had attended the same prestigious university in coastal France, and once they'd graduated, all of Bella-Moritz seemed to hold its breath in anticipation of a royal engagement.

Henry had been happy to oblige. He'd known Jolie his entire life, and marrying her had just felt right, even though they'd been ridiculously young and naive at the time. Less than eighteen months into the marriage, Rose had been born—a precious royal heir.

And then Jolie had fallen ill, and Bella-Moritz's fairy-tale romance had crumbled to the ground.

That was the thing with fairy tales, though, wasn't it? They were only imaginary. Henry and Jolie's relationship had always been based on friendship, and in the months before she'd passed away, Jolie had become disillusioned with life in the palace. She'd even mentioned divorce, but once she'd been diagnosed, Jolie and Henry had put on a brave face. The word had never been uttered again.

The months Jolie had been sick had been the loneliest of Henry's life. He'd never mentioned his marital troubles to his mother, but nearly two years after Jolie's passing, the queen had confessed to him his wife had come to her and asked about the possibility of ending the marriage. She'd been prepared to give up her title and leave both Henry and Rose.

A new sort of loneliness had settled over him then. What was he supposed to do with that information, years after the fact?

According to his mother, Ian, and everyone else in his life, he should simply start over. Find someone new, someone he could fall crazy in love with. He deserved that, didn't he? Didn't everyone?

Henry disagreed. Vehemently. He'd tried marriage, and it'd been a spectacular failure. If a literal Prince Charming couldn't make it work, the prospect seemed hopeless. He was perfectly fine on his own. He had Rose and he had his role as heir to the throne. That was more than enough to keep him occupied.

But as time marched on, the rumblings began. His subjects wanted to know who he was dating. After all, Henry was too young to live the rest of his life as a widower. Every woman who crossed his path was analyzed in terms of her suitability as future queen. These days, he couldn't even speak to a female over the age of twenty-five without the press insisting a royal wedding was in the works.

Ian shot Henry a serious dose of side eye. "Did you really dance with this Sweet Pea queen?"

Henry kept walking without a word. He'd danced with a pretend princess, just like he'd waltzed a million other times at royal balls—one of his many princely duties. There was really nothing more to say about the matter.

Except he'd felt a very strange, very *real* jolt of electricity when he'd taken the pretend princess's hand in his...

And leading her around the ballroom had been the most fun Henry had had in quite some time. She'd expected him to bumble his way through the waltz like her theme park prince had done. Henry had winced during their entire dance. It had been *painful* to watch. Sweet Pea had noticed Henry's silent critique, of course, and calling him out to participate in the dance lesson had been a challenge.

No one challenged Henry. Ever. Part and parcel of being the Crown Prince meant people deferred to him, day and night. Even Ian was guilty of it. Truth be told, it got a little old. "Princess" Sweet Pea's little test had given Henry a wholly unexpected jolt of adrenaline. He rather liked being treated as a regular person, and her utter astonishment at his ability to put one foot in front of the other had made him feel like he was smiling from the inside out.

But neither of those things were any of Ian's business, and now that Henry had exited the saccharine-sweet castle and was back in the very real light of day, he realized he'd made a terrible mistake. There had been at least fifty people at that tea party. Fifty *strangers*, armed with phones and cameras. It would be a miracle if he didn't end up on the worldwide news, waltzing with a theme park princess. The optics would be borderline insane. The press would eat it up with a spoon.

Oblivious to Henry's massive lapse in judgment, Rose prattled on. "Princess Sweet Pea had a giant crown she wears all the time, even when she takes a bath, and her dress looked like pink cotton candy. Daddy twirled her all over the ballroom, and everyone clapped like crazy." Rose clapped her little hands.

Ian regarded Henry and appeared to be doing his level best not to laugh. "Shall I alert the Queen? She's been trying for a while now to pair you with a nice eligible princess."

Henry arched a brow. "Are you quite finished?"

Ian shook his head, and he raked his dark-blond hair from his eyes. "No. I'm definitely going to need to hear more about this cotton candy princess."

Rose was only too happy to elaborate. "She has pretty blond hair all piled up on top of her head, and she's friends with birds and butterflies. Her footman is a bunny rabbit."

Ian nodded. "Naturally."

"And she loves to read books."

"Ah, a well-read woman of royal lineage." Ian slid Henry another glance. "Princess Cotton Candy sounds rather lovely."

"Her name is Princess *Sweet Pea*," Rose said, tiny brow furrowing. "While she was dancing with Daddy, the clock started bonging, and she ran away. Her shoe fell off, and then the tea party was over."

Ian cocked his head. "Hmm, for some reason, this story sounds vaguely familiar."

Henry's memory snagged on what he'd said the moment Princess Sweet Pea had pulled away from him. *Wait, where are you going?* The words had slipped right out of his mouth as if he were an actor playing the part of Prince Charming, right out of central casting. Worse yet, he'd had the wholly irrational urge to chase her.

Maybe Henry actually *had* landed right in the middle of a storybook. Thinking about it was giving him a headache of the highest order.

He rubbed his temples. "Am I the only one feeling jet-lagged?"

Ian glanced at his ever-present smartwatch. "We're due to meet with the park manager in an hour, but I could always reschedule for first thing in the morning if you'd rather get some rest. We've been on the go for almost twenty hours straight."

Henry was accustomed to powering through time changes and travel stress, but little Rose wasn't. Despite her tea party excitement, she was beginning to yawn every few minutes.

He rested a hand on her tiny shoulder. "What do you say, sweetheart? It's your birthday trip, but we've got days ahead of us. Maybe you'd like to take a nap, or call it day and hit the ground running in the morning?"

Rose glanced around the bustling theme park until her gaze landed on a gift shop, conveniently situated mere steps from the Ever After Castle. A child-sized version of Sweet Pea's puffy ballgown hung in the window, covered in bits of glitter that twinkled in the Florida sunshine. Rose gasped. "Look, daddy! It's her dress!"

"Shopping it is, then, birthday girl. Followed by a nap and a quiet night in." Henry nodded. They could order room service and have a picnic on one of the hotel beds—something they could never do on Rose's fancy four-poster bed in the palace.

Rose sprinted toward the gift shop and gazed up at the window display in wide-eyed wonder.

"Rose is having a ball." Ian's expression turned tender as he lowered his voice. "As much as it upset Her Majesty, I think this birthday trip was an excellent idea—if you don't mind my saying so."

Henry felt the tense set of his shoulders relax just a bit. "I haven't been spending as much time with her as I should. The queen will understand, eventually."

Unless Rose refuses to ride in the royal procession at the Flower Festival...

It was going to take more than a waltz to get Henry's mind off the pony problem. The queen wasn't just his mother—she was his monarch. His sovereign. He'd made her a promise, and if he didn't live up to it, there would be consequences. Not just for him, but for his daughter, too. The queen wasn't going to let the matter of Rose's education go, not if he continued to let her avoid getting back in the saddle. Henry didn't want Rose to spend all day shut inside a palace. He wanted her to learn with children her own age. Yes, she was a princess, but she was also just a little girl. She wouldn't sit on the throne for years. She deserved to have a life first.

Henry's gut tightened. Was that how he felt about this own existence? That he didn't have a life?

He glanced at Ian. "You might want to postpone the meeting with the park manager. Something tells me Rose is going to be a while in the shop, and afterward, I wouldn't be surprised if she wants to check into the hotel and take a bubble bath."

Which was exactly as it should be. She was behaving as any normal seven-year-old girl would, and it warmed Henry's heart. For better or worse, he'd deal with the fallout when they returned to Bella-Moritz.

"Very well." Ian pulled his cell phone out of his pocket. "And later, I'm assuming you'll require my assistance."

Henry felt himself frown. Had he forgotten something? "Remind me what for, please."

The corner of Ian's mouth hitched into a sardonic half-grin. "For roaming the theme park far and wide in search of the fair maiden whose foot fits into the shoe the princess left behind. That's how the story goes, isn't it?"

Henry glared at him.

Ian waved a hand at Henry's athleisurewear. "I'm assuming you pocketed the glass slipper in question."

"Ian." Henry sighed. His head pounded. He could really use an ibuprofen...or three.

Ian pulled a face. "Too far?"

"A little bit, yes." Henry held his thumb and forefinger a fraction of an inch apart.

"Duly noted, Your Royal Highness."

By the time Lacey had finished her princess shift and was back home in her favorite gingham pajamas and sharing Chinese takeout with Ava, she'd forgotten all about her royal waltz with Grumpy Baseball Cap.

Mostly, anyway.

Maybe she'd kept an eye out for his sweet daughter's pigtails for an hour or so post-tea party, but with three meet-and-greet sessions dotted throughout the park and a private party for children visiting from a summer camp for kids with special needs, she'd had more pressing things to think about than a semi-professional ballroom dancer disguised as a moody dad.

She still did, apparently, because as usual, Ava was brimming with gossip about the behind-the-scenes goings on at Once Upon A Time.

"Gretel and the Big Bad Wolf are an item now. Can you believe it?" Ava said as she dug into her half of their sesame chicken. Over the years, they'd fallen into the habit of referring to most of their theme park friends by their character names. In the beginning, it had been easier than trying to connect actual names to so many faces. Plus, now there were no less than three Brittanys on the Once Upon A Time roster. Character names just worked better all around.

Lacey blinked. "What? I thought Gretel had a crush on the Frog Prince."

Practically *everyone* had a crush on the Frog Prince. There was a lot going on underneath that warty green costume of his.

"She did, but you know what a sweetheart Wolf is. He won Gretel over when she forgot her basket of bread crumbs on the way to her meet-and-greet and Wolf ran back to the dressing room to fetch it for her. He sprinted clear across the park and back in that furry costume. He's lucky he didn't get heat exhaustion. It's the middle of summer." Ava stabbed her fork at her chicken for emphasis.

Ava and Wolf did a lot of appearances together in the park, given that their characters were from the same fairy tale. Contrary to the enmity of their costumed personas, they were very close friends. For Thanksgiving last year, Ava had even gone to Wolf's parents' house for turkey dinner. Since Once Upon A Time was open three hundred sixty-five days a year and the holiday season was so popular with tourists, days off for Thanksgiving and Christmas were often hard to come by.

Lacey had of course spent last Thanksgiving with Mark and his parents. That obviously wasn't going to be an option this year.

Weird. Lacey frowned into her plate of yummy, sesame goodness. This was the first time all day that she'd thought about Mark, and they'd only broken up twenty-four hours ago. Was that normal for someone who was supposed to be heartbroken?

Her stomach churned.

Granted, Lacey been the breaker-upper and not the other way around, but still. She'd expected to *marry* Mark. Somewhere under her bed there was a stack of dog-eared bridal magazines. Which, come to think of it, she really needed to dump into the recycling bin. She sort of wished she could dump the memory of her last dinner with Mark in there too.

"Earth to Lacey." Ava snapped her fingers in front of Lacey's face. "You disappeared there for a minute. You completely missed my other Once Upon A Time romance update. Sneezy and Doc are engaged."

"Oh, wow. Good for them!" Lacey grinned and tried her best to ignore the fact that she suddenly felt more invested in her co-workers' upcoming nuptials than she did in the wedding she thought she'd be planning for herself right about now.

All the more reason to swear off dating for a while.

Clearly she'd made the right decision about Mark, but now she felt weirdly adrift. Heartbroken or not, the memory of their painful dinner conversation still hurt. A lot. Mark had been one hundred percent right about one thing, though— Lacey couldn't work as a theme park princess for the rest of her life. She needed to enjoy every minute of her dream job while she still could.

"I've saved the most intriguing news for last," Ava announced, leaning closer to Lacey across the sofa cushions.

"I hope this isn't put-down-my-fork news, because I'm starving," Lacey said as she took another bite. How did the old saying go? Feed a cold, starve a fever...and feed a breakup as much comfort food as possible. If that wasn't a real adage, it should be.

"Keep eating." Ava waved a hand. "It's nothing earth-shattering, just a special visitor."

"Really? Who?"

Ava shrugged. "I don't know. Nobody does. That's the intriguing part."

"Is it a VIP?" Lacey said.

Like other popular theme parks, Once Upon A Time offered private VIP tours. The service offered a personalized tour guide who accompanied the VIP and their guests on all the rides and attractions throughout the day. Sometimes special guests were even given the opportunity to stay at a private suite on the top floor of Ever After Castle.

"Yep." Ava nodded.

"Who's in charge of the tour?"

"Charles, apparently," Ava said, indicating the tour guide with the highest level of seniority at Once Upon A Time. "So it must be someone really big."

"Agreed. Charles always gets assigned to escort the most important of the important people." Lacey arched an eyebrow. "Remember that time the Vice President came? There were as many secret service agents in the park that day as there were fairy-tale characters."

"Oh my gosh, what if it's that big Broadway producer? The one who won the Tony last year for best musical." Ava's fork clattered onto her plate. "He's got kids! It could totally be him."

"For your sake, I hope it is." Lacey couldn't help but laugh. Ava's dream was to perform on Broadway one day. "What if it's the star of that new romcom you're dying to see? She has kids too."

"Don't make me choose between a romcom and Broadway. That's just cruel." Ava clutched her heart. "I'll bet it's neither of those people, though."

Lacey shrugged one shoulder. "Probably not, but it's still fun to think about."

"True."

They sat quietly for a minute, until Lacey reached for the television remote. It was just about time for their nightly *Friends* ritual.

"You know who I think it's really going to be?" Ava said as the sitcom's familiar theme song started up.

Lacey stood to gather their empty plates and put them in the dishwasher. "Who?"

"Someone we least expect."

CHAPTER FIVE

It's Raining Peas

S POILER ALERT: ONCE UPON A Time's very important visitor wasn't a Broadway producer. Nor was it a glamorous-yet-relatable romcom star. It was, in fact, someone Lacey and her roommate never expected.

"Wait a minute." Lacey paused from sliding on one of her white satin gloves the following morning in the dressing room of Ever After Castle. "You're saying a prince is coming? As in *actual* royalty?"

Lacey had been playing the part of fairy-tale princess for so long, she'd almost forgotten that being royal was a real job. Not so much a job as a birthright, in the case of genuine royalty. Either way, it was a thing.

And according to word on the cobblestone streets of Once Upon A Time, it was coming to Florida.

Big Bad Wolf—whose real name was John, but he seemed to enjoy going by Wolf—nodded and leaned against the makeup table, where Lacey and Ava were busy getting ready for their shifts. Wolf was always ready early. There were certain advantages to simply having to crawl into a furry lupine ensemble as opposed to applying princess makeup and styling an updo around a massive tiara.

"Yes! Prince Henry of Bella-Moritz. You've heard of him, right?" Wolf's gaze swiveled back and forth between Lacey and Ava.

Ava nodded. "Of course. He's the third most eligible bachelor in Europe."

Lacey laughed. "Says who?"

"The internet, obviously." Ava dabbed at her Riding Hood-red lips with a tissue. "*And* the world at large. Don't tell me you don't know who he is."

"The name sounds vaguely familiar," Lacey said. As usual, Ava was one step ahead of her in the news department.

"He's a pretty big deal," Wolf said. "Not as well-known as the British royals, because Bella-Moritz is so tiny. But he's going to be a king someday. Right now, his mother is the reigning monarch."

"He's got the cutest little girl." Ava pressed her hand to her heart. "Princess Caitriona. Her mother died when she was just a tiny baby."

"Oh, wait. I think I remember that." Lacey paused from jamming a last-minute bobby pin into her hair.

Hadn't there been a photo of the widowed prince, holding his tiny infant princess, splashed on the covers of all the grocery store magazines? The prince's head had been bowed, and something about his posture as he'd stood in a blue shaft of light beneath a stained-glass window in the grand cathedral where his wife's funeral had taken place had tugged hard at Lacey's heart.

He'd looked so alone. So human, despite the loftiness of his position. Lacey had gotten tears in her eyes thinking about his baby girl. She knew what it was like to lose a parent at such a young, tender age. All the wealth and power in the world couldn't replace a mother's love.

"That had to be six or seven years ago," Lacey said, doing the math. "Is his daughter coming too?"

Wolf nodded, and his furry wolf snout slid in front of his eyes. He pushed it out of the way. "Yep. According to Charles, the trip is to celebrate Princess Caitriona's birthday."

Ava stood and tied her red hood in place. "I'll bet Charles is beside himself, the lucky duck. This could be the biggest VIP tour Once Upon A Time has ever seen."

"I've never seen him so happy," Wolf said. "You ready? We can walk to our meet-and-greet together."

"Sure, let's go." Ava gave Lacey's shoulder a squeeze. "Have a great tea party this morning! Don't forget to keep your eyes peeled for the prince."

Lacey grinned.

A real prince...

She wondered if she'd recognize him. Doubtful, seeing as he probably wouldn't be walking around the theme park with a crown and scepter. He'd seemed so sensitive in those famous pictures. Vulnerable, almost. Lacey couldn't imagine him being anything but kind and gracious. A true Prince Charming—the very opposite of Grumpy Baseball Cap.

Sure, he'd been a great dancer, but Lacey had spotted the undeniably smug gleam in his eye when he'd dipped her low and then twirled her back into a waltz hold. He'd been so pleased to prove her wrong.

Granted, she'd made some pretty big assumptions about his waltzing abilities. But how could she not, after all his eye-rolling during her dance with Charming, and his third degree about her rules of proper princessing and her enchanted footman?

Today, she'd select a sweet, innocent child to dance with. No more cranky dads, period.

Lacey took a final glance in the mirror, puffed up her

tulle skirts, and headed down the hidden castle hallway to the ballroom's secret entrance. Her tea party progressed in a blessedly normal fashion this time. The nine-year-old little boy she chose as her dancing partner grinned from ear-to-ear for the duration of their waltz. When the clock struck twelve, Lacey dashed out of the ballroom, feeling much more tranquil than the day before.

She really shouldn't have let Grumpy Baseball Cap rattle her so much yesterday. Frankly, it wasn't like her. She'd been mocked plenty of times during her tenure as Princess Sweet Pea. People who dressed like a cake topper for work every day developed a surprisingly thick skin.

Lacey had just been a little tender after her breakup with Mark, that was all. Grumpy Baseball Cap's dry tone and his questions about her fictitious royal life had been like pressing a fresh bruise. Or, more to the point, like a princess sleeping on a rock-hard pea.

Today was a new day, though—not a pea in sight.

"Lacey, good." Simon Dole, Once Upon A Time's general manager, walked toward her as the double doors to the ballroom closed behind her. "We've been waiting for you."

"You have?" Lacey glanced around.

The stagehand from the day before was the only other person present in the secret hallway. He gave her a nearly imperceptible shrug.

Weird.

Double weird, actually. Lacey had never bumped into Mr. Dole in any of the employees-only staging areas of the park. He tended to either stick to his corporate office, which Lacey had never set eyes on, or wander the park grounds to make sure things were running smoothly. In fact, she wasn't sure if she'd even spoken to him before, other than the occasional greeting at Once Upon A Time's holiday party.

"Yes. I knew Sweet Pea's Royal Tea Party was almost over, so it only made sense to wait until you were available.

Come along." He turned around and began bustling in the other direction, leaving Lacey no choice but to follow.

She gathered heaps of tulle in her arms and scurried after him. Wherever he was going, he was in an awfully big hurry to get there.

"Now, I know this is rather unprecedented. Nothing about this situation is ordinary, I'm afraid. We've been working day and night to get everything in order, and we had all of our i's dotted and our t's crossed." Mr. Dole waved his arms as he spoke, and Lacey had to duck a few times to prevent her crown from becoming a casualty of his enthusiasm. "We had a plan—a *proper* plan." They exited the Ever After Castle and turned down the cobblestone path that led to the sleek glass executive offices near the park entrance. "Everything would've worked out just fine, but you know, in a delicate situation such as this one, fine isn't quite good enough, is it?"

Once again, she struggled to keep up as he marched toward the office door and held it open for her.

He glanced at her. "Well, is it?"

A heads up regarding the nature of said situation would've been helpful, but Mr. Dole seemed awfully wound up. She wasn't sure if she should ask him to elaborate. "Definitely not," she said.

"Right. I knew you'd agree. We'll have to adjust your schedule a bit, but the second they walked in and I saw that little girl all dressed up as Princess Sweet Pea, the idea hit me. You're absolutely perfect for this."

"Thank you," Lacey said. *I think.*

The office receptionist smiled politely at them as they entered the building. "Excellent, you're both here. The guests are waiting in your office, sir. We've served them tea and Sweet Pea cookies, as you requested."

"Very good," Mr. Dole said and motioned for Lacey to follow him to the elevator bank.

The elevator doors parted, and once Lacey had managed to cram the entirety of her princess gown into the small space, her boss—more like her boss's boss's boss—pressed the button for the top floor.

What was going *on?*

Anticipation fluttered in the pit of Lacey's stomach, and her hands started to shake as the elevator climbed from one floor to the next. The journey to the top of the building seemed to take forever, until at last, the elevator spilled them out onto a red-carpeted space with swirling gold lettering on the wall.

Welcome to Once Upon A Time
The Land Where Fairy Tales Come True

A massive white door with Mr. Dole's name on it stood just to the left—the only office within sight.

Lacey swallowed. This was silly. She needed to know what she was walking into, didn't she? "Mr. Dole, if you could just—"

"Don't forget." He gave her a curt nod. "Cinderella hands at all times. I'm counting on you, Lacey. You're the only princess we have who I know without a doubt is up to this task."

Then he pushed the door open, and Lacey was ushered into the largest office she'd ever seen in her life.

It was decorated in varying shades of white and gold, offset by the same crimson carpet from the hallway. Definite fairy-tale castle vibes, but Lacey barely had a chance to notice the pristine decor before her attention was drawn to the floor-to-ceiling windows that stretched from one end of the office to the other, affording a stunning panoramic view of the entire park. She could see every ride and attraction Once Upon A Time had to offer, from Jack's Towering Beanstalk to Rapunzel's Fantastical Ferris Wheel and everything in between. In the center of it all stood Princess Sweet Pea's home—the grand, glittering Ever After Castle.

Lacey had never seen the theme park like this, and for some silly reason, it put a lump in her throat. She was truly lucky, wasn't she? She got to come to work every day at a place that was, for lack of a better word, magical. If only she could go back in time and give her six-year-old self a glimpse of this moment.

But then Mr. Dole cleared his throat, catapulting Lacey back from the past to the very real present, where a small group of people sat around an ornate conference table. She took a deep breath. Every pair of eyes in the room was trained on Lacey and her Cinderella hands.

"Hello, everyone," she said, dropping into a princess-y curtsey, as her character did about a thousand times a day.

"Please don't," someone said in posh British accent. "It's really not necessary."

Wait, wasn't she supposed to be in character?

Lacey stood, looking back up and her gaze immediately fixed on a familiar pair of swoony blue eyes.

Grumpy Baseball Cap?

It was him. She'd know those eyes anywhere—even here, in her boss's boss's boss's office, no longer hidden beneath the brim of a navy-blue cap.

The fluttering in Lacey's belly tightened into a knot of anxiety. What on earth was he doing here? Was she in some sort of trouble? Had he lodged a complaint about her tea party? Was he seriously *that* angry that she'd dragged him onto the dance floor, his ballroom-worthy moves notwithstanding?

She blinked, willing him to disappear. But when she opened her eyes, he was still there, rising to his feet as if to greet her. Right beside him, his little girl—dressed head-to-toe in a perfect replica of Lacey's Sweet Pea costume—bounced up and down on her tiptoes.

Mr. Dole's baffling words from earlier drifted back to the forefront of Lacey's consciousness.

We'll have to adjust your schedule a bit, but the second they walked in and I saw that little girl all dressed up as Princess Sweet Pea, the idea hit me. You're absolutely perfect for this.

No. No, no, no, no, no.

Lacey felt like she might faint. This couldn't mean... *He,* of all people, couldn't be...

She shook her head as if she could somehow stop whatever absurdity was about to transpire. She wouldn't have been the least bit surprised if hard little peas started raining down from the heavens. A full-on hailstorm of peas.

Just *no.*

"Princess Sweet Pea." Mr. Dole beamed, oblivious to her suffering. "It's my pleasure to present to you Their Royal Highnesses, Crown Prince Henry Frederick Augustus Ranier and Princess Caitriona Rose of Bella-Moritz."

Henry was rather accustomed to extreme reactions upon being introduced to new people. It kind of went with the princely territory.

When he went on engagements—the generic royal term for duties ranging from state responsibilities and acts of charity to overseas visits—Henry was often greeted by cheering crowds, particularly in and around his home kingdom. Groups of schoolchildren often broke out in painstakingly rehearsed songs, toddlers offered him bouquets of flowers, teenage girls screamed as if he were a one-person boy band, and more than one woman had fainted dead at his feet. But never before had he prompted such an expression of shocked dismay as the one currently showing on Princess Sweet Pea's face.

"How do you do?" he said and offered her his hand.

She stared blankly at it as every drop of color drained from her face.

An irrational surge of disappointment coursed through Henry. *Unflattering* didn't even begin to cover Sweet Pea's reaction, but since when did he care so much about the opinion of a total stranger?

Since waltzing with said stranger made you feel like a man for once, instead of just a prince.

"Ahem. Perhaps Princess Sweet Pea needs a moment to collect herself," Simon Dole said. "I'm sure she's quite excited."

Excited clearly wasn't the word for whatever Sweet Pea might be feeling at the moment. Annoyed, perhaps? Angry? Upset?

Disappointed, most certainly. But *excited* was nowhere on the list of possibilities.

"So sorry," she said, collecting herself. "It's a pleasure to meet you both." Sweet Pea flashed Rose a wink before sliding her gloved hand into Henry's. After the dance they'd shared, her touch was instantly familiar. All softness and light.

He ducked his head a bit to catch her gaze, and when their eyes met, he tried as hard as he could to impart a silent message. *This wasn't my idea.*

The last thing Henry wanted was for her to think he was trying to force her into something she clearly didn't want to do. Henry would've been just fine with a regular VIP escort. In fact, he would've preferred no escort at all. But Ian wouldn't hear of it. Neither would the palace or Simon Dole. A stolen hour or two at the tea party yesterday was one thing, but the numbers one and two in line to inherit the Bella-Moritz throne couldn't simply roam around one of the most popular tourist spots in southern Florida, all on their own. Still, Henry would never have demanded that Sweet

Pea climb down from atop her pile of imaginary mattresses to be his unwilling companion for the next four days.

It was the dress. Rose had pranced into Simon Dole's office this morning, proudly showing off her Princess Sweet Pea costume, and Simon Dole had gotten the crazy idea into his head that the "real" Sweet Pea should be their guide. *Anything for the princess! It's her royal birthday, after all!*

Henry had done his best to gently object. As much as he loved his daughter—and contrary to what her *grandmère* believed—he tried not to spoil her. Also, this birthday trip was a chance for Rose to be as much like a regular girl as possible, and Henry hadn't seen private, Princess Sweet Pea-guided tours anywhere in the park's brochure. Not even the VIP section.

For once, though, no one cared what Henry thought. Simon, apparently eager to do anything and everything to make Once Upon A Time the new royal vacation hotspot, had already decided this was the way it was going to be. And Rose was bubbling over with excitement. The Crown Prince didn't get a vote.

Having so little control over the situation—*any* situation, really—was a new experience for Henry. Truth be told, he didn't quite care for it.

This was a lot of information, however, to try and impart with nothing but a meaningful glance, as evidenced by the bewildered look in Sweet Pea's soft brown doe eyes. A hurt frown tipped her lips for a fraction of a second—barely long enough for Henry to catch a glimpse of it—and then she carefully arranged her delicate features back into her innocent, happy princess expression.

"Princess Sweet Pea will be your personal guide for the duration of your visit here at Once Upon A Time. She'll escort you on all the rides and attractions and accompany you anyplace you'd like to go in the park. Anything you need, she can make it happen. After all..." Simon Dole glanced at

Sweet Pea, obviously prompting her to finish his sentence.

"This is the land where fairy tales come true," she said.

And then she flashed a dazzling grin at Rose and tipped her head to Ian, but seemed to ignore Henry—the living, breathing Prince Charming—altogether.

CHAPTER SIX

Mermaid Tails and Unicorn Horns

S OME FAIRY TALE.

It feels more like a nightmare, Lacey thought as she took her seat beside Prince Henry in one of the mechanical sleighs on the Snow Queen's Mountain Sleigh Ride.

The sleigh ride was the third attraction they'd ridden since leaving Mr. Dole's office, but the first where she'd ended up seated directly next to her royal companion. So far, they'd ridden in swan boats topped with huge golden crowns along the Swan Princess River that wound its way along the outer perimeter of the park, followed by a virtual reality tour through Tom Thumb's Adventure, where enormous 3-D screens made guests feel as if they'd been shrunk down to mere inches tall. Just like in the famous fairy tale, they'd fallen into a bowl of batter for Christmas pudding, gotten swallowed by a red cow, and carried off by a raven. In the end, the king placed everyone into a tiny coach pulled by cheerful gray mice and they were carried outside the ride, where they "miraculously" turned back to normal size.

Their foursome had turned a few heads as they'd walked throughout the park, particularly when Lacey had walked them past the queue, toward the unmarked VIP entrances. It was only a matter of time until word spread that actual royalty was on the premises. A baseball cap could only do so much.

Rose, which was apparently Princess Caitriona's middle name, insisted on sitting next to Lacey on the first two rides, which was just fine with her. Nothing would've pleased her more than to somehow avoid any alone time with Prince Henry. Every time Lacey looked at him, she kept remembering all the ridiculous things she'd said at the tea party.

She'd asked an actual princess if the footmen in her castle were bunnies, squirrels, or frogs. She'd told real royals they should always wear their crowns in a bubble bath. She'd asked Prince Henry if the reason he knew how to waltz was because he was a fan of *Dancing with the Stars*!

It was mortifying, and the very worst part of all was that Prince Henry had egged her on. He'd probably gotten a royally huge laugh out of the entire episode.

Lacey had never considered she might one day meet a prince, but if she had, never in a million years would she have guessed how humiliating it would be.

"Why do I get the feeling you're angry with me?" Prince Henry murmured after she'd gotten situated next to him on the bench seat of the sleigh. The sled in front of them carrying Ian and Rose surged ahead until they were a speck in the distance.

Lacey had noticed Henry murmuring something to Ian while she'd been escorting them through the VIP entrance to the ride, and she'd had the impression he'd specifically arranged for them to ride together this time. She just wasn't sure why.

Lacey took a deep breath. *This* was why the prince had

wanted to share a sleigh with her? He wanted to have a royal heart-to-heart?

Her dress took up so much room in the small, two-person sled that it spilled over onto Prince Henry as if it were trying to swallow him whole. He regarded her over the pile of glittery tulle in his lap. "You're going to have to talk to me eventually, Princess Sweet Pea."

Lacey felt a hot flush creep up her neck. Every time he called her *Princess,* she wanted to crawl in a hole. "Whatever you like, Your Royal Highness."

How had Mr. Dole put it? *Anything you need, she can make it happen.*

"Call me Henry," he said gently. "Please?"

She met his gaze for the first time since she'd first been bowled over by the sight of him in Mr. Dole's palatial office. "Um…"

"That's a royal order," he said in a preposterously over-the-top swanky accent.

Lacey laughed despite herself. "Very well, Henry."

Their sleigh surged into motion, crawling in a slow, winding ascent up the Snow Queen's mountain. The man-made peak was tipped with copious amounts of white paint and glittering glass beads to make it feel like they were really traveling through a snowy pass in the Swiss Alps.

"You never answered my question," he said as they approached a cluster of flocked blue spruce trees. "Why do I get the feeling you're angry with me?"

Lacey wasn't touching that question with a ten-foot scepter. "I'm sure I don't know what you're talking about," she said in her sweetest possible Sweet Pea voice. "Henry."

The shadow of a snow-laden fir tree fell across his chiseled face. He shook his head. "Can we pretend I'm not a prince? I much preferred the honest way you spoke to me yesterday at the tea party."

"Is that why you lied?" Lacey clamped one her white

gloved-hands over her mouth the second the words escaped her.

What was she *doing?* If she wasn't careful, she was going to get herself fired. And he hadn't lied to her at all. He just hadn't announced his royal status ...which Lacey could sort of understand.

Still, it would've been really great if he'd stuck a name tag to his innocent-looking athleisurewear. *Hello, My Name Is Prince Henry of Bella-Moritz, so maybe refrain from making silly royal jokes. You'll only end up embarrassing yourself.*

"Skulking around beneath a baseball cap and pretending to be someone you're not isn't technically lying, princess." He flashed her a wink.

Her stomach did a fluttery little flip-flop. Lacey wished she could blame it on the motion of the sleigh, but the Snow Queen ride was one of the tamer attractions at Once Upon A Time.

"So you admit you were skulking," she heard herself say.

Did Bella-Moritz have a tower, like the one in London? If so, Lacey was definitely going to end up imprisoned there.

The sleigh pulled away from the blue spruce forest into a darkened tunnel as it made its way inside the mountain. A rush of cool air washed over Lacey, and goosebumps broke out over every inch of exposed skin from the sweetheart neckline of her ballgown.

"No more skulking. You have my word," he said, his voice dropping to a near-whisper in the darkness.

Lacey snuck a glance at him. She could just make out his profile against the interior of the mountain tunnel, frosted with crushed crystals and faux pearls, and again, the moment felt strangely intimate, like when they'd waltzed together in the ballroom.

She drew in a shaky breath and faced forward. Their sleigh was approaching a hollowed-out cave where two animatronic reindeer pawed at the snow and tossed their huge heads against a backdrop of aquamarine gemstones and stalactites, hanging from the ceiling like snowy chandeliers. "I supposed skulking is indeed out of the question now," Lacey said.

Henry was dressed slightly more regal today in a pressed linen button-down shirt with the sleeves rolled up to his elbows and a pair of tailored khaki trousers—high fashion for a theme park. Most guests wore shorts, but perhaps there was a rule against exposing his royal kneecaps.

"I just wanted to give my daughter an hour as a regular person before word got out that we were here. I wasn't trying to deceive you." He turned toward her in the darkness, and Lacey could hear the bittersweet smile in his voice.

"You don't need to explain yourself to me, Your—" Lacey had to bite her tongue to stop herself from using his title. "It's your vacation. You have every right to spend it as you please."

"I found your tea party quite charming. Let me guess—it seemed like I was mocking you."

"A little bit, yes," she admitted, instantly feeling acutely vulnerable. She stared hard down the dark tunnel in front of them. "But I might have overreacted. I've been a tiny bit out of sorts lately." Why, oh why was she being so honest with him? She was supposed to be playing a fairy tale character, not baring her soul.

"Can I ask why?" he said, sounding impossibly tender against the piped-in howling wind noises that had just begun swirling through the ride.

Lacey could feel her pulse in her throat all of a sudden. She took a deep breath and hoped he didn't notice that the gentle tone of his voice had just made her go all soft inside. "It's nothing, really. Not even worth talking about." No way was she going to tell him about her recent break-up. He was a royal prince, not her BFF. She already had one of those.

"Fair enough, but can I ask you one last thing?"

They'd reached the part of the Snow Queen's Mountain Sleigh Ride where huge crystal snowflakes hung from the ceiling, and the wind gave way to distant yodeling. Soon they'd come upon a shaggy animatronic St. Bernard perched atop a snowy cliff—the last thing they'd see before the sleigh exited the mountain tunnel and plunged them back into the Florida sunlight.

"Probably. That depends on what the question is," Lacey said.

The St. Bernard came into view, looming over them with a brandy keg fastened to his neck as snow made from foam drifted down from the ceiling.

"What's your real name?" Henry turned toward her with delicate snowflakes dotting his hair as they made their way toward the light.

Warmth spread through her, as if she'd been sipping from the St. Bernard's keg.

She couldn't tell Henry her name. Doing so would break every rule in the theme park princess handbook. He was a guest, and she was Princess Sweet Pea. Period.

But he'd asked her to call him Henry, and they were about to spend the next four days together. Was she really supposed to expect him to address her as *princess* that entire time? And technically, wasn't she supposed to be catering to his every whim? Even the ones that broke the rules?

"It's Lacey," she heard herself say. "But I'm not supposed to tell you that, so it has to stay our secret."

The sleigh slowed to a stop, their journey through the magic winter wonderland officially over. Ian and Rose stood on the platform, waiting for Lacey and Henry to climb out of the sled and accompany them on their next adventure.

"Your secret is safe with me, Lacey," Henry said.

Then he climbed out of the sleigh and offered her his hand, as if she were descending the steps of Cinderella's grand coach instead of a mechanical sleigh at the base of a mountain made of glass and steel.

Lacey placed her hand in his and reminded herself that even though the prince in this land of make-believe might be real, everything else was still just pretend.

Henry's seatmate for the remainder of the day was Ian. Rose practically glued herself to Lacey's side, and Henry had to admit they looked awfully cute together in their matching cotton candy ballgowns. He snapped a sweet picture of them together in front of the glittering Ever After Castle, and in a moment of rare familial sentimentality, he texted it to his mother. But the second after he pressed send, an email popped up on his phone from her private secretary.

Henry read the email three times in a row, a metaphorical bomb dropped into his inbox. The secretary's message included a list of governesses Her Majesty considered to be appropriate choices for Rose's upcoming school year. Would Henry take a look and return the list to his mother's assistant, ranked according to preference?

No, Henry would not. He and Rose were on vacation, not a royal tour. Tomorrow was her seventh birthday, and the absolute last thing he intended to do on such a special day was to break the news to his sweet daughter that her grandmother wanted to yank her out of school and have her educated at home.

At least now Henry knew what he was dealing with. The queen was digging her royal heels in about Rose's education. Removing Rose from school would be the consequence his daughter would face if she continued to refuse to ride her horse in the upcoming procession. He'd known the palace officials wouldn't take a breach of royal tradition lying down.

His mother had made that clear, and Henry had suspected she might dangle the possibility of a governess over her head.

He understood the queen's point of view. Historically, heirs to the Bella-Moritz throne were taught by a succession of governesses when they were young and private tutors once they became teenagers. Henry himself had never darkened the door of a group classroom until he'd gone to university at Oxford in England.

But when the time had come for Rose to begin her schooling, Henry had gone another route. He remembered how envious he'd been of other children who'd gotten to attend real school and make real friends—friends who, at that age, didn't care a bit if one of their playmates was the heir to the throne. He'd wanted a real school experience for Rose. After losing her mother, the last thing she needed was to be stuck in the palace twenty-four hours a day without any playmates.

So he'd dug in, just as he'd insisted upon taking Rose to America for her birthday, and Henry had no regrets about either decision. The Flower Festival was vitally important to Bella-Moritz, though. Florists from all over the world came to compete in the flower show, and the day of the royal procession was a national holiday. The good people of his kingdom would be severely disappointed if they didn't get to see Rose riding her pony. The principality's newspapers and magazines had been anticipating her big royal debut for months already. All she had to do was sit atop the sweet horse for the length of the wide avenue that stretched from Bella-Moritz's Grand Flower Park to the palace—five city blocks.

Henry planned to ride alongside her, of course. If necessary, he'd even prop her in his own saddle, and they could ride together.

But he'd rather see Rose conquer her fears and learn that she could do anything she set her mind to. He wanted his little girl to thrive, both inside and outside the palace.

"Everything okay?" Ian asked as they stood at the edge of the Little Mermaid Magic Fountain while Lacey and Rose visited the nearby ice cream cart. "You look slightly green around the gills."

Henry slid his phone back into his pocket. "Green around the gills?"

"Fish humor." Ian waved a hand at the fountain, where a costume mermaid sat inside an enormous pink clamshell. Water danced around her in sea glass hues of blue, green, and turquoise. "'When in Rome' and all that."

"Sometimes I think you're enjoying this vacation as much as Rose is," Henry said as his lips twisted into a smirk.

Ian's gaze narrowed. "Don't pretend you're not having a good time. You and Princess Sweet Pea looked awfully cozy when your sleigh swished out of that crazy mountain."

Henry felt his smirk slide off his face. "Stop. I just wanted to talk to her in private for a few minutes about...theme park logistics."

"'Theme park logistics.' Got it." Ian crossed his arms.

Henry averted his gaze. "And to answer your previous question, everything is just fine—or it will be once Rose resumes her riding lessons. She just needed a break."

"She's a brave, spirited girl, Henry. Give her time."

Henry shot him a look.

Time is the one thing we don't have.

What limited time Henry *did* have felt borrowed. So far, they'd been able to roam the grounds of Once Upon A Time with little intrusion. Park goers had aimed curious glances in their direction a few times, but their presence had yet to cause a stir, and for that, he was immensely grateful. He just wasn't sure how long such good fortune could possibly last.

"Daddy, we got you a treat," Rose said in a sing-song voice that sounded uncannily like Lacey's princess persona. She skipped toward Henry with a mermaid tail ice cream bar in one hand and a frozen unicorn horn in the other. "Which one do you want?" She held them both up for inspection.

The unicorn horn appeared to have been rolled in pastel-colored sugar. Henry's teeth ached just looking at it. "I think I'll choose the mermaid tail."

"An excellent choice," Lacey said as she joined them, her massive skirt billowing behind her. She waited until Henry bit into it and then grinned. "It has a bubble gum center."

"So it does." Henry laughed as he chewed. And chewed. And chewed.

"We got one for you too, Uncle Ian." Rose pointed her unicorn horn bar at Lacey.

He plucked a mermaid tail treat from Lacey's hand and winked. "Thank you very much, Your Royal Highnesses."

No titles, remember? Henry very nearly said it, until he realized Ian had been addressing Princess Sweet Pea and her mini-me. Not him.

He took another bite from his ice cream bar to prevent himself from sticking his foot in his mouth. He'd done enough of that at Sweet Pea's Royal Tea Party, apparently.

Henry and Lacey had moved beyond that royally awkward encounter, though, hadn't they? They seemed to have reached an understanding during their sleigh ride. He hoped so. It was crazy how fast their journey through the Snow Queen's Mountain had passed. Why did it suddenly feel like time was slipping through his fingers when the previous four years had crawled by at a snail's pace? Already, their first full day at the theme park was coming to a close.

You still have three more days.

He took another bite of his ice cream. Ian's tongue appeared to be turning bright blue from the frosty mermaid scales, which meant Henry's probably was too.

"Have you had a good time today, sweetheart?" Henry glanced at Rose and stuck his tongue out at her.

She nodded, giggling at him as her pink ice cream dripped

onto her white-gloved fingertips from her unicorn horn—a fatal flaw of Princess Sweet Pea's white glove rule, as far as Henry was concerned.

"Do you have something to say to Princess Sweet Pea?" he said, prompting a thank you.

"Thank you, Princess Sweet Pea," Rose said softly, leaning into the puff of Lacey's ballgown.

"Of course, my darling. We'll have fun tomorrow too." Lacey bent to give Rose an affection squeeze around her slender shoulders.

When she stood back up, Henry smiled at her, but Lacey's attention strayed to a spot over his shoulder.

He took a backward glance and at first couldn't tell what had captured her interest, but then he noticed a child in a wheelchair, dressed in the same Princess Sweet Pea costume Rose was wearing.

The girl appeared to be a year or two younger than Rose, and she waited in line with her family for a ride in the swan boats. She had the gown, the gloves...the whole deal, except for the crown.

When Henry turned back around, Lacey was once again refocused on Rose, but every so often, she snuck a glance in the other child's direction.

Henry felt a tightness in chest. He didn't need to ask why Lacey's gaze kept flitting to the little girl in the wheelchair. He just *knew*. If Princess Sweet Pea hadn't been assigned to accompany Henry and his royal entourage and cater to his every whim, she would've been over there in a heartbeat.

"Go," he said quietly, while Rose and Ian debated the virtues of unicorn ice cream versus mermaid tails.

"What?" Lacey's eyes went wide. She blinked, clearly worried she'd been caught doing something wrong.

"The child in line at the swan boats." Henry tipped his head in the direction of the Swan Princess River. "I know you want to go talk to her. Please don't let us stop you."

She shook her head. "But..."

"Don't worry about Simon Dole. I'll deal with him, if necessary." He shot her a wink. "Go."

"Thank you! I'll be right back," she whispered, beaming at him as she shoved her ice cream bar into his hand, gathered her skirts, and floated toward the queue for the swan boats.

The girl's face lit up when she saw Lacey coming toward her. Lacey went into full princess mode, posing her hands just so and dropping into a deep curtsy in front of the girl's chair. Then she bent down to eye-level with the child and chatted animatedly with her. Henry was too far away to hear the conversation, but he would've bet money that it involved bubble baths, fanciful footmen, and sleeping on piles of mattresses atop a troublesome pea.

A lump lodged in his throat.

"Daddy, you have ice cream dripping down your arm." Rose tugged at Henry's shirt sleeve, then pointed to a garish trail of blue and green melting down his forearm.

"So I do," he said, voice going thick. "Oops."

Rose's tiny forehead crinkled. "Where did Princess Sweet Pea go?"

"She's over there, talking to another young visitor who's wearing a ballgown just like yours." Henry pointed toward Lacey with one of the rapidly melting ice mermaid tails.

"Oh." Rose's face fell.

The ache in Henry's chest felt cavernous all of a sudden. Was his mother right? Had he doted on Rose to such an extent that she didn't want to share Princess Sweet Pea with anyone else?

But then Rose shook her head. "She's missing her crown."

Henry blinked. "What?"

"That little girl." The crinkle in Rose's forehead grew deeper. "She doesn't have a crown."

Before Henry could truly grasp what was happening,

Rose shoved her unicorn ice cream bar at him, much like Lacey had just done, and ran toward the Swan Princess River, where a crowd had begun to gather around Princess Sweet Pea.

Ian launched into motion, intent on following for the young princess's protection.

"No, it's okay," Henry said. "Let her go."

And then he watched as his sweet daughter removed her own plastic crown and gently sat it atop the other child's head.

CHAPTER SEVEN

What's the Opposite of Royal?

"TELL ME *EVERYTHING*." AVA PUMPED her arms as she strode beside Lacey on the walking path at Fort Lauderdale Beach Park after work.

Since they couldn't exactly afford an apartment right on the water, Lacey and Ava tried to get out to the public park a few evenings every week. Sometimes they sipped iced frosés in fancy coup glasses at their favorite sidewalk café overlooking the ocean, and sometimes they made a picnic dinner to enjoy on a blanket in the sand. But when one of them had a problem or just a surplus of nervous energy to burn off, they liked to hit the brick path that ran along the shoreline for a power walk.

Currently, Lacey had both—a problem *and* plenty of nervous energy fizzing through her veins. Usually, simply taking a few deep breaths of salty sea air and listening to the waves crash against the shore was enough to bring her a sense of peace. So far, she and Ava had walked nearly a mile along the white wave wall that separated the walking path from the sandy shore, dotted with tall palm trees, and Lacey still felt all jumbled up inside.

"There's nothing to tell, really," she said, squinting into the sunset.

Ribbons of pink and lavender stretched across the blue Florida sky, and the sea glittered with bits of gold. Lacey wondered if the sunsets in Bella-Moritz were anywhere near as glorious as the ones in south Florida.

Probably. In fact, Henry could probably summon them on command, given his royal status.

"Lacey, please. You just spent an entire day with a real-life prince and his adorable daughter. There's got to be *something* to tell." Ava gave her a sideways glance. "Wolf said he saw you and the prince riding together in one of the sleighs at Snow Queen Mountain. Is that true?"

"Of course it's true. It's my job at the moment. I'm the personal park guide for his group." How insane was this situation? She still couldn't wrap her head around it.

"Well, what's he like? The prince?"

Lacey picked up her pace, even though Ava was already struggling a bit to keep up with her. "He's very...um..."

Charming.

She couldn't say it. True as it might be, it was just too cliché.

"He's nice," she finally said.

"Nice? That's an awfully bland description for a royal prince." Ava pulled a face.

How exactly was Lacey supposed to elaborate?

I can't stop thinking about our waltz.

When his fingertips brush against mine, I get butterflies.

I told him my name.

She wasn't about to admit any of those problematic facts out loud—not even to her best friend. Especially the part about telling Prince Henry her real name. Ava would think it meant something, which it didn't. He'd asked Lacey to call him by his first name. It seemed only fair to reciprocate.

But reciprocity didn't have anything to do with the butterflies. Or the waltz that kept spinning on an endless loop in her head. Which summed up Lacey's royally huge problem—the reason she'd stepped out of her glass slippers and into her favorite pair of running shoes and dragged Ava to the beach—in a nutshell: Lacey's feelings toward Prince Henry were beginning to thaw. After spending the day with Grumpy Baseball Cap, she'd realized he wasn't very grumpy at all.

"He seems like a really good dad," Lacey finally said as the palm trees swayed overhead. "The reason he's here is to give Rose a chance to have a normal birthday. And she did the sweetest thing this afternoon."

Lacey gave Ava a play-by-play of her interaction with Molly, the little girl who'd been dressed up as Princess Sweet Pea in her wheelchair, including the moment when Rose had removed her plastic crown from her head and offered it to the other child.

In her tenure as Princess Sweet Pea, Lacey had been privy to many encounters that tugged on her heartstrings. Children and adults alike often shared private struggles with her, and she regularly visited with people who were grieving a loved one or dealing with heartbreaking medical diagnoses. Those encounters were Lacey's favorites—the very reason she'd wanted to become a theme park princess to begin with.

Lacey was used to keeping her composure during such bittersweet interactions with guests at Once Upon A Time. So many people she met at the park had an emotional connection to her character or to fairy-tale princesses in general, and she never wanted to let anyone down. Lacey had always seen her job as an opportunity to bring peace, light, and comfort to people who needed it most. So she always kept things positive and never cried—*ever*.

But she'd almost had to blink back tears as she'd watched Rose and Molly become friends. She wasn't sure what had gotten into her lately.

"It sounds like Rose will make a wonderful working royal when she gets older," Ava said, panting as they slowed to a stop in front of the wave wall to watch the sun dip lower on the horizon.

Lacey nodded. "Like her dad."

Waves lapped at the sugary white shore, and close to the water's edge, a family built a sandcastle together. Colorful buckets and tiny plastic rakes lay scattered on the sand beside a young boy pressing seashells into the castle walls—cat's paws, scallop shells and bleached white sand dollars. A man who Lacey guessed was the boy's father dug a moat while two small girls filled buckets with sea water. The mother dripped wet sand from her loose fist into a tall, drippy turret.

Caught up in the nostalgia of their beach tableau, Lacey didn't even notice Ava studying her until she gave Lacey a gentle shoulder bump.

"Wait a minute. You like him," Ava said.

"Of course I do. I said he was nice."

"No." Ava shook her head, grinning from ear to ear. "I mean you *like* him."

"What?" Lacey's stomach churned. "That's crazy."

"No, it's not. It makes perfect sense, actually. He's a prince and you're a—"

Lacey held up her hand. "Don't say it. I'm not a princess. I work at a theme park, same as you. I don't belong in a castle any more than you belong in a forest village plagued by wolves."

Ava tightened her ponytail. The breeze was really picking up, like it always did on summer evenings at the beach. "Fine. You're not royal. You're *un*royal, but you can still like

Prince Henry. It's not against the law or anything."

"I think the word you're looking for is *common*," Lacey said. "I'm a commoner."

Ava's eyes twinkled. "Oh, hon. You're anything but common."

The churning in Lacey's stomach calmed just a little bit. "You know what I mean. I can't like Prince Henry—not in that way. Besides, I'm taking a break from dating, remember?"

This entire conversation was ridiculous. Had she just mentioned *Prince Henry* and *dating* in the same breath?

Ava sighed, clearly unconvinced. At the shoreline, high tide rolled in, sending foamy waves crashing over the family's carefully built sandcastle. In a matter of seconds, it was nothing but a muddy mound of sand littered with seashells.

"I can't like Prince Henry," Lacey repeated. "And I don't."

Maybe if she said it enough times, she'd believe it.

Henry stood on the balcony of his suite of rooms at the Ritz-Carlton and watched the sun disappear into the horizon. It looked as though it were melting right into the bright-blue layers of the sea, gilding the crests of the waves with shimmering gold light.

Simon Dole had offered Henry and his guests the use of a special, private suite in the Ever After Castle on Once Upon A Time's premises, but Henry had politely declined. Ian had security concerns about staying on park property twenty-four seven, and Henry thought Rose might like to spend some time at the beach while they were in America. Like most of the coastline near the French Riviera, Bella-Moritz's beaches were covered in small pebbles instead of sand. Not so in Florida. The beach beyond Henry's terrace looked like an upturned bowl of sugar—fine white sand as far as the eye could see.

After their first full day at the park, they'd come back to the hotel and eaten room service on the balcony—a traditional American cheeseburger for Henry and chicken tenders shaped like stars for Rose, a delicacy she never would've had the opportunity to enjoy back in the palace.

Henry smiled to himself as he gathered the plates and silverware and piled them back on top of the room service tray. His feet ached from walking around the park all day. He had no idea how Lacey did it in faux glass slippers. But it had been a good day—no, a *great* day. Over dinner, Rose had mentioned her cheeks hurt from smiling so much.

"I'm ready for bed, Daddy," she said as she padded onto the terrace in her new Princess Sweet Pea pajamas and comically oversized hotel bathrobe, trailing behind her like the train on a queen's coronation mantle.

Henry bent to press a kiss to the top of her little head. She smelled like fresh soap and no-tears shampoo, which made his heart twist for some strange reason. "Good night and pleasant dreams, sweetheart."

"Good night, Daddy." She let out a wide yawn and turned to go back inside, a storybook dangling from her fingertips.

Henry paused for a beat and then followed. At the palace, he was often still in governmental meetings or attending royal social engagements this time of night. Most evenings, when he went to bid Rose goodnight, he either found her fast asleep or struggling to keep her eyes open so she wouldn't miss her bedtime kiss. "How about I read you that story?" he said, gesturing toward the slender book in her hands as she crawled onto one of the beds in their vast suite.

"Yes, please!" She hugged the book to her chest. "It's new. Princess Sweet Pea gave it to me for my birthday."

"Did she, now?" Henry had seen Princess Sweet Pea slip a flat, wrapped package into Rose's hands as they'd been leaving the park earlier, but at the time, Simon Dole had been busy shaking Henry's hand and checking to be sure they'd had a wonderful day in the Land Where Fairy Tales Come True.

Rose pointed at each word in the book's title and read it aloud. "The...Princess...and...the...Pea."

Henry felt himself smile.

Of course. What else would it be?

The book's slim gold spine cracked as he lifted the cover. Inside, Lacey had written an inscription to Rose in swirly pink lettering.

Sweetest Rose,

Wishing you a birthday filled with dreams come true.

Love, Princess Sweet Pea

Rose traced the handwriting with the tip of her finger, and Henry's chest felt as though it were being squeezed in a vise. How was it a woman they'd known for only two days had made such a profound impression on his daughter?

Henry frowned to himself. Who was he kidding? Lacey had made quite an impression on *both* of them.

He cleared his throat and began reading. "Once upon a time, in a kingdom far, far away, there lived a handsome prince."

"Just like you, Daddy," Rose said, burrowing further into the covers.

Henry turned the page. "But the prince was—" his voice cracked, "—very, very lonely." He hadn't seen that coming, nor the empty feeling in the pit of his stomach as he'd read the words out loud.

"Are you lonely, Daddy?" Rose peered up at him, her blue eyes huge in her dainty face.

Yes.

The word nearly tumbled right out of his mouth before he could stop it.

"Not right now, sweetheart. How could I be lonely when

we're here together?" He pressed the tiny furrow in his daughter's brow with a gentle touch of his finger.

She nodded, but didn't appear convinced. "This story is about a prince searching for his perfect princess. Did you know that?"

Sort of? He mostly remembered the part about the pea. But he was beginning to think that reading Rose a bedtime story hadn't been such a brilliant idea, after all. "Let's see how it turns out, shall we?" He forced a smile.

Coward.

"Okay." Rose nodded and focused her attention back on the story book.

He moved on to the next page, where the prince indeed embarked on a journey to find the perfect princess, because "only a real princess would do," which seemed rather snobbish to Henry. But he refrained from dwelling on that fact, lest Rose ask more questions. Her comments were beginning to feel like a thinly veiled commentary on his own life rather than the fairy tale at hand.

"The prince met many princesses, but in his heart, none of them seemed right to the prince," Henry read.

He paused again as Lacey's generous smile flitted through his mind. How was it that he felt more himself around her than any other woman he'd ever met, when Lacey was playing a fictional part? Their entire interaction had been based on make-believe.

It defied logic. Henry didn't know anything about the real Lacey, did he? All he knew was a princess persona that wasn't even real.

Except every now and then, he caught a glimpse of the woman behind the ball gown and the white satin gloves— like when they'd shared a sleigh together on Snow Queen Mountain and when she'd been so eager to leave the royal group behind to go talk to Molly at the swan boats. As much as Henry didn't want to admit it, those tiny glimmers of reality had left him longing to know more.

When he started reading again, his voice sounded rusty—even to his own ears—as if he hadn't used it in a long, long time. "So the prince returned to his kingdom with a heavy heart..."

He swallowed, and it was a relief when Rose's breathing became heavy and her little chest lifted and fell with the steady rhythm of sleep.

Because even though Henry was pretty sure he knew how this story ended, he simply wasn't quite ready to turn the page.

CHAPTER EIGHT

Faster Than a Spinning Teacup

THE FOLLOWING MORNING AT ONCE Upon A Time began with The Ugly Duckling's Boat Parade, a grand procession of boats that wound its way through the Swan Princess River. Every boat in the flotilla was duck-themed, laden with colorful feathers and sparkling, golden eggs, except for the final watercraft, which was, of course, a beautiful white swan with enormous outstretched wings.

Lacey had arranged for her regal guests to watch the parade from a platform at the top of Jack's Towering Beanstalk, a twisty, multi-level treehouse flush with climbing ivy and dripping with Spanish moss. The tiptop of the attraction overlooked the river, affording park-goers a perfect view of the parade. Rose was mesmerized, and she and Ian had a contest going to see who could most accurately count the number of golden eggs aboard the various boats.

"My lips are sealed," Lacey said, pretending to zip her mouth closed.

Was it her imagination, or did Henry's gaze flit briefly to her lips? She felt herself blush, all the way from her tiara to the toes of her glass slippers.

"Don't give any hints." Ian wagged his finger. "At the end of the parade, Rose and I will make our guesses, and you can let us know who came the closest to spotting all the eggs."

Lacey crossed her heart with a sweep of her Cinderella hands. "You have my solemn word."

"I see one!" Rose squealed, pointing at a white duck boat with a huge yellow beak covered in bright yellow Gerbera daisies as it made its way down the river. A glittery golden egg was tucked beneath one of its wings.

"Very good, Princess Rose," Lacey said.

Henry leaned forward and advised his daughter in a stage whisper. "Perhaps you shouldn't announce every egg you see, in case Ian doesn't notice it. You could be helping him cheat."

Ian gasped in mock outrage. "I wouldn't dare."

Henry arched a brow.

Ian smirked and directed his gaze back toward the boats, floating serenely below.

Lacey loved the way they seemed like an ordinary family—even Ian, who wasn't technically related to Henry and Rose, but had clearly worked in the palace for many years. Every once in a while, she almost forgot they were royal—emphasis on *almost*. Every time she met Henry's gaze, she heard Ava's voice booming in the back of her head.

You like *him.*

And then Lacey would remember Henry lived in a real castle with real servants who didn't run around wearing bunny ears like hers did. *Reality check.*

The castle in Bella-Moritz probably had dozens, if not hundreds, of footmen, and they no doubt wore fancy uniforms instead of bunny ears. Lacey didn't know a thing about Henry's kingdom, except that it looked like the sort of dreamy location where Grace Kelly would've driven along a rocky seaside cliff in a vintage convertible with Cary Grant in the passenger seat as a fluttery pink scarf trailed behind her in the wind. Okay, yes, maybe Lacey had watched a few too many Grace Kelly movies with her mom when she'd been bedridden during Lacey's childhood.

And maybe, just *maybe,* Lacey had looked up Bella-Moritz on the internet after she'd gotten home from her power walk the night before. But that had purely been for research purposes. It only made sense to know a little bit about her guests, didn't it?

Keep telling yourself that, commoner.

Lacey stared intently at the boats winding their way down the river.

"You look awfully introspective all of a sudden," Henry said in his undeniably regal-sounding, princely accent.

Lacey turned to glance at him and noticed Ian and Rose had moved to stand along the railing at the edge of the beanstalk's upper terrace. She and Henry were out of earshot, alone together at opposite ends of a bench designed to look like a giant, twisted green stem. "Oh." She gave him a wobbly smile. "I was just thinking about my mom."

He slid a bit nearer, lessening the wide gap between them. "Do your parents live here in Fort Lauderdale?"

If he'd been anyone but Prince Henry, Lacey would've found a way to deflect his question and ask about his family instead. Talking about her mom always felt a little bittersweet, even after all this time.

But knowing what she did about Henry and the loss of Rose's mother, she couldn't do that now.

"Um, no. My dad and my stepmom live in Dallas, where I grew up." She swallowed. "And my mom passed away from Leukemia when I was seven."

"I'm so sorry, Lacey. I wouldn't have asked if I'd known."

Henry rested his hand on hers with a featherlight touch.

Goosebumps broke out over Lacey's arm beneath her satin gloves. She didn't dare move. "No need to apologize. It was a long time ago."

Neither of them said anything for a minute or two, but it suddenly seemed like they were in their own little world among the cheery noise and hoopla of the boat parade. Lacey's heart thump thump thumped in her chest.

Sharing such a personal part of herself with Henry should've felt surreal. He was a prince, and here she was, telling him things about herself that she normally only shared with her closest friends. Not to mention the fact that she was flagrantly violating theme park rules by breaking character.

But the more time Lacey spent with him, the harder it was to keep pretending to be someone she wasn't. He treated her like a person, not a character. And the way he looked at her sometimes made her breath bottle up in her throat. Playing make-believe had never seemed quite so real before.

Say something.

Henry dragged his hand away from hers, until just their pinky fingers were touching.

Lacey cleared her throat. "I think that's one of the reasons Rose and I get along so well."

Had she really just said that? It seemed horribly intrusive, but was she supposed to sit there and pretend she hadn't seen that famous photograph of Henry and Rose? Doing so would've felt disingenuous. It seemed better to just acknowledge the elephant in the room.

Henry nodded slowly, and Lacey felt compelled to keep talking to fill the loaded silence. "Losing my mom is actually what inspired me to be a theme park princess."

His eyes met hers, and her insides immediately tumbled like she was on a tilt-a-whirl. For a pretend princess and a real prince on holiday, this moment was beginning to seem far too real.

He angled his head closer, so close that she could see tiny flecks of gold in his blue irises beneath the brim of his baseball cap disguise. "How so?"

"She was sick for a long time before she passed away, in and out of the hospital for almost a year. My dad and I spent a lot of time there, and on Fridays, princesses from a local theme park would come visit the hospital playroom."

A warm glow filled Lacey, like it always did when she thought back on those rare glimmers of happiness during such a confusing and difficult time.

"I was enraptured. Those stolen moments with the princesses every week made me believe everything would be okay in the end. They were always so cheery and kind, and they told me I was beautiful and strong and that even the saddest stories eventually had happy endings." Lacey gave Henry a lopsided smile. "And I believed every word. Those princesses might've been pretend, but they were a ray of light to me when I needed one most. I like to think I can do the same for guests here at Once Upon A Time."

Henry's gaze bore into hers until his mouth curved into a smile that reached all the way to his eyes.

Lacey's pulse fluttered in her throat. "I know it probably seems silly to someone like you, but—"

"No, not at all." He shook his head. "It seems lovely. I can't think of a better reason to be a princess—the theme park sort or any other variety."

Lacey went all fizzy inside.

"Really and truly?" she asked in her Sweet Pea voice.

"Really and truly," Henry said, and the softness in his tone made her head spin.

His hand moved closer to hers again, and just when Lacey thought he was about to weave his fingers through hers, a gravelly voice boomed from the nearby loudspeakers.

Fee-fi-fo-fum!

The huge, man-made beanstalk began to shake.

Henry looked so alarmed that Lacey couldn't help but laugh. "Don't worry. That's just the giant."

Henry glanced over his shoulder. "He's not about to grind my bones to make his bread, is he?"

Ah, so the prince was well-versed in fairy tales. How adorable was that? If Lacey had been standing, she would've definitely been weak in the knees. "You can rest easy. It's just a special effect that happens up here every hour on the hour." She winked.

"Daddy, I heard the giant!" Rose scampered back toward the bench with Ian trailing behind her. "Did you hear him?"

"I think they heard the giant all the way back in Bella-Moritz," Henry said.

"No, they didn't." Rose giggled.

Henry stood and stretched his arms over his head, Frankenstein-style, and began chasing Rose around the terrace. "Fee-fi-fo-fum!"

They'd been plunged back into the land of make-believe, but a rebellious piece of Lacey's heart lingered in the real world with a real prince and real feelings she couldn't wish away.

No matter very how hard she tried.

After the parade, Henry and his group followed Lacey down Jack's Towering Beanstalk, back to the cobblestone promenade of the park. For lunch, they feasted on something called sausage-on-a-stick at a wood-paneled tavern straight out of Beauty and the Beast. It seemed as if most theme park food came served on some sort of skewer, which Henry rather liked—even if Lacey seemed amused when he'd ordered seconds.

After lunch, with the Florida sun high in the robin's egg-blue sky, Rose's round little face became flushed, and Lacey suggested they cool themselves off with a ride on The Three Billy Goats Gruff Wild Water Crossing. They followed colorful signs held aloft by sparkly fairy wings pointing in the direction of the attraction. Rows of carnival games lined either side of the pathway, where giant stuffed animals hung from the ceiling, waiting to be claimed as prizes. Players tossed footballs through hanging tires and threw darts at a wall of colorful balloons, lined up in the happy hues of the rainbow.

Not one person gawked at Henry. For once, he could walk through a crowd of people without being met with endless requests for selfies or having his every move recorded on cell phone videos. Henry was the center of attention everywhere he went in Bella-Moritz. Here, in this place where people came to feel like kings and queens, Henry reveled in being just a regular nobody. A dad. A man...

A man who was starting to remember what it felt like to be drawn to a beautiful woman, even if that woman's job was to dress up as a cartoon version of his very real existence. He couldn't seem to stop looking at her, and every time Rose snagged the seat next to Lacey on a ride, his chest ached. Henry had forgotten how tortuous attraction could be. It seemed he'd forgotten a lot of things in recent years.

Just as the swishing waters of the Billy Goat ride came into view in the distance, Lacey paused. She looked up at Henry, and warmth spread through him. "Did you hear that?"

He glanced around. "Hear what, exactly?" They were surrounded by all manner of sounds and unique noises that made up the very specific soundtrack of a theme park—the clanging of ride chains, the whoosh of rollercoasters, happy screams, lilting music streaming from speakers overhead and, above all, laughter. He had no idea which one she could possibly be referring to.

"That chirping sound." Lacey's brow knitted, then she bent down to inspect a small grassy area beside the spot where they were standing.

Rose followed her, of course, imitating Lacey's exact posturing. "Look!" His daughter pointed a finger toward a tiny, squirming, feathery lump in the lush green grass. "It's a bird."

Lacey gasped. "A hummingbird! See its long, narrow beak. It looks like a needle."

Henry and Ian exchanged a glance. Was this real, or some sort of the theme park magic? Henry honestly didn't know.

He crouched down beside Rose for a closer look. It was a hummingbird, all right—a real one, with green feathers and cherry-red coloring on its throat.

"He's got something stuck on one of his wings." Lacey pointed to a tiny wad of pink at the tip of the bird's feathers.

"I think it might be gum," Ian said.

"Oh, no." Rose peered up at Lacey. "We should help him."

"Of course we should," Lacey said. Then she dropped to her knees, and her ballgown puffed up around her like frosting on a cupcake.

A crowd began gathering around them. Henry's body tensed. He kept his head down and pulled his baseball cap low over his eyes.

"I don't think you have anything to worry about," Ian murmured, barely loud enough for Henry to hear him. "They're not here for you. They're here for her."

Henry glanced over his shoulder. Ian was right. Every set of eyes in the vicinity was trained on Lacey, awestruck by her handling of the delicate bird. She gently went to work disentangling the gum from short blades of grass until she was able to cradle the tiny creature in the palms of her hands.

Henry couldn't tear his gaze away from her graceful

hands. The tenderness in her touch made his throat grow thick.

"Here, can you hold him while I the gum off his wing?" Lacey angled her head toward Henry as if asking him to hold onto a hummingbird was an everyday occurrence.

He held out his hand. "Of course."

The colorful bird was as light as air, and Henry held his breath, worried about hurting the little guy. But his new feathered friend stayed perfectly still, tiny black eyes fixed on Henry's.

"He's so cute," Rose whispered.

"Isn't he, though?" Lacey said, gently prying the bits of chewing gum from the bird's wing. "Let's see if he's good to fly again, and if not, we can take him to the first aid station and see about getting him to a veterinarian."

Once free, the hummingbird rolled to his feet, blinked, and then sprang from Henry's outstretched hand, flying in a buzzy loop de loop over their heads before disappearing.

Lacey stood and shielded her eyes with her hands, looking up into the sky as Rose cheered.

"Wow," Ian said.

"That was—" Henry paused, swallowing. "That was really something."

"Like I said." Lacey grinned at him over her shoulder. "Always make friends with birds and butterflies."

Henry's heart leaped inside his chest.

Who was this woman? And where did the make-believe character end and the real Lacey begin?

Shortly after the impromptu hummingbird rescue, Henry found himself strapped into a hollowed-out log with Ian situated behind him and Rose and Lacey seated directly in front of him.

As the log meandered slowly down a stream of impossibly bright turquoise water, Henry's gaze kept shifting from the banks of the meadow on either side of the log to the back of Lacey's head. Her buttery-blond hair was fashioned in its usual updo, swept off her graceful neck with soft tendrils framing her face. One of the pins holding her enormous crown in place was poking out just a little, and Henry had the completely inappropriate urge to tuck it back into place.

He balled his hands into fists in his lap to keep himself from doing so. He'd already almost held her hand in plain view of everyone on Jack's beanstalk—just the sort of mistake he knew better than to make. He wasn't sure what had come over him all of a sudden or when exactly he'd begun to consider Lacey more of a friend than someone who'd been ordered to be his companion for the duration of his stay in America. All Henry knew was that her story about why she'd become Princess Sweet Pea had moved him and made him feel things he hadn't known he was capable of anymore.

You're a prince. You can't be attracted to a woman who, for all practical purposes, is in your employ.

That was the very definition of un-princely behavior, wasn't it? Henry was pretty certain it was.

The log swished beneath a waterfall, spraying Henry and the rest of the group with water. It was cool against his skin, a relief from the warm Florida sun. He didn't have time to dwell on the pleasant sensation for long before his attention was dragged to more urgent matters, such as a fierce-looking troll that lunged toward their log as they passed beneath a rickety bridge. The clip-clop sound of billy goat hooves crossing the bridge echoed overhead.

At the front of the log, Rose let out a squeal, and then Lacey wrapped her arms around his daughter as they tumbled down a steep drop. The ride ended with an enormous splash, drenching almost everyone aboard—especially Ian, who got the brunt of the tidal wave, thanks to his seat at the back of the ride.

They scrambled out of the log and back onto dry ground. Tiny droplets of water were caught in the delicate tulle of Lacey's dress, glittering like diamonds in the bright summer sunshine. Miraculously, she didn't have a hair out of place. Ian's soaked athletic shoes sloshed with every step he took.

Henry did his best to swallow his laughter as Ian pushed wet hair from his face.

"At least I'm no longer hot," Ian said, arching an eyebrow at Henry. "And I'm not sure what you're laughing at, considering you just lost your precious baseball cap."

Henry froze in his tracks and reached for the brim of his disguise, but Ian was right. His cap was no longer there.

"Oh, no." Lacey's white-gloved hand flew to her mouth. "It must've flown off on the drop after the bridge."

Henry glanced back toward the ride, half hoping to find his hat bobbing nearby in the water. No such luck.

"Don't worry. There are souvenir stands all over the place. Surely we can find you something suitable." Lacey turned to gesture toward a kiosk farther down the path but stopped and bit back a smile.

The cart contained row after row of royal-themed head coverings, from oversized, plush purple king's crowns with faux ermine trim to plastic knight's helmets and replicas of Princess Sweet Pea's elaborate tiara.

Lacey cringed. "As far as disguises go, I don't suppose any of those would be effective."

"I think not," Henry said, raking back his damp hair. "Let's not worry about it. I'm sure we'll stumble upon something."

Rose skipped toward the next closest ride—the spinning teacups. If Henry's baseball cap had managed to survive the log ride, it definitely would've been a casualty of the centrifugal force of a whirling china cup. Rose turned the wheel in the center of their teacup as fast as her dainty arms could, and when Lacey pitched in, Henry began to regret his second sausage-on-a-stick.

Blessedly, the whimsical music faded and the ride ended while the contents of his stomach were still intact. Rose, however, was ready for more.

"Can we go again?" She bounced on her toes, spinning in circles on the pavement just outside the lime-green iron gates of teacup territory.

"Already?" Lacey said, sounding a bit wobbly.

Henry shook his head. "Why don't we take a break for bit, sweetheart?"

"It's okay. I'll take her. I think all the spinning is helping me to wring out. Why don't you two do something a bit tamer?" Ian said, as his gaze flitted over Henry's right shoulder.

Henry turned to see a tall, white Ferris wheel looming behind him, turning gently to a lyrical piano tune.

"Rapunzel's Fantastical Ferris Wheel. It's definitely tame," Lacey said, and then her perfect princess smile slipped a bit. "But if you'd rather not, we don't have to—"

"No, let's do it. That sounds—" Henry cleared his throat. *Lovely,* he'd almost said. *It sounds absolutely lovely.* He shouldn't say such things, though, should he? Not when they might hint at the feelings he was beginning to have for her. "Like a great idea."

Rose was already tugging Ian back toward the line for the teacups.

"See you soon," Ian said, flashing Henry a wink.

He'd wondered why his protection officer seemed so eager to give him a few minutes of freedom. Now it seemed as if Ian was trying to add royal matchmaker to his resumé.

Lacey and I are friends, Henry reminded himself. Maybe if he kept dwelling on that fact, he wouldn't keep crushing on her like a schoolboy. He didn't have a clue if she was attracted to him or not. She was supposed to be at his beck and call, so of course her face lit up every time their eyes met. It didn't necessarily mean anything.

But then Lacey smiled at him, and he became hyper-aware of his heartbeat in a way that didn't feel altogether friendly. "We should get some cotton candy," she said, floating in her puffy gown toward a pink stand with a striped awning situated near the entrance to the Ferris wheel.

Henry followed and stood beside her, watching a man dressed in an old-fashioned barber shop quartet-style costume spin a puff of cotton candy on a rolled paper cone.

"More food on a stick." Henry nodded. "I'm in."

Laughter leaped in Lacey's big brown doe eyes. "It's peppermint-flavored. It'll calm your stomach after the teacups."

"This sounds like something only a theme park princess would know."

She wiggled her eyebrows. "Just one of the perks of the job."

Juggling their newly acquired cotton candy in one hand, Henry used his other to help Lacey into one of the Ferris wheel's gondolas. Once she and her dress were all tucked in, he slid onto the narrow bench seat beside her. The door shut with a click, and they lifted a few feet off the ground and hung suspended in the air while the couple behind them in line climbed into next gondola.

On and on it went, until the lilting piano music started up again and the ride began to turn, ever so slowly—a graceful white wheel against the pinkening light of the evening sky.

Down below, the park shimmered in a whirl of color, spinning rides and flashing lights. As the Ferris wheel carried them higher and higher up, it all blended together like a watercolor painting.

"It's so quiet up here," Henry said in a near whisper.

"It is, isn't it?" Lacey plucked a bit of cotton candy

between her finger and thumb and let it melt on her tongue.

Henry followed her example. A rush of sweet peppermint filled his mouth, and then the candy floss vanished.

"I have to thank you, you know." Lacey grinned. "It's been a while since I've had a chance to enjoy the park like this. The past couple of days have been so much fun."

Warmth filled Henry's chest. "Please. I should be the one thanking you. Last night, Rose told me this has been the best birthday she's ever had."

"Did she really?"

"Yes, but she didn't need to. It's been obvious. She's having a ball. This trip has been a happy break from her royal life."

Lacey tilted her head and regarded him over the puff of cotton candy. "What's her life back in Bella-Moritz like? Does she attend regular school with other children?"

"Yes." Henry gave a firm nod. *For now, at least.* "I try to give her as normal a childhood as possible, but I've been working a lot lately. I haven't spent as much time with her these past few years as I should."

"She adores you, though. Surely you know that." Lacey regarded him. "Are you sure you're not being too hard on yourself?"

"Possibly, but she's been having an especially hard time lately. I thought it was time for us to take a little break together." Henry's eyes flickered to Lacey and then back to the horizon, where a blazing sunset was spreading across the sky.

He knew he should stop talking. He'd probably already said too much, but it felt good to share a part of himself with Lacey, especially after she'd told him about her childhood.

"The Bella-Moritz Flower Festival is in less than two weeks. It's a very important annual event for our country, with a royal ball and a special procession. This year, it's also Rose's royal debut. She's expected to ride her pony in the parade, and it's not going so well." He sighed and met Lacey's gaze again. "She fell off a horse last year and broke her arm. Since then, she'd been struggling with her riding lessons."

Her princess-y smile slipped. "Oh, no. Poor thing. And wow, two weeks isn't very much time."

Henry shook his head. "It's not. I can only hope when we go home the day after tomorrow, she'll feel refreshed and ready to give it a try."

"That's right. Tomorrow's your last day at the park." Lacey bit her lip. "It's gone by rather fast, hasn't it?"

Henry nodded.

Faster than a spinning teacup.

But he didn't want to think about what little time he had left in America—not now. He felt as light as air, pirouetting in the twilight with this most unusual princess by his side. For once, he just wanted to live in the moment.

So he smiled, sat back, and did his best to simply enjoy what was left of the ride.

CHAPTER NINE

Cotton Candy Dreams

"Do people still have pen pals?" Lacey asked Ava later that night as she chopped lettuce for the salad they were making for dinner.

Ava looked up from the bell pepper she was cutting into slender pieces. "You mean the old-fashioned kind? Like, actual letters?"

"Yes."

"I suppose so." Ava scraped the bell pepper into the large wooden salad bowl on the kitchen counter and reached for a tomato. "Why do you ask?"

"I just thought exchanging letters might be nice if people still did that sort of thing." Lacey shrugged. Something about the fact that she was considering communicating with a person who lived in a palace seemed to mandate pretty stationery and crisp, thick envelopes.

Ava stopped chopping to peer at her. Her eyes narrowed. "Might this proposed pen pal be a royal prince?"

"No, don't be silly. I'm sure Henry is far too busy for that sort of thing." Lacey scooped a handful of lettuce into the salad bowl.

Ava gasped. "You called him Henry! Not Prince Henry, but just plain Henry."

There isn't anything remotely plain about him, Lacey thought as her face went warm. "He asked me to call him that. He's trying to fly under the radar, remember? Anyway, I was actually thinking about writing letters to Rose."

"Aw." Ava tilted her head and smiled. "That's really sweet, Lace."

"She's such a sweet little girl. I know she's royal, but I can relate to what she's going though, you know?" Lacey's chopping slowed.

Rose was such a spirited child. Lacey had loved spending time with her these past few days...Henry too. They might've gotten off to a rocky start, but now Grumpy Baseball Cap's impending departure was looming over her head like one of Florida's infamous thunderstorms.

It was raining right now, in fact. The sky had opened up shortly after Lacey and Henry had ridden the Ferris wheel together. Lacey's Sweet Pea costume was currently hanging from the shower curtain rod, dripping onto the towel-covered bathroom floor.

She was going to have to do something about the wet ballgown after dinner. She might even have to blow dry the tulle skirt, but Lacey couldn't think about that right now. Tomorrow was Henry and Rose's last day at Once Upon A Time. Lacey wanted to make it extra special, but she wasn't sure how.

"I'll bet if you asked her, she'd love to exchange letters with you after she goes back to Bella-Moritz." Ava grabbed a bottle of rosé from the refrigerator and started working to remove the cork.

"I wish we had horseback riding at the park," Lacey

heard herself say.

"Horseback riding?" The cork popped and Ava reached for two wine glasses from the cabinet. "It's probably the one thing we *don't* have at Once Upon A Time. Why?"

"No reason in particular. It was just a thought." Lacey focused intently on her head of lettuce, which by now, was practically shredded on her cutting board.

She didn't want to betray Henry's confidence, but she couldn't stop thinking about Rose's pony problem. It must've been really weighing on him if he'd brought his daughter all the way to America to give her a break.

A few days away was probably just what Rose needed. People usually came home from vacations feeling relaxed and de-stressed, didn't they? That was what Lacey always heard, anyway. Other than quick trips to Dallas to visit her dad and stepmom, it had been years since she'd taken an actual vacation. She always joked that she worked at one of the world's most popular vacation spots, so why would she want to go anyplace else?

Lacey had never even gotten around to going away for a romantic weekend trip with Mark. They'd talked about it all the time, and Mark frequently traveled for work and often went on trips with his family, but something had always come up that had prevented Lacey from tagging along. Yet another red flag she should've spotted from a mile away. If she'd really wanted a weekend away with Mark, she could've found a way to make it happen. Lacey had loads of accumulated vacation time at work that she'd never used.

It was strange how easily Mark had slid right out of her life. She'd hardly thought about him at all the past few days, and already, the thought of Henry leaving and going back to Bella-Moritz made her feel a little panicky deep inside.

All along she'd been telling herself not to get attached, and she'd gone and done it anyway. This was why there were rules against breaking character. If she'd managed to stick to her Princess Sweet Pea role instead of letting Henry get to know the real her, she probably wouldn't be worrying about Rose and her pony or dreading their last day at Once Upon A Time.

But she couldn't quite bring herself to regret a thing.

"I guess we sort of have a horse." Ava sipped her wine and handed Lacey a glass filled halfway to the top with blush-colored liquid.

Lacey swirled her glass and laughed. "How so?"

"Well, we've got a donkey suit in the costume department. It got retired when Once Upon A Time discontinued the Pinocchio ride." Ava gave a little shudder. "Rightfully so, in my opinion. That attraction was straight-up terrifying."

"Not the same. At. All." Lacey shook her head. "Donkeys aren't horses, and I'm talking about *riding* them, not dressing up like one."

If the park offered horseback riding, she might be able to help Rose get over whatever anxiety she had about her pony. The little girl liked to imitate everything Lacey did. She'd worn her Princess Sweet Pea costume every day, and it seemed as if she'd been practicing the fine art of Cinderella hands. When Lacey picked up her skirt to step onto a ride, so did Rose. When Lacey curtseyed, Rose curtseyed. She ordered the same snacks and meals when they stopped for lunch, and except for the few times Lacey had ended up seated beside Henry on park rides, Rose was always nestled right next to her. If only Lacey had access to a horse, she might've been able to help Henry with his dilemma.

"I've got it!" Ava pointed at Lacey with her wine glass. "The carousel."

Lacey gasped. "The carousel!"

Once Upon A Time's Fairy Tale Carousel sat on the far right side of the park, kitty-corner from the Ferris wheel she'd ridden with Henry. Since it wasn't located anywhere near Ever After Castle, and park guests tended to favor more modern attractions over the carousel's quaint, old-fashioned simplicity, Lacey sometimes forgot about it.

"The carousel totally has horses." Ava grinned in triumph.

"It does, doesn't it?" Lacey nodded.

A few years ago, the park had even had all the carousel horses restored by a special preservationist. Before the ride had found its home at Once Upon A Time, it'd been an attraction at one of the oldest state fairs in the country. When the theme park had opened, it purchased the carousel and had it moved from New England all the way to Florida. The graceful horses that bobbed up and down on the carousel's brass poles had been carved from smooth mahogany way back in the early 1900s. They were gorgeous—hand-painted with painstaking, whimsical details and buffed until they shone like sparkly bits of confetti.

Best of all—they were completely non-threatening.

"Ava, you're a genius." Lacey clinked her wine glass against her friend's. "You've just given me an idea for the perfect way to end Rose and Henry's trip."

If she was going to have to say goodbye, she could at least do it in fanciful-theme-park-princess style.

Rain beat down on the windows in Henry's suite at the Ritz-Carlton. The leafy palm trees that surrounded the hotel's infinity pool overlooking the Atlantic Ocean fluttered madly in the wind. Every few minutes, swollen gray clouds boomed, and flashes of lightning stretched from sky to sea.

Lacey had warned him Florida was known for its summer thunderstorms—a function of the state being surrounded by water on almost every side. The rain had started up mere minutes after their Ferris wheel ride, once again preventing Rose from seeing Once Upon A Time's nightly fireworks display.

She still has one more chance, Henry thought as another boom of thunder rattled the windows.

Dramatic rainstorms were almost unheard of in Bella-Moritz, outside the French Riviera's tropical cyclone season. The weather was usually mild in Henry's modest little kingdom, in keeping with the principality's reputation as a picturesque summer paradise. Bella-Moritz was best known for its rocky, jagged cliffs overlooking vivid turquoise waters dotted with houseboats and its charming, hillside pastel cottages. Like Florida, it boasted an abundant amount of palm trees. They lined either side of the wide avenue that stretched from Grand Flower Park to the palace. On the night of the royal ball, twinkle lights were strung from palm tree to palm tree, crisscrossing their way to the castle.

Henry watched the storm churn the deep blue sea, feeling every bit as tossed about as the lawn furniture on the deck of the infinity pool.

Tomorrow was their last day, which would've been fine, if not for the fact that a certain phrase from Rose's bedtime story keep dancing through Henry's thoughts.

So the prince returned to his kingdom with a heavy heart...

His jaw clenched. Why was he letting a children's book mess with his head so much?

"Daddy, it's not going to rain tomorrow, is it?" Rose said, blinking at the scene outside the window with concern etched in her dainty features.

"I don't think so, sweetheart. Tomorrow is supposed to be bright and sunny all day long." Henry lifted his daughter into his arms and squeezed her tight. Fresh from yet another bubble bath, she was dressed in her Sweet Pea pajamas again and had a book pressed to her chest. He knew without asking exactly which storybook it was. "You're not worried about missing out on your last day at the park, are you?"

She nodded, and her damp hair brushed against Henry's cheek.

He pressed a kiss to the top of her head. "Don't you worry. We have another fun day planned, and we won't let anything stop it. Our trip isn't over."

Yet.

Rose yawned and rubbed at her eyes with her free hand.

"It looks like someone is ready for bed," Henry said as he set her back down.

The toes of her bare feet wiggled, and she held the book out toward him. "Can you read more of the story to me? Please?"

"Absolutely."

Henry tucked the book under his arm and followed Rose as she dashed toward the big bed where she'd been sleeping during their stay. Her bedroom in the suite was situated directly opposite Henry's. If he was really still, he could sometimes hear her at night, shifting beneath the covers or breathing softly in her sleep. It was such a stark contract to the palace, with its expansive hallways and thick, heavy walls.

He liked being close to his daughter like this. He told himself it was because he wanted Rose to feel a little bit less isolated, less lonely. But sometimes he wondered if he was the one who missed having someone he loved so near.

"Do you remember where we left off?" he asked as he settled beside Rose on the downy white duvet and she rested her head against his shoulder.

Rose flipped through the book until she landed on the page with the illustration of the forlorn prince, back in his lonely castle after his fruitless search for the perfect princess to marry.

"Right. That's the one," Henry said, sighing. "Let's see what happens next." He turned the page. "One night, a terrifying storm settled upon the kingdom. Lightning crackled in the sky, and dark clouds poured buckets of rain onto the royal castle."

Henry glanced at the windows overlooking the choppy sea. Thunder rolled in the distance while Rose flipped to the next page. He reminded himself—again—that the story was only a fairy tale, not any sort of commentary on his personal life. But he could've done without the more striking similarities.

He continued reading. A princess showed up at the castle in the middle of the rainstorm, because of course she did. The royal household invited her inside, even though she looked more like a drowned rat than royalty. The prince took an immediate liking to the dripping-wet stranger, but the queen wanted to make sure she was indeed a "real" princess.

"Look, she put a pea in the princess's bed." Rose pointed to a drawing of a tiny pea being placed on the mattress.

The next page showed the queen heaping twenty more mattresses plus twenty feather beds on top of the pea, which definitely seemed like overkill to Henry. But of course, the following morning, the princess woke up black and blue from the offending pea, which had caused her a terrible night's sleep, despite the abundance of cushioning.

"The prince was delighted and asked her to marry him right away, because he knew he'd at last found his real princess," Henry read.

"Her dress is pink, just like Princess Sweet Pea's," Rose said, tracing the illustration of the royal newlyweds with the tip of her pointer finger.

"Indeed it is." Henry nodded and felt a nonsensical stirring deep inside his chest. "That's because this is Princess Sweet Pea's story."

"So Princess Sweet Pea is a real princess, just like me," Rose said without an ounce of doubt in her tone.

Henry swallowed. How the heck was he supposed to

respond to that? "There are a lot of things that make someone a real princess," he finally said. "Things like bravery..." He was tempted to slip in a mention of Daisy the pony, but decided against it. They were still on holiday, and he didn't want to push—not yet and not here. "And kindness too. Like when you gave your crown away the other day. That was very kind."

Rose nodded against his chest. "Princess Sweet Pea is brave," she said in a sleepy voice. "She loves all the rides, even the scary ones."

Henry smiled to himself. "Yes, she does."

"And she's kind too," Rose murmured, finally letting her eyes drift shut.

"Very, very kind," Henry whispered.

He closed the story book and set it gently on Rose's night table. Rain pitter-pattered against the windows, and the moon cast shimmering light over the ocean. He wondered where Lacey was right then and what she was doing. The more she opened up to him, the more he wanted to know about her.

Henry crossed his feet at the ankles and made no move to slip out from beneath the soft weight of Rose's sleeping form. He wanted to suck all he could out this vacation—to make each moment last as long as possible. Maybe he'd close his eyes for just a minute...

And maybe he'd dream of cotton candy and peppermint and being lifted so high in the sky that he could no longer see his troubles waiting for him down below.

CHAPTER TEN

Gallant Is Just Part of His Job Description

THE SUN CAME UP THE following morning and bathed the shore in pale golden light, melting away all traces of the previous night's storm. Rose popped out of bed and zipped herself into her Sweet Pea costume before Henry managed to finish shaving. She was so anxious to get to back to the park that he practically had to tie her down in order for her to finish their breakfast of American-style pancakes and fresh Florida orange juice.

But before they left the room, she tore one of the croissants that had come with their room service order into tiny bits and arranged the crumbs in a neat row on the balcony railing. Just as she finished, a small sparrow sporting wings tipped with yellow plucked one of the torn pieces of bread from the railing. Rose turned toward Henry and her entire face lit up.

He had an expansive feeling in his chest as she tore another croissant into pieces, covering the railing from one end to the other.

Rule number one: always make friends with birds and butterflies.

Ian accompanied Henry and Rose to Once Upon A Time and, just as she had the day before, Lacey met them at the special VIP park entrance. As usual, she was in full theme-park-princess mode, with her elaborate Sweet Pea crown, white gloves, and billowing gown. Henry really should've been used to the sight of her by now, but something about her generous smile turned his knees to water.

He'd developed feelings for her over the past few days. There was no more denying it. His heart beat faster whenever she was near, and for the first time in his life, he'd begun to let his guard down. The anonymity the theme park afforded him had allowed him to drop his royal mask and be his true self—a luxury he hadn't experienced in years, if ever. He was going to miss that sense of freedom, but he was beginning to realize he was going to miss Lacey even more.

"Good morning," she said, greeting Rose with her customary Princess Sweet Pea curtsey.

Henry had lived in a palace his entire life, and he'd never witnessed as many curtseys as he had in the past few days. It was rather endearing.

Rose mirrored Lacey's greeting, and Lacey flashed her a wink.

"I have a special surprise for everyone this morning," Lacey said as she guided them through the white wrought-iron gate, decorated with elaborate swirls and scrollwork.

"A surprise?" Ian said, glancing at Henry. "That certainly sounds intriguing."

Rose reached for Lacey's hand. "I love surprises."

"Me too," Lacey said.

She led them down the wide promenade at the entrance of the park, toward the lush, green space where the words *Once Upon A Time* were spelled out in lavender, violet, and cherry-red chrysanthemums. The heady perfume of the flowers reminded Henry of home, and for a brief, fantastical moment, he wished he could show Lacey what Bella-Moritz was like this time of year. He wanted to walk with her through Grand Flower Park and watch her close her eyes and tip her face toward the warm Mediterranean sun. He wanted to tuck a daisy behind her ear. He wanted so many things, none of which were remotely possible.

Henry blinked hard and commanded himself to focus on the here and now and whatever surprise Lacey had up her glittery, puffy sleeves. Henry himself had never been overly fond of surprises, which he supposed was a result of his royal upbringing. Not only was everything in the palace meticulously planned, it had also been set in stone since what felt like the beginning of time. Nothing was as important to a royal court as tradition.

Henry's family had been a source of comfort and good will for the people of Bella-Moritz for thirty generations. In good times and bad, the monarchy had been a consistent, reliable presence in their quaint principality. The citizens knew they could count on the Chevaliers. The noble family stood for resilience, especially in times of stress or uncertainty. The economy in Europe had been turbulent lately. People weren't traveling as much they used to, and tourism was the backbone of Bella-Moritz. So far, they'd been fortunate enough to avoid any serious layoffs or unemployment. But people were scared, and if Henry and his family could make people forget their worries for a day by showing up with smiles on their faces and riding down the promenade toward the palace, then that was what they needed to do. Their traditions weren't about just going through the motions—they meant something.

Which was precisely why Rose riding in the royal procession was so important. God willing, there wouldn't be any surprises during that esteemed occasion. But for now,

Henry would do his best to embrace the joy of the unexpected. Rose was sure to love whatever Lacey had in mind.

It was Henry, though, who was rendered speechless by her surprise. At first, he saw what looked like a circus tent in the distance, a striped awning in pink and purple shades to match Ever After Castle. A gold flag perched at the very top. But as they moved closer, he spotted horses—so *many* beautifully carved, wooden horses—moving up and down on shiny brass poles. There were white horses, gray horses, brown, and black. Henry even saw a pink one, and they were all painted with whimsical flowers, streaming ribbons and tassels in every shade of the rainbow. No two were alike.

He slowed to a stop in front of the carousel, his throat growing thick with emotion. Lacey's special surprise couldn't have been a coincidence. This was intentional. He'd confided in her about Rose's fear of riding in the procession, and now she was trying to do what she could to help.

His heart jerked as his eyes met Lacey's. A look passed between them—some unspoken sentiment that wrapped around Henry like a blanket.

Lacey cleared her throat and crouched down to Rose's eye level. She took both of Rose's petite hands in hers. "Would you like to ride one of the carousel horses with me, Princess Rose? I thought it might be fun if we shared one and rode together."

Rose nodded, although she seemed a little more hesitant than she'd been on most of the other rides.

"The carousel has over ninety horses to choose from. You can pick whichever one you want. Why don't we take a look?" Lacey stood and waited for the carousel to grind to a stop before she walked onto its base, hand-in-hand in with Rose.

They wove in between rows of carousel horses pawing at the air, mid-prance. Following Lacey's lead, Rose ran her fingertips along their smooth, glossy backs.

Beside Henry, Ian nodded, a smile tipping his lips. "You told Princess Sweet Pea about Rose's difficulty with her riding lessons, didn't you?"

"Maybe," Henry said. "It's not a state secret."

"I know it's not. I'm surprised, though. You don't usually share that kind of thing with..." Ian's voice drifted off and his brow furrowed.

"With whom, exactly?" Henry lifted a brow.

"With anyone," Ian finally said. "It's about time you started opening up to someone. Other than your favorite protection officer, of course."

"Don't read anything into it," Henry said, unsure who he was trying to convince—Ian or himself. "It was just a conversation."

"Well, it certainly seems as if Princess Sweet Pea took it to heart." Ian jerked his head in the direction of the carousel, where Lacey was lifting Rose onto the back of a pale silver horse with painted pink ribbons woven through its mane and decorated with a huge wreath of red-and-pink roses around its neck. "That horse looks a little bit like Daisy, doesn't it?"

Henry nodded, not quite trusting himself to speak as Lacey climbed onto the horse behind Rose and wrapped her arms around his daughter's waist.

"Are you two going to join us?" Lacey called, beckoning to Ian and Henry with a wave.

"Wouldn't miss it," Ian said. He positioned himself astride a sleek black carousel horse with its head tossed back and tail held high.

Henry chose a snow-white horse right next to the gray one Lacey and Rose shared.

"Ready?" Lacey asked as the organ in the center of the carousel began to play and the horses slowly started bobbing up and down.

"Ready," Henry said. "Aren't we, sweetheart?"

He winked at Rose. She had a white-knuckle grip on her horse's brass poll, but as the ride began moving round and round, and as the carousel horses pranced in place, she gradually began to relax. Little by little.

Rose's big breakthrough came when the organ in the center of the carousal launched into a sonorous version of "Happy Birthday to You." Her eyes flew open wide and she gasped. Too stunned to remember to be afraid, she bounced on her carousel horse's back and swayed in time with the music, grinning from ear to ear.

They rode the carousel four times in total. By the end, Rose rode solo, and Lacey switched places to a pink horse just to the left of Henry's white steed. As the organ music wound down a final time, he caught Lacey looking at him with her head tilted and her eyebrows squished together.

"What?" Henry said, narrowing his gaze at her. "Is something wrong?"

"No. I just realized that you're—" she dropped her voice to a whisper, "—well, you're a *prince* and you're riding a white horse right now." Her bow-shaped lips tipped into a frown.

"Too cliché?" Henry asked, a smile tugging at the corner of his mouth.

"Not at all. Someone recently told me a prince wasn't about to come charging into my life on a white horse, and yet, here you are." Lacey blinked.

"Here I am," Henry said. He had a feeling there was more to the story, but she didn't seem to want to elaborate.

She cleared her throat. "It's kind of funny, don't you think?"

"I suppose it is," he said, although why would a person say such an insensitive thing to her? The thought of anyone hurting her feelings made every muscle in his body tense.

Lacey was kind—kinder than anyone he'd ever come across before, and after spending so much time with her these past few days, he could tell it wasn't just an act. She was beautiful, inside and out. Rose worshipped her, and her adoration didn't have a thing to do with Ever After Castle or the princess trappings. Rose was royal in her own right. It took more than a pretend castle and pretty dress to impress her. His daughter liked Lacey because Lacey understood her in a way no one had before. Lacey empathized with Rose. She genuinely cared about people. She'd taken the time to help a tiny little bird. Who *did* that sort of thing?

He slid off his horse and helped Lacey down from hers while Ian made sure Rose disembarked safely. Lacey placed her hand in Henry's and landed on the platform of the carousel in a swish of tulle and satin.

He gave her hand a gentle squeeze and held it until she met his gaze. "I can't thank you enough for this," he said quietly. Words seemed inadequate.

"All in a day's work," she said, eyes glimmering with tiny bits of light from the carousel.

When they'd talked on the Ferris wheel the night before, he'd simply been unburdening himself in a rare, unguarded moment. Lacey had been so open with him, so willing to let him get to know the real her. Henry had wanted to do the same.

He'd never expected her to try to help Rose want to ride her horse. He'd never expected a lot of things he'd felt or experienced in the past few days. He'd never expected *her*.

Henry had been a prince his entire life, white horse and all, but it had taken a story book princess in a plastic crown to make him realize surprises weren't so bad, after all.

Lacey never should've said what she did about Henry and his white horse. She'd wanted to reel the words back in the very moment they'd flown out of her mouth.

What had she been thinking? He probably thought she had some bizarre Cinderella complex or something—as if the ballgown, the tiara, and glass slippers weren't already evidence enough.

She'd been so struck by the sight of him sitting on that white carousel stallion, though. The memory of what Mark had said to her on the night of their breakup had nearly knocked her off her own wooden horse. If Lacey hadn't known better, she would've thought maybe fate had tossed Henry into her path.

That was crazy, though. She was Henry's glorified tour guide, a grown woman who played dress-up for a living. Fate was probably laughing its head off right now.

The morning had been such a success up until the moment she'd put her foot in her mouth. Lacey had had doubts at first, particularly as Rose had gone quiet when she'd realized Lacey wanted her to ride one of the colorful horses. But by the time her first turn on the carousel was over, the little princess had been happy and smiling. Lacey had no clue if Rose would feel any better about riding her pony when she returned to Bella-Moritz, but at least she'd have a pleasant equine-related memory...even if the equine in question hadn't quite been real. Sort of like everything else at Once Upon A Time.

Don't think about it.

Lacey forbade herself from dwelling on her pretend royal status and the embarrassing prince-on-a-white-horse comment as she did her best to cram as many attractions as possible into Rose's final day at the park. She didn't want the sweet little girl to miss a thing. Lacey ticked off her mental list of all the rides and attractions, one by one. Only a few remained.

By lunchtime, they'd gone through Hansel and Gretel's Haunted Forest, where Rose had grabbed Lacey's arm and scream-laughed every time one of the eerie green ghosts that were projected onto the attraction popped out from behind a tree. Then they hollered their way through the mini-roller coaster that wound its way through the Three Bears' Woods.

Rose stayed glued to Lacey's side throughout the day, which was probably for the best. So long as she and Henry didn't have another moment alone together, Lacey could avoid further embarrassment. A part of her couldn't help but feel disappointed, though. Time seemed to be passing at warp-speed. Tomorrow, they'd be on their way back to their kingdom, and Lacey would once again be waltzing with a theme park Prince Charming instead of the real deal.

Which is perfectly fine, remember? All appearances to the contrary, Lacey was no delusional Cinderella.

Still, the thought of going back to her regular life made her stomach squirm. She wasn't ready to return to hosting tea parties and doing meet-and-greets. Lacey had made a real connection with Henry and Rose. She'd gotten to know them—*really* know them—which was rare. She typically spent five minutes or fewer with each guest, not days.

Then again, she'd never been quite as drawn to a guest as she'd been to Henry and his precocious daughter. She didn't even think of them as guests anymore. Rose was her friend, and Henry...

Well, as unbelievable as it seemed, sometimes Henry felt like more than a friend.

Lacey had no business thinking like that, though. Doing so would only leave her with a broken heart. *I work at a theme park, and he rules a country...a country he's returning to in just a matter of hours.*

But when Henry spoke up as their foursome approached their last ride, a rebellious swam of butterflies took flight in her stomach. "Rose, would you mind if I rode with Princess Sweet Pea on this one?" he said, resting his hand on his daughter's shoulder. "I'd like to chat with a her a bit while I still have a chance."

"You can ride with me. We'll have a nice time, won't we?" Ian ruffled Rose's hair. "Besides, I don't think your daddy and I would fit into one of those small boats together."

Ian cast a dubious glance at the line of miniature pirate ships floating just inside the entrance to the Wild Pirate's Ghost Ship Experience. They were indeed small, built to carry guests through a dark, eerie haunted shipwreck scene, two at a time.

Rose nodded. "Okay." Then she slipped her hand into Ian's and they made their way toward one of the tiny pirate boats.

Lacey glanced at Henry, and when his eyes flashed over to her, the corner of his mouth curled into a grin. He'd procured another baseball cap since losing the navy blue one he'd worn when they'd first met. The new one was charcoal gray, with the image of Ever After Castle stitched onto it in deep purple embroidery. He looked far less grumpy than he had at the tea party—probably because it was near impossible to look cranky while rocking a fairy tale castle hat. But Lacey couldn't help hoping she had a little something to do with the smile on his face.

Her heart skittered. She wasn't imagining things, was she? There really was something happening between them.

"Shall we?" Gallant as ever, he motioned for Lacey to go in front of him.

She reminded herself that being gallant was part of his job description. A ride that featured a ghostly pirate who liked to knit scarves for his pet parrot aboard his sunken ship was hardly a recipe for romance. This wasn't a *date*. Henry was simply being nice. Charming was built right into his DNA.

They took their seats in the boat behind Rose and Ian's. Lacey's gown spilled over into Henry's lap, just as it had on the very first day when they'd ridden in the Snow Queen's sleigh together. But now there was an ease between them that hadn't been there before, a quiet intimacy as familiar as it was beguiling. Lacey forced herself to face forward and ignore the nonsensical impulse to rest her head on Henry's princely shoulder.

The boat floated forward, headed for a cave illuminated with deep blue lighting and dripping with sparkling gemstones and ropes of pearls hanging from the ceiling.

She felt Henry's gaze on her—as real as if he'd reached out and touched her cheek—so she swiveled to glance in his direction. Blue and purple shadows moved across his chiseled face, making his eyes glitter like sapphires. He smiled a lopsided smile, looking far more like someone she might bump into on the walking path at the beach than an actual, future king, and Lacey melted a little bit inside.

Maybe she hadn't been imagining things in recent days. Maybe there really was something happening between them, something real.

Lacey swallowed hard, and as their boat ventured deeper into the cave, she could no longer see Henry's expression. But somehow she could feel still feel his boyish grin.

Had she really been indignant when Mr. Dole had informed her she'd be showing Henry and Rose around the park during their stay?

She had, hadn't she?

"What did you want to talk to me about?" Lacey said while flashes of fake lightning lit up their surroundings and wind whistled through their watery cavern.

"I just wanted to thank you for everything you've done for Rose over the past few days." Henry shifted beside her.

"Of course. I got the idea for the carousel from my roommate, Ava. She works here at the park too." Lacey lowered her voice to a whisper. "She's Red Riding Hood, but her identity is supposed to be a secret, so maybe keep that under your hat." She shot a meaningful glance at Henry's head. "Or in your case, crown."

His handsome face split into a wide smile. "Cute."

Lacey took a deep breath. She was *flirting*...with royalty, which, when you were a commoner, was probably the literal equivalent of flirting with danger. "You already thanked me this morning," she said, turning to face the depths of the watery cave again. "And last night, remember?" She caught another glimpse of Henry as streaks of rain were projected onto the walls of the cave.

He regarded her thoughtfully. "Well, it bears repeating. And..." He took a deep breath. The air between them felt swollen all of a sudden, full of things neither one of them would let themselves say.

"And?" she prompted. Lacey's heart hammered in her chest. What was happening?

Their boat drifted past a vignette of a shipwrecked pirate ship with ripped sails. A chest of gold coins lay scattered onto the sand beside the wreckage. Lacey barely noticed any of it. Her body was inside the tiny pirate boat she shared with Henry, but in her imagination, she was back on the dance floor in the ballroom at Ever After Castle, waltzing one last time with the Crown Prince of Bella-Moritz.

"Well, I was wondering—" Henry began.

And then Jack the Knitting Pirate popped out of nowhere, a ghostly apparition that seemed to crawl right into the boat beside them, thanks to a dash of theme park magic and high-end special effects.

They both jumped in their seats, caught completely off guard by the spooky interruption. Lacey heard someone scream, and she realized the noise had come from her very own mouth. Worse yet, the ridiculous pirate had given her such a start that she'd grabbed onto Henry and was clutching the front of his pristine polo shirt in both of her fists.

"Oh, um." She tried to apologize, but the words wouldn't

come. Henry's face was *right there*, mere inches from hers. Beneath handfuls of Ralph Lauren fine knit fabric, she could feel his heartbeat, pounding like mad.

Or was that frantic boom-boom her own heart, galloping wildly in her chest? She honestly couldn't tell.

Henry's gaze dropped to her mouth, and she licked her lips. He was going to kiss her, like they were a pair of completely normal teenagers riding in a pirate-themed tunnel of love instead of what they were. Mismatched royalty.

He lowered his head, ever so slowly, and Lacey tipped her face toward his. She'd never identified with her theme park character more in her life.

This is craziness!

And yet, it felt right, somehow. It really did...

Until Henry pulled away in the moment right before their lips touched.

CHAPTER ELEVEN

Are Platonic Goosebumps a Thing?

HENRY BLINKED.

He was sure he'd just seen a flash of cell phone camera. It had come from somewhere to the left, but when he scanned the dark recesses of the pirate cave, he came up empty. The flash of light must've been one of the ride's many special effects.

He shook his head and turned back toward Lacey. "Sorry, I—"

"You don't want to miss Jack the Knitting Pirate's ghost parrot." Lacey's gaze was fixed straight ahead, and her lovely mouth was curved into her practiced Princess Sweet Pea smile, but Henry could detect a slight tremor in her voice. "Look, there he is."

Henry didn't care about the parrot. He didn't even care about why a ghost pirate had any interest in yarn crafts. He did, however, care about the kiss they'd very nearly just shared. "Lacey," he said.

Look at me. Please.

"Ahoy, mateys," a spooky voice echoed throughout the cave.

When Lacey finally glanced over at him, she scrunched up her face and made a silly pirate noise.

Clearly she preferred to laugh things off and pretend the almost-kiss had never happened, and Henry certainly wasn't going to force the issue. He told himself that ignoring it was for best, anyway. The flash of light he'd mistaken for a camera had been a blessing in disguise. It had saved him from a terrible lapse in judgment.

He was a prince. A *father*. He couldn't just go around kissing people...

No matter how very badly he'd wanted to kiss Lacey Pope.

Henry *still* wanted to kiss Lacey, but the moment had passed, and there was no getting it back—not even if he tried. The rest of the boat ride passed in awkward silence. When they floated out of the cave and back into the salty beach air, he realized he'd never gotten a chance to tell her why he'd wanted to speak to her in private to begin with. He'd started to, but then everything had become a blur of pirates and phantoms and Lacey's perfect, bow-shaped lips, and the speech he'd prepared in his head while traversing the Three Bears' Woods via roller coaster had fallen by the wayside.

Rose and Ian stood on the platform beside the cave's exit, waiting for Henry and Lacey to disembark. It was now or never. The park would be closing soon, and his trip to the land of fairy tales would be over for good. The next time he set foot in a castle, not a single footman would be sporting bunny ears.

"Lacey, I—" Before he could finish, the sky overhead exploded into glittering light. Bursts of red, white, and blue shimmered against the velvety night, one right after another.

"Daddy!" Rose cried. "The fireworks!"

Henry and Lacey climbed out of the boat as quickly as they could and raced toward the promenade for a better view. Earlier, Lacey had mentioned a special VIP balcony at Ever After Castle, where they could see the grand fireworks display up close, unobstructed. Time had gotten away from them, though, especially after so many repetitive rides on the carousel.

Henry was sort of glad, though. He liked being crammed into the crowded space with the regular park-goers, faces tipped up toward the sky. This was why he'd come here—to blend in and be a regular person for a change. It was the best possible way he could conceive of to end their trip.

Ian lifted Rose off her feet and let her sit on top of his shoulders for a better view. Looking at her sweet face, lit with wonder and the reflection of the dazzling sky, made Henry's throat go thick.

Lacey turned toward him and grinned, but he could already see the goodbye in her eyes. "Beautiful, isn't it?"

"Very." Henry nodded.

The fireworks came faster now, crackling in dizzying succession. Light filled the heavens, like falling stars, and Ever After Castle—Once Upon A Time's crown jewel—twinkled beneath the display. Henry had the same panicky feeling in his chest that he'd gotten when the clock at Sweet Pea's Royal Tea Party had struck midnight.

He didn't want to be the sort of prince who was left standing with an empty glass shoe in his hands. Not this time.

He leaned toward Lacey and whispered in her ear. "Would you do me the honor of coming to Bella-Moritz next week for the Flower Festival?"

Her mouth fell open and she stared at him, the fireworks all but forgotten. "What did you just say? I think I must've misheard you."

Henry glanced at Rose to make sure she wasn't listening. The last thing he wanted was to get his daughter's hopes up if Lacey didn't want to make the trip. Thankfully, she was too enamored by the park's spectacular closing ceremony to notice her father was asking a woman on a date for the first time in over a decade.

Because that was what this was, wasn't it? He wanted to see Lacey again. He wanted to take her on a proper date. He wasn't ready to say goodbye for good, not by a long shot.

"I asked if you'd like to come to Bella-Moritz for the Flower Festival. You can see Rose ride in the parade, and afterward, attend the royal ball." Henry swallowed hard.

He hadn't known he'd actually go through with the invitation until the words had left his mouth. He'd wanted to ask her all day, and he just couldn't hold it in any longer.

"The royal ball?" she sputtered. "A *real* royal ball."

Henry gave her a half shrug. "We've danced in your castle. It seems only fair that we should dance in mine."

A burst of laughter flew out of Lacey's mouth.

She still hadn't said yes yet, though. A flare of panic spread through Henry's chest—a firecracker of anxiety.

Why isn't she saying yes?

"As friends, of course," he heard himself say, but he wasn't entirely sure he believed it. He just knew he wanted her there, on whatever terms would make her feel comfortable. "You can bring a guest if you like. Perhaps your roommate would like to join you?"

"Ava?" Lacey laughed again. "Trust me, Ava would never let me go to a royal ball without her. She'd insist on coming, whether she was invited or not."

"In that case, Red Riding Hood is officially invited as well."

Lacey narrowed her gaze at him as the fireworks began to fade away. "You're serious, aren't you?"

"Absolutely." Henry nodded. "My treat. I'll make all the travel arrangements, and you and Ava can stay in the palace."

"The palace." Lacey inhaled a shuddering breath. "I don't know what to say."

And then, for the first time since their almost-kiss on the boat, her gaze softened, and Henry saw Lacey smiling up at him again. Not Princess Sweet Pea.

Happiness surged through him. "Say yes."

"Well, of course you said yes," Ava said, giving a mighty eye roll as Lacey told her about the surprise invitation later that night in their apartment.

Waiting until they'd gotten home had been torture, but she didn't dare say a word about going to Bella-Moritz in the dressing room at Once Upon A Time. This definitely seemed like the sort of thing that required discretion. After all, George and Amal Clooney hadn't run to Facebook to tell people they were on the guest list for Prince Harry and Meghan Markle's wedding the minute their invitation had arrived, had they?

No, they hadn't.

"Wait a minute. You *did* say yes, didn't you?" Ava's eyes widened and her voice went a little panicky. "*Please* tell me you said yes."

Lacey bit her lip. "I said yes." Happiness coursed through her, with a heavy dose of nerves. She felt like she'd just consumed three espressos in rapid succession.

"Thank goodness." Ava clutched her heart and fell backward onto the sofa in dramatic relief.

Lacey began pacing back and forth in their tiny living room, which seemed tinier than ever now that she was about to go stay in an actual palace. "Do you really think we should, though? Because I feel like it's a completely crazy idea." She pressed a hand to her abdomen as her stomach churned.

Lacey didn't know a thing about royalty. The only thing she had to go by was the theme park princess handbook, and suddenly that seemed to be wholly inadequate. Was she supposed to curtsey when she saw Henry and Rose on their home turf? How was she supposed to address them? Somehow, calling them by their first names no longer seemed appropriate.

Ava propped herself up on her elbows and shook her head. "It's not crazy at all. You obviously like Prince Henry. Apparently, the feeling is mutual."

"It's not like that. Henry made that very clear." Lacey felt her giddy smile begin to wobble off her face.

"As friends, of course."

Those had been Henry's exact words when he'd invited her to the ball—no doubt because Lacey had made the mortifying mistake of thinking he was going to kiss her on the haunted shipwreck ride.

"What do you mean?" Ava frowned.

Lacey cleared her throat. "He said we'd danced together in my castle, so it only seemed fair we should dance in his."

Ava's eyes about bugged out of her head. "Oh em gee, that's the most romantic thing I've ever heard."

"And then he added, 'as friends.'" Lacey arched a brow. "I rest my case."

"I'm still not convinced. He's flying you and your best friend—" Ava paused to point to herself, "—all the way to the French Riviera for a Petunia Party."

Lacey felt herself smile again. "Flower Festival."

Ava frowned in mock concentration. "Are you sure? I thought you said Daisy Dance."

"Flower Festival and Royal Ball." Lacey picked up a throw pillow and swatted Ava with it, but at least she was no longer thinking about almost accidentally kissing a prince.

Not much, anyway.

"We're *friends*. Period." Still...a royal ball. Just the

thought of it gave Lacey goosebumps—completely platonic, completely unromantic goosebumps.

Right. Because those are totally a thing.

"What are we going to do if Mr. Dole won't give us the time off?" Ava scrunched up her face.

Lacey winced. "Don't be mad, but I already asked him."

"You're saying the park manager found out I was going to Bella-Moritz before I did?"

"I didn't want you to get your hopes up if it was going to be impossible, but don't worry. Mr. Dole is so eager to make the royal family happy that he said yes on the spot." Every role at the theme park had backup players. In fact, Lacey's understudy had been hosting Sweet Pea's Royal Tea Party the past few days so Lacey could devote her time to Henry and Rose. The key to preserving the magic of the theme park's make-believe was making sure two Sweet Peas or two Snow Whites were never, ever seen together. Lacey plopped down on the sofa beside Ava and grinned. "So I guess we're really going!"

Ava spent the next two minutes screaming into the throw pillow Lacey had recently weaponized.

Lacey wanted to join her—oh, how she wished she could simply shake off her humiliation over the non-kiss and just bask in the excitement of Henry's invitation to Bella-Moritz. He'd seemed so sincere, and the way he'd looked at her as the sky had erupted into glittering light had made her feel all bubbly and fizzy inside.

"As friends, of course."

The words kept coming back to her, even though she had no reason whatsoever to feel disappointed in the qualifier. Lacey adored Rose and wanted to spend more time with her. She couldn't wait to see the little princess ride her pony in the royal procession. She could totally be *just friends* with Prince Henry. That was completely doable.

Wasn't it?

"Oh, nooo." Ava groaned into the pillow and then popped her head up. "I just thought of a complication."

Lacey wilted. She was almost afraid to ask. *You mean in addition to the fact that I'm a pretend princess who might be having feelings for a real-life prince?* She shifted her gaze toward Ava. "What is it?"

"We're leaving in just a few days, right?"

"Yes. Ian, Henry's bodyguard, is supposed to send our itinerary and all the other necessary information as soon as they get back to the palace." In the meantime, at least Lacey would have a few days of waltzing practice at her Sweet Pea tea parties.

Ava threw her hands up. "What are we going to wear to the ball?"

In keeping with fairy tale traditions dating back to the 1600s, one of the perks of being a theme park princess was having a theme park fairy godmother. At Once Upon A Time, the fairy godmother role was played by a former kindergarten teacher named Madeline Martin.

Madeline had been popping up in surprise locations around the park, waving her magic wand and sprinkling guests with a dash of her fairy godmother dust—cupcake-scented glitter, if you must know—for the past three years. With her beaming smile and glorious singing voice, she'd become a park favorite practically overnight. Madeline often belted out humorous fairy tale songs in an operatic voice at her appearances. Park goers loved it, kids and adults alike.

Lacey and Ava often invited Madeline to tag along on their trips to Fort Lauderdale Beach Park. One night, over frozen peach Bellinis, she'd told them how she'd become such an accomplished vocal performer. As it turned out, before Madeline had become a kindergarten teacher and *way* before she'd taken on her fairy godmother persona, she'd been a pageant queen. She'd started off winning crowns in tiny local pageants, gradually making her way to the Miss Florida stage, where she'd performed an aria from *La Traviata* in the talent portion of the competition.

Madeline hadn't walked away with the crown, but after years on the pageant circuit, she'd walked away with an impressive collection of evening gowns. Lacey had never seen anything quite like it.

"Whoa," she said as she stood staring at the contents of Madeline's packed walk-in closet. "This reminds of me of the closet scene in that movie *27 Dresses*."

Madeline laughed. "I'm pretty sure there are more than twenty-seven gowns in there. And you and Ava are welcome to borrow whatever you like. I haven't worn any of them in years, but I can't bear to part with them."

"You're a lifesaver." Ava clapped her hands. "A real-life fairy godmother."

"Where are you two going again?" Madeline asked as Lacey ran her fingertips over the soft tulle overlay of a violet-colored mermaid gown.

Lacey's gaze darted to Ava. This was the hard part about asking to raid Madeline's closet. She still didn't feel comfortable telling anyone except her boss's boss's boss about the royal ball, but how was Lacey supposed to explain their urgent need for two fancy ballgowns? "It's just a fancy black-tie thing." Lacey let go of the mermaid gown. It seemed like it might be a tad dramatic for the occasion. She was going for more of a Duchess of Cambridge vibe—soft and graceful without being too daring.

Ava waved a hand. "Right. We'll probably be bored out of our minds, but we still want to make an appearance."

"Oh." Madeline sighed, looking a little deflated. "I was hoping this had something to do with Lacey showing that prince around the park all week."

Lacey somehow resisted the urge to bury her face and hide in a rack of sequins and organza.

"He's gone back to his kingdom already, didn't you hear?" Ava shrugged. "He and his entourage left after the fireworks tonight."

"Thinking it had something to do with the prince seemed a little too good to be true, but a girl can dream, right?" Madeline shrugged.

"Right," Lacey said, forcing a smile.

Too good to be true.

This entire upcoming trip seemed too good to be true. She was beginning to think maybe she'd dreamed the entire thing. What if she never heard from Ian? What if Henry forgot all about her once he left American air space?

Her stomach tumbled. Maybe she should've tried harder to convince Ava not to call Madeline until everything was set in stone.

But then Madeline reached inside the closet and pulled out a beautiful pale lilac gown made of miles and miles of floaty chiffon. It had a gathered bodice and cap sleeves. A delicate rhinestone belt decorated the waistline—perfectly elegant, perfectly regal. It seemed just like something Kate Middleton would wear.

"This would look gorgeous on you," Madeline said. She held the dress up to Lacey and turned toward Ava. "What do you think? Should she try it on?"

Ava nodded. "*Definitely.*"

"I can't wait to see it on you." Madeline offered her the hanger.

Lacey took it. The gown was as light as a feather, as if the delicate organza had been spun from air. The complete and total opposite of her over-the-top Princess Sweet Pea ballgown in every possible way.

She carried it to the bathroom to try it on while Madeline dug around her closet for the right dress for Ava. When she slipped the lilac organza over her head, it fell around her body with an elegant whisper.

Lacey smoothed down the bodice of the gown, marveling at how soft the organza felt against her skin. Best of all, it fit like it had been made for her. Even the sparkly rhinestone belt sat snug at her waist, not too tight and not too loose.

When she opened the door and stepped back into Madison's bedroom, the bed was covered in a heap of discarded silk, satin, and lace. Ava held a hanger in each hand as Madison appeared to weigh the pros and cons of two very different red dresses. One of them was a one-shouldered, Grecian-style gown, while the other had a sequined bodice, a prim bow at the waist, and a long, ruffled skirt.

"I like the ruffles," Lacey said, gently interrupting with her opinion.

"I think so too but—" Ava froze mid-sentence when she swiveled her head in Lacey's direction.

Madison followed her gaze and gasped as soon as she set eyes on her in the pale lilac gown. "Oh, my."

"That dress is The One," Ava announced.

It seemed crazy to settle on the very first gown she tried on, considering Madison's closet could've doubled as a high-end dress shop. But Lacey agreed. The gown felt right, and as she caught a glance of herself in the full-length mirror on Madison's closet door, her breath caught in her throat.

Madison stepped forward to give the belt a tiny adjustment and arrange the floaty skirt in a billowing train behind Lacey's feet. "You look perfect," she said when she stood up. "Classically beautiful, just like Audrey Hepburn."

"No." Ava shook her head. "Just like a princess."

Lacey *felt* like a princess, or at least like the sort person who might get invited to a royal ball. "I can't thank you enough for this, Madison."

Madison waved a hand. "It's no trouble at all. These poor gowns never get to go anywhere anymore. Just try not to get too bored at your fancy event."

"I'll do my best," Lacey promised.

After all of this was over and she and Ava returned from Bella-Moritz, Lacey was going to have to tell Madison the real truth and swear her to secrecy. She'd very nearly caved and spilled the beans right then and there, but she didn't want to betray Henry's trust. He hadn't specifically asked her not to tell anyone, but so little in his life was private. Talking about it just didn't seem right.

"Now we just have to choose a gown for Ava," she said.

"I think I'm going to have to try both of these on." Ava's gaze flitted toward a navy-blue satin tuxedo dress lying on the bed. "And maybe that one too."

"Something tells me we're going to be here a while." Lacey laughed. "I'm going to go ahead and take mine off."

"Here, use this. I have extras." Madison tossed her an empty ivory garment bag with Once Upon A Time printed on it in swirly gold lettering. It was just like the hanging bags Lacey used to carry her Princess Sweet Pea costume back and forth from the park, home and the dry cleaners.

"Thanks."

Back in the bathroom, Lacey took a mirror selfie to send to her parents. Her dad and stepmom were going to flip when they found out she was going to Bella-Moritz. She'd have to swear them to secrecy, but there was no way she was going to travel halfway across the world without telling her family where she was going. After she got a good shot, she removed the dress and hung it back up with great care, smoothing down the delicate fabric inside the garment bag before she zipped it closed. Just as she placed it beside her purse, her phone pinged with an incoming email.

Her heart gave a little zing. Surely it wasn't from Ian.

They couldn't have already arrived back in Bella-Moritz. She couldn't help checking, though, just in case.

Henry's name, not Ian's, popped up at the top of Lacey's inbox.

All arrangements have been made. Airline confirmations for you and Ava are attached, and a car from the palace will meet you upon your arrival. Rose is delighted you'll be joining us.

As am I.

xx Henry

Lacey re-read the message and then read it again a third time, turning each word over and over in her mind. He'd already made her travel arrangements. He was delighted she was going to Bella-Mortitz. And those flirty little x's were *kisses*, weren't they?

A shiver zinged up and down Lacey's spine.

She re-checked the time on her phone. There was no way Henry was already back in his home country by now, which meant he must've made the reservations from the plane. And he'd done so himself. Maybe being friends with a prince wasn't such a bad thing, after all.

Then she thought about the x's again. They seemed more than friendly. Surely he didn't sign his messages to Ian the same way.

"Lace-y." Ava stood just a few feet away, waving her arms in an apparent effort to get Lacey's attention. "I need you to look at this dress."

"Sorry." She shoved her phone back into her handbag and grinned at the sight of her friend in the pretty red gown. "You look gorgeous."

Ava twirled in front of the mirror. "I still think I should try on a few more. What do you think?"

"Try on as many as you like. We're not in a rush," Madeline said.

"Absolutely." Lacey nodded. She wanted Ava to be as

thrilled with her gown as Lacey was with hers.

So she joined Madeline in the closet while Ava slipped into the next sparkly option. The trip was all set. They were really going to Bella-Moritz. In just a few days, Lacey would see Rose and Henry again. She'd get to stay in a palace and watch Rose ride her pony in the royal procession. And thanks to her theme park fairy godmother, she had a fabulous dress to wear to the royal ball.

After years of playing the part of a princess, Lacey Pope had never felt so much like Cinderella.

CHAPTER TWELVE

It's Not All Crowns and Curtseys

Henry, Rose, and Ian arrived back at the palace in the wee hours of the morning. While Ian made his way to his quarters, Henry carried a sleepy Rose to her bedroom and got her all tucked into bed, rather glad the valets and housekeeping staff had gone home for the night.

While they'd been away, he'd gotten accustomed to doing simple things for his daughter—things like making sure she brushed her teeth before she went to bed and planning what they ate for breakfast. He wasn't quite ready to forego such hands-on parenting.

The following morning, however, there was no sipping fresh-squeezed Florida orange juice or eating a towering stack of American pancakes on the balcony overlooking the pure turquoise waters of the Atlantic Ocean. Breakfast in the palace was typically a rather formal affair, served at the long mahogany table in one of the castle's formal dining rooms. It was the only meal of the day the entire family always enjoyed together, without fail. Henry's mother, and frequently Henry himself, were often away, attending to royal duties in the evening. Breakfast, as stuffy as it could be at times, was reserved for family.

Henry popped by Rose's suite on his way to the dining room, but she was in the middle of getting her hair combed and arranged into two perfect French braids by Miss Marie, her favorite ladies' maid. So much for Henry's meager attempts at pigtails. He left his daughter sitting at her vanity in her pajamas—chattering away to Marie about her birthday trip—and strode down the wide, crimson-carpeted hall toward the rich scents of fresh-ground espresso, flaky croissants, and hearty breakfast cassoulet.

The queen was already situated at the head of the table, flipping through the stack of newspapers she read religiously every morning, when Henry entered the room.

"Good morning, Mother," he said, pausing to kiss her cheek on his way to his seat.

She looked up from the pages of *Le Figaro* and smiled. "Ah, you've returned, and not a minute too soon."

Henry unfolded his napkin and spread it across his lap. "Yes, and Rose had a lovely time. We both did."

He waited for her to comment on the photo he'd texted her. Henry thought it might be the best way to bring up the fact that he'd invited Lacey for a stay at the palace during the Flower Festival, but his mother clearly had other concerns.

"My secretary tells me you never responded to her email about the list of potential governesses for Rose," she said, reaching for her teacup.

Henry was going to need caffeine for this conversation. Lots of it. A footman set an espresso in front of him, and Henry shot him a grateful smile. "That's because she's not getting a governess. Rose will be returning to school in the fall. She's a future monarch, but she also needs a real childhood. Our time away has made that clearer than ever."

The queen raised her eyebrows. "Is that so?"

"Yes." Henry nodded and drained his cup. Then he added in a gentler tone, "I wish you could've seen how happy she was in Florida. I know you'd understand."

His mother studied him for a moment, her expression softening a bit. "And you? Did you have a good time as well?"

"Very much." He nodded.

Here was his opening, served right up on a silver platter. Henry wasn't sure why he was suddenly nervous about telling his mother about Lacey's visit. If her past comments about his love life were any indication, she'd probably be thrilled.

But Lacey's just a friend, remember?

Right. Why did he have such a difficult time remembering that significant detail?

Henry cleared his throat. "In fact, I wanted to tell you—"

But then Rose bounded into the dining room and threw herself at the queen as if she hadn't seen her for a year, rather than just a few days. "Grandmère! We're back."

Henry's throat grew thick as his mother smiled and returned Rose's enthusiastic embrace. The queen took her role as the monarch with the utmost seriousness, and she was committed to the people of Bella-Moritz and upholding their traditions, but she also loved her granddaughter and wanted what was best for Rose—even if Henry didn't always agree with what that might entail. It was easy to lose sight of that sometimes. Perhaps getting away had been good for his perspective, among other things.

"Did you have a nice birthday, Caitriona?" Queen Elloise asked, frowning slightly as she took in her granddaughter's attire. She was wearing her Princess Sweet Pea gown...*again.*

Rose nodded. "It was the best birthday ever. We went to a tea party at Ever After Castle."

Henry's mother shot him a look, as if to remind him he needn't have dragged his daughter to America for a royal tea party when she could've attended the real deal right here at home.

Henry shook his head. "Not the regular sort of tea party."

"Daddy waltzed with Princess Sweet Pea, and everyone clapped." Rose spread her arms out wide.

Henry probably should've seen this coming, particularly since Rose had issued a similar recounting of the tea party when she'd told Ian about it.

That had been days ago, though. So much had happened since then.

Henry glanced at the queen, whose eyebrows had shot clear up to her hairline. "Not the regular sort of waltzing, either," he said.

His mother smiled in the serene way that queens through-out the ages had mastered, but Henry knew better than to trust outward appearances. Her face could be a perfect mask when she wanted it to. "The last time I checked, the assorted varieties of waltzing were somewhat limited."

"It was just a waltz," Henry said for clarification, but his heartbeat kicked up a notch.

The queen's gaze narrowed ever so slightly before she turned her attention back toward Rose. "And what is this lovely dress you're wearing?" she asked, fluffing one of the puffed sleeves of Rose's Princess Sweet Pea gown.

She'd obviously dragged it out of her suitcase and zipped herself into it after Marie had finished braiding her hair. Henry didn't see the harm in letting her wear it around the palace. In fact, it warmed his heart to think she'd enjoyed their trip to Once Upon A Time so much that she still wanted to wear the costume here at home.

"It's my Princess Sweet Pea dress. Isn't it beautiful?" Rose stepped back and twirled three times before dropping into an exaggerated theme-park-princess curtsey.

"Quite beautiful," the queen said with her usual diplo-matic flair.

"It's just like Princess Sweet Pea's gown, except I don't have my crown anymore. I gave it away." Rose climbed onto the dining chair beside Henry's.

He motioned for her to put her napkin in her lap.

Rose talked throughout the entire meal, giving her grandmother a detailed play-by-play of everything they'd done in Florida, placing heavy emphasis on the time they'd spent with Lacey. It was *Princess Sweet Pea* this and *Princess Sweet Pea* that for the better part of an hour, until Rose was excused to go change for her riding lesson.

His daughter had been gone a grand total of two minutes when Queen Elloise brought up the subject of Lacey again.

"Rose seems quite enamored with this Princess Sweet Pea character," she said, arching a brow. "Would this be the same 'princess' who was in the photograph you sent me a few days ago?"

So she'd gotten the text, after all. A reply would've been nice, but Henry refrained from saying so.

Still, he bristled at his mother's unspoken air quotes around the word *princess*. "Yes, she was our guide at the theme park. Her real name is Lacey Pope. Rose took quite a shine to her."

"I can see that." The queen sipped her tea.

Again, Henry tried to tell her that Lacey would soon be visiting Bella-Moritz. In just a matter of days, she'd be sitting at one of the empty places around the polished mahogany dining table. And despite the fictional nature of her royal title, Henry had no doubt she'd fit right in.

Beneath the table, Henry's foot jiggled. He felt like he was going to jump out of his skin. He couldn't wait for Lacey to arrive. "Actually..." he began.

But the queen stood, indicating the conversation was over. "I'm pleased you and Caitriona had a nice trip, but you two are home now. It's time for both of you to turn your attention back to our family duties." She squared her shoulders, even though Henry had never once seen his mother with anything but perfect posture. "You chose a most inopportune time to whisk your daughter off to fantasy land. I realize it was her birthday, but the Flower Festival begins in three days. There's much business to attend to, and Caitriona needs to realize that royal life comes with real responsibilities. The sooner she learns that lesson, the better. It's not all crowns and curtseys."

Henry counted to ten in his head so he wouldn't say something he'd later come to regret. A million objections spun round in his mind. His daughter had been born into privilege, but her life had also been marked by sadness when she'd lost her mother. Despite it all, Rose had a heart of gold. She deserved a real childhood.

Most of all, though, the time she'd spent with Lacey at Once Upon A Time had taught her more about being a princess than she could possibly learn from being shut inside the palace with a governess. Henry wasn't sure he'd realized it until right that second, but tucked among Princess Sweet Pea's silly rules had been the most important one of all—the rule Rose had truly taken to heart.

Always, always be kind.

"Rose will make a wonderful princess someday," he said quietly. "She's a special girl, and she's braver than you realize."

Braver than Henry had been in recent years, that was for sure—braver in ways that had nothing to do with climbing atop a pony. His little girl lived her life with her heart open wide.

"She is indeed special, but I worry about this new obsession she has with a fictional princess character. Surely you agree," his mother said.

Henry's stomach hardened. "Lacey plays a part at the park, but I assure you—she's a real person."

A real person who'd soon be showing up at the palace

doors...but now clearly wasn't the time to break this news.

Part of being a prince was mastering the fine art of diplomacy, and Henry possessed this particular attribute in spades. He'd dealt with stubborn heads of state on numerous occasions and mediated arguments between politicians and the citizens of Bella-Moritz to ensure everyone felt they'd been represented fairly and their voices had been heard. Experience had taught him when to hold his tongue and wait for a better moment to make his case most effectively. Now was definitely one of those times.

Even so, not speaking up was torturous.

"In any case, Caitriona doesn't need to become so attached to someone who'll never be a part of your permanent life," Queen Elloise said as she walked briskly out of the room. Then she paused in the gilded doorway for a final word. "I think you've come home just in time."

Somehow, Henry got the feeling her comment had nothing at all to do with the upcoming royal parade.

In the days that followed, Henry got back to his working royal routine. He sat in on a legislative meeting with the Bella-Moritz council. He went over the annual reports from several of the nonprofit organizations that listed him as their royal patron. He presided over the investitures honoring citizens of the principality who'd been awarded special honors for emergency medical services and rescue efforts.

Henry's impromptu trip to America with Rose meant his work diary was piled with rescheduled meetings, one right on top of another. And since the Flower Festival was just days away, he also attended daily strategy sessions for the parade while his mother handled all the details for the flower show and the royal ball. Other than family breakfast, Henry's only glimpses of the queen were the few times they passed one another in the palace hallways as they each rushed off to business meetings.

Worse yet, he rarely had time to see Rose, either. The minute he returned to the palace every evening, he went straight to her room so he could read her a bedtime story. On the third night after they'd come home, she yawned her way through a page or two of "The Princess and the Pea" and then fell asleep with her head on Henry's shoulder as he lay in the dark, staring at the dried breadcrumbs she'd scattered on her windowsill overlooking the palace courtyard.

He missed the long, uninterrupted days spent together in Florida. Henry hadn't even had a chance to look in on any of Rose's riding lessons. This particular week was always the busiest of the year in Bella-Moritz, though. His schedule would calm down soon enough. Once the Flower Festival began, all work would cease for the entire principality. The three days of the festival had always been observed as traditional holidays.

Henry still felt strangely empty inside, even as he reminded himself the work he was doing on behalf of the kingdom was meaningful to the little principality that held such a special place in his heart. And the reason for his malaise was even more worrisome than his long work hours. He didn't simply miss being on holiday. He missed Lacey.

He missed the sound of her laugher. He missed the gentle way she had with Rose and the way her eyes danced every time she teased him about his baseball cap. He missed her honesty and the way she talked to him as if he were a regular person instead of a prince.

He missed the tender intimacy of sitting beside her on a darkened ride and having to call on every last shred of his willpower not to hold her hand or take her lovely face in his hands and kiss her silly.

But most of all, Henry missed Lacey's joyful spirit. Being around her made him want to experience every moment of the day as if it were something to be treasured, not simply tolerated.

He let his gaze travel over the words on the page of the book spread open on his lap.

So the prince returned to his kingdom with a heavy heart.

He scrubbed a hand over his face. This wasn't a fairy tale; it was real life. But how many times in the past few days had his mother's warning come back to him and burrowed deep inside his chest?

"Caitriona doesn't need to become so attached to someone who'll never be a part of your permanent life. I think you've come home just in time."

Perhaps his daughter had come back to the palace just in time, but Henry was beginning to think he was a lost cause. He'd already grown attached.

The morning after Lacey chose her gown for the royal ball, she was back at work, playing her regular part at Once Upon A Time. No more escorting royalty around the park, and no more quiet, tender moments with Henry as they sat side by side in the dark in a sleigh or on a Ferris wheel. It was back to tea parties, meet-and-greets, and waltzing with a pretend Prince Charming instead of the real deal.

At one point, Prince Charming stepped on her toe so hard that her fake glass slipper broke with an audible crack. When the clock struck twelve and Lacey dashed out of the ballroom, she made sure to leave the other shoe behind so it wouldn't look like she'd stepped out of a pile of tiny glass shards.

Back to reality. As she limped toward the castle's backstage dressing room, she felt more like Alice returning to the real world after her magical adventures in Wonderland than a princess, poufy ballgown notwithstanding. She hobbled toward one of the benches beside the lockers where the performers kept their personal belongings.

The wardrobe supervisor, a stout woman named Sally who'd worked there since before Lacey had been born, peered at her. "Everything okay?"

"Yes, but one of my shoes cracked." Lacey lifted the hem of her princess gown to show off her shattered slipper. "We have a spare around here somewhere, don't we?"

"Of course. Sit down for a minute, and I'll find it." Sally winced at the sight of Lacey's foot. "I'll grab you ice pack too."

"Thanks." Lacey's foot throbbed. The pain wasn't excruciating, but she'd be on her feet for at least six more hours today. She'd take all the help she could get.

After Sally left, Lacey propped her foot up on the bench and extricated it from the broken shoe. The dressing room, ordinarily a hive of activity, was eerily silent. The characters were all off interacting with guests or performing at their scheduled mealtimes or shows. Furry costumes and glitter-encrusted princess gowns hung on the costume rack, looking forlorn.

Then a familiar little chirp sound pieced the air. Lacey's gaze swiveled toward the lockers. Someone's phone was going off.

Another chirp sounded. It was the same exact tone Lacey's cell made when she got a text. Had she forgotten to turn her ringer off?

Characters weren't supposed to carry their phones while they were in costume and on duty, for obvious reasons. Hansel and Gretel wouldn't have needed to toss breadcrumbs if they'd been in possession of a phone with GPS. Seeing the Big Bad Wolf or one of the princesses with a phone in their hand would put a serious dent in the park's magical, whimsical atmosphere.

But Lacey wasn't out in one of the pubic park areas at the moment. She was temporarily laid up with a glass slipper-related injury. So she scooted toward her locker and dug around in her purse to check and see if her phone was the one making so much noise.

Sure enough, she was the guilty party. The display on her iPhone showed a little red number two by the green text message icon. She set her phone to vibrate and then tapped the icon to see who was messaging her.

An unfamiliar number flashed across the top of the screen. It started with a plus symbol and a one, followed by a longer-than-normal string of digits.

Lacey gasped. This was a European phone number, wasn't it? Her hands shook as she read the first message, even though she fully expected the text to be from a palace official or someone in Henry's office. She'd given Henry her phone number for her travel arrangements and fully expected the text to be something official about trip logistics.

It wasn't, though.

Do I hear waltz music?

Lacey pressed her hand to her chest and laughed. Those words could've only come from Henry himself. The second message was even more flirtatious than the first.

It's evening here, but something tells me my favorite princess is dancing with another prince at a tea party right about now.

His favorite princess? Lacey's heart did a little flip-flop, even though she knew he was just being sweet. His daughter was a princess, after all. Lacey knew he wasn't serious. Still, she liked to think that maybe, just maybe, she was in the running as second favorite.

But that was ridiculous. He probably knew dozens of actual princesses. Maybe even hundreds. *You're not real, remember?*

But the way her breath hitched in her throat as she

reread Henry's words was real. And so was the smile that tugged at her lips.

She texted him back right away so she wouldn't be tempted to overthink what she should say.

Don't worry. I have a midnight curfew, remember? I left Prince Charming standing in the ballroom all by himself.

Three little dots appeared and then a single word, followed by more x's. Three this time instead of two.

Good. xxx

Was this really happening? Were they flirting across multiple time zones? Lacey glanced up and spied her reflection in one of the dressing room makeup mirrors. Her cheeks were flushed and her eyes, bright. She felt drunk with happiness.

They were just friends, though.

Weren't they?

Lacey tapped another message into her phone. *This isn't fair. You know exactly where I am and what I'm doing, but I don't know a thing about your life at home.*

She pressed send, hoping he'd say he was doing something ordinary like watching a movie or playing a board game with Rose. If he was wearing a crown right now, she would die.

I have a lot of business dinners in the evenings. Tonight, I'm dining with the ambassador from Monaco.

Right, and Lacey usually had dinner with Little Red Riding Hood. What a pair she and Henry made.

That sounds fancy, Lacey typed.

Henry sent back a yawning emoji, and then more words popped up on the screen. *You know me...I prefer my food on a stick.*

"What's got you so smiley, Sweet Pea?" Sally's voice boomed as she walked back into the room, carrying a glass slipper in one hand and a plastic baggie full of ice in the other.

Lacey shoved her phone out of sight, hidden among the folds of her gown. "Nothing. Just texting with a friend. I forgot to silence my phone and I heard it going off inside my locker."

Sally winked as she offered her the ice and the replacement shoe. "Whatever you say. I'm not sure I've ever grinned that big in my life. This friend of yours must be really special."

You have no idea.

"Thank you for the ice." Lacey rested it gently on her toes. "And the glass slipper. I should probably hurry and get back out there."

Sally nodded. "Indeed. You don't want to miss out on the fairy tale."

No, she didn't. Although she was starting to believe her own fairy tale might just be waiting for her somewhere on the other side of the park gates.

Lacey typed out a final goodbye to Henry before stashing her phone back inside her locker, letting her gaze linger on the first part of his most recent message.

You know me…

Strangely enough, she felt like she *did* know Henry. And now they were continuing to learn more about each other, even though they were a world apart in every possible way.

"Oh, good. I've caught you," Queen Elloise said the following morning as she breezed into the dining room for breakfast as Henry rose and pushed his chair away from the table.

He sat back down. "Good morning, Mother. You just missed Rose. She had another riding lesson this morning."

Never mind the fact that, according to Ian, Rose hadn't

seemed any more thrilled lately about riding in the procession than she'd been before they'd gone to Florida. She'd managed to get on her pony but froze every time Daisy moved a muscle. Thankfully, the queen had been too busy with Flower Festival preparations to monitor her granddaughter's equestrian progress. No doubt she was relying on Henry's assurance that Rose would do her duty and ride. He'd made a promise, and he intended to keep it. He simply needed to figure out how. And soon.

"I had an early meeting this morning with the planning committee for the ball," the queen said, stirring cream into her teacup. "I'm glad you're still here. I wanted to go over the guest list with you."

"For the ball?" Henry smoothed down his tie. "I don't recall you ever asking my input on the guest list before."

"Well, this time is different." The queen sipped her tea and then placed her china cup down on its saucer. "There will be several suitable women at the ball I thought you might be...interested in."

Henry reached for his espresso cup, but it was empty. *Not this. Not now.*

"I've been thinking about Caitriona's fondness for this Princess Sweet Pea character. Perhaps it's time you think about finding a proper royal wife and mother for sweet Caitriona. It's been years, darling. Maybe it's time?"

"You think Rose's attachment to Lacey means she needs a new mother? That I need—" he cleared his throat, "—a new wife? And now you've made a list of potential prospects who'll be at the royal ball?"

Brilliant. As long as his life was beginning to resemble a fairy tale, fate may as well toss in a matchmaking parental monarch for good measure. Somewhere in the afterlife, the author who'd penned Cinderella was probably having a good laugh right about now.

Henry's mother regarded him with one of her serene

smiles. "I know you might not feel you're ready, but perhaps you can give it some thought."

"I have, actually," he said, surprising himself as much as the queen.

"You have?" Her eyes widened, and then she pulled a sheet paper from the stack in front of her. "Excellent. Here are the names..."

"Thank you, but I won't be needing your help. I've already invited a guest to the ball."

His mother sat back in her chair. "I see."

"It's Lacey," he said.

"The theme park princess?" The queen's mouth dropped open.

"Yes. I've invited her and a friend to stay at the palace and attend the Flower Festival, the royal procession, and the ball. They're scheduled to arrive later today." Henry felt a weight lift off him as he gave his mother the details. He should've done this days ago—right when he'd first come home.

He hadn't been ready yet, though. He'd needed time to figure out why he'd been so keen to invite Lacey to Bella-Moritz. The more time that passed since he'd seen her, the more he realized it hadn't been merely a thank-you gesture. He'd been fooling himself if he'd ever thought otherwise. And in the days that had passed since they'd seen one another, he and Lacey had started texting each other. It had begun with the brief exchange of messages when he'd looked at the clock and realized she was at her tea party, waltzing around the ballroom at Ever After Castle. Henry had felt a wholly irrational stab of jealousy at the thought of her dancing with someone else, and before he'd been able to stop himself, he'd sent her a text.

That simple exchange of words had blossomed into something else—something more meaningful. Last night after he'd tucked Rose into bed, he'd lain awake in his bedroom, staring at the glow of his phone as he and Lacey exchanged intimate details about themselves, like favorite childhood memories and their hopes and dreams for the future. Henry reiterated he wanted to take a more active role in Rose's upbringing, but he also wanted to spend less time at ceremonial functions and more time serving the people of his kingdom in a concrete, meaningful way. Lacey understood exactly what he meant. She too was trying to figure out a plan beyond her own castle walls.

The more they messaged back and forth, the more Henry longed to hear her voice. He'd finally called her, just to tell her good night.

"Henry, I don't think you need me to tell you that a theme park princess is hardly a proper match for a royal prince." Queen Elloise picked up her teacup again, and this time, it rattled a nervous tap-tap-tap against the china saucer. "You barely know this person, and you and Rose have been through enough."

"I think once you meet her, you'll like her very much," he said simply. "And I certainly know her better than any of the names on your list."

His mother's gaze narrowed.

"Not that she's my 'match,' as you insist on saying. We're..." Henry swallowed, "...friends."

When he'd asked her to the ball, Henry hadn't even been certain Lacey would accept his invitation.

"When was the last time you invited a friend to visit the palace?" his mother countered.

Point taken. Henry usually kept to himself. He worked, he attended to his royal duties and didn't do much else. But he wasn't altogether sure that was all he wanted any more. And he definitely didn't care to be on the receiving end of any more curated columns of names—not of governesses, and especially not of potential wives.

He rose from the table as his mother continued eyeing

him with no small amount of astonishment. "Thank you for your concern, but I won't be needing your list."

CHAPTER THIRTEEN

X's and Oh No's

THE JOURNEY FROM FORT LAUDERDALE to Bella-Moritz was a fifteen-hour haul, and when Lacey and Ava stepped off the plane, they weren't even in Henry's kingdom yet. The closest airport to his "quaint little principality," as he'd called it in his email, was in Nice on the southeast coast of France.

A driver met them near the baggage claim area, just as Henry had indicated. He wore a finely tailored black suit and carried a placard with *Miss Lacey Pope* printed on it in boldfaced lettering. Ava and Lacey exchanged a glance as they walked toward him.

"Fancy." Ava waggled her eyebrows.

Lacey somehow resisted the urge to laugh. She felt like she was in a scene in a romcom movie, especially when the driver took their luggage and escorted them to a sleek black car with tiny flags mounted on either side of the hood, like the ones she'd seen on diplomats' vehicles. Only, instead of stars and stripes, these flags featured an elegant coat of arms overlaid with a banner that read *House of Chevalier, Bella-Moritz.*

Something about the sight of the royal crest gave Lacey pause. After they were buckled into the plush backseat of the car and had started cruising alongside a coastal highway overlooking the glittering Mediterranean Sea, she grabbed hold of Ava's arm.

"Are you sure this is a good idea?" she said under her breath.

Ava's eyes widened. "Are you serious right now? Look around."

She gestured toward the passenger side window, where lavender bloomed beneath the heat of the summer sun. Wasn't lavender supposed to be calming? Lacey wondered if the driver would notice if she unrolled the window to stuck her head outside like a dog and took a big whiff.

Probably so. And then tomorrow morning, her picture would likely be splashed on the front page of every newspaper in Bella-Moritz. She could see the headlines now: *Prince's Girlfriend Shows Canine Tendencies on Ride from Nice.*

"I'm not his girlfriend."

"I know." Ava rolled her eyes. "You've said so a million times, but I'm still not sure I believe you."

Had Lacey just uttered that denial out loud?

She really needed to get herself together before they arrived at the palace. She was excited to see Henry again. Rose too, obviously. But what would it be like spending time together away from the cobblestone utopia of Once Upon A Time? Everything was so happy and friendly at a theme park. She'd spent the past few days trying to tell herself that nothing out of the ordinary was happening between her and Henry, but who was she trying to fool? A prince had just flown her halfway across the world, and every time she thought about the triple xxx's at the end of his text, she went a little swoony.

"I can practically see the wheels spinning round in your head," Ava said. She reached into her carry-on bag and pulled out the slim mint-green box of French macarons she'd purchased at the Ladurée boutique at Charles de Gaulle during their layover in Paris. "Here. Relax, have a treat, and try to enjoy the fact that you aren't about to accompany Prince Henry on an amusement park ride right now. Let him show you around for a change."

Lacey plucked a pink macaron from the box and let the delicate meringue melt on her tongue. She closed her eyes and gave in to the decadent taste of confectioner's sugar, culinary rose petals and just a hint of sweet almonds. They hadn't even made it to the Flower Festival in Bella-Moritz yet, and already everything was coming up roses.

Lacey texted her parents to let them know she'd arrived safely and then tried to take Ava's advice and enjoy the scenery instead of second-guessing whether or not she belonged here.

The ride was short—just under half an hour—and as the driver glanced over his shoulder and said, "Welcome to Bella-Moritz," he maneuvered the car beneath a huge arch made entirely of flowers—blooms of various shades of purple, from pale lavender orchids to brightly-hued tulips to deep, rich hydrangeas.

Lacey gasped. There were flowers everywhere she looked, spread in layered fields as far as the eye could see on either side of the car and overflowing from baskets suspended from the dozens of ornate, iron street lamps that lined the avenue. Palm trees stretched toward the clear blue sky, their bright green leaves providing shelter for the colorful blooms below.

"What is this place?" Ava asked, pressing her face to the window.

"Grand Flower Park. You've come at the perfect time of

year. Flowers bloom year-round in Bella-Moritz, due to the mild temperatures and our close proximity to the sea, but summer is always something special." The driver smiled at them in the rearview mirror. "During the Flower Festival, vendors set up booths here in the park, selling handmade soaps, essential oils, and perfumes. The day after tomorrow, the greenhouse at the royal palace will be open to visitors, and the following day the festival parade will travel down this very street, all the way from Grand Flower Park to the castle."

"When is the ball?" Ava said, unable to help herself.

Lacey bit the inside of her cheek to keep from laughing.

"The royal ball is the grand finale of the festival. It takes place the day after the parade—in the evening, of course. Gardeners, florists, and representatives from all the local charities supported by the palace are invited, along with assorted royal guests."

Assorted royals. Does that include theme park princesses?

At least she'd look the part, thanks to Madeline. The Once Upon A Time garment bag containing Lacey's borrowed gown was tucked neatly into the trunk of the car, along with the rest of her luggage.

Lacey did her best to take everything in as they crawled along the wide avenue that led to the palace. Pretty shop windows lined the street, decorated with floral themes in celebration of the upcoming festivities. At the corner of every intersection, flower cart vendors sold fresh-cut bouquets—tiny nosegays with stems wrapped in tightly wound satin ribbon, all the way to magnificent bunches of glitter-tipped roses with petals that looked as if they'd been rolled in diamond dust.

Below the cliffside town center, perched at the edge of a jagged mountain covered in adorable cottages in soft watercolor hues, the Mediterranean Sea shone like a rare sapphire. Lacey had never seen water so blue, not even back home. It reminded her of Henry's soulful eyes.

Which was a super-platonic, non-romantic thought to be having as she sat in the backseat of a fancy town car on the way to his palace.

She couldn't dwell on her feelings much, though, because the castle had suddenly come into view. The crown jewel of the charming principality, it stood at the end of the avenue, behind an enormous fountain that created a roundabout at the palace drive. Beyond the dancing water, the glamorous Belle Époque-style building rose against the backdrop of the deep blue sea. It was so breathtaking that Lacey could've cried. She wasn't sure what she'd expected—something cold, gray, and made of stone, maybe?

But this was the very opposite of whatever medieval structure she'd conjured in her head. The Bella-Moritz Royal Palace was the color of a sun-bleached seashell—soft white, with just a touch of peachy pink—and it made Lacey want to put on a pair of dark, heart-shaped glasses and tip her face toward the sun.

As grand as it all was, there was no line of servants awaiting her at the doors to the enormous building. Clearly Lacey had watched too much *Downton Abbey* last year when she'd been sick with the flu. The lack of uniformed staff waiting to greet her was a relief, more than anything, especially when she caught sight of a familiar trio walking down the palace's wide steps toward the car when the driver pulled to a stop. Her heart felt like it was going to pound right out of her chest in the moment her eyes met Henry's.

"Um. Lace?" Ava peered out of the vehicle's tinted windows. "Who is *that*?"

"Henry and Rose," Lacey said, swallowing. After days of anticipation and more text messages than she could count, she was finally here.

"Obviously." Ava rolled her eyes. "I mean the other one."

"That's Ian, Henry's protection officer. I told you about him, remember?"

"You failed to mention how cute he is, which is a flagrant violation of the girlfriend code. How could you possibly forget to tell me he looks like a long-lost Hemsworth brother? You'll have to explain yourself later, over budget rosé, when we get back home. Meanwhile—" Ava dabbed her lips with gloss while Henry approached the car, "—I'll settle for an introduction."

Lacey laughed. Thank goodness this journey was beginning to feel more like a normal girls' trip than a royal fairy tale...except for the ridiculously handsome prince who grinned down at Lacey and offered her his hand after he'd opened her car door.

"Henry." She beamed up at him and suddenly had no idea what to do with her hands. Instinct told her to hug him, but was that allowed right here in his royal front yard?

"Princess Sweet Pea!" Rose, dressed in a prim white blouse with a Peter Pan collar and a pair of tan riding breeches instead of the Sweet Pea ballgown she'd worn every day at the park, threw herself between them and hugged Lacey's legs. "You're here."

Sorry, Henry mouthed. Then he leaned closer and whispered, "She's a little excited to see her favorite member of the nobility."

Henry smelled like sun-drenched lemons, sea salt, and fresh Mediterranean air. Lacey's stomach did a little tumble. Without his baseball cap and casual theme park clothing, he looked every inch a prince.

I am in so much trouble.

The theme park princess handbook didn't offer a single word of warning against developing a crush on a real-life prince, which definitely felt like a glaring omission.

She bent to peel Rose's arms from her knees and wrap her arms around the little girl. "You know what? While I'm here, why don't you call me Lacey instead of Princess Sweet Pea?"

"You mean like how Daddy calls me Rose instead of Caitriona?" Rose tilted her head. Her hair was arranged in tight French braids rather than the lopsided pigtails that had been her trademark at Once Upon A Time. "Is Lacey your secret princess name?"

"Um..." Lacey didn't know to answer that question. She'd been there less than a minute and already she was beginning to feel weirdly self-conscious about all the princess talk.

"Yes." Henry gave Rose a solemn nod. "Lacey is definitely her secret princess name."

"Only my favorite little girls get to call me that," Lacey said, playing along.

Henry smiled until his eyes crinkled in the corners, and it felt like they were back at Once Upon A Time, where royal titles were just pretend and a simple change of clothes could turn a person into anything they wanted to be—Goldilocks, one of the Three Little Pigs, the Big Bad Wolf. Even a princess who showed up on a castle doorstep and turned a lonely prince's life completely upside-down.

So very much trouble, indeed.

After introductions were made and Lacey noticed definite chemistry between Ava and Ian—whom she realized did indeed look like a Hemsworth brother, now that Ava had mentioned it—Henry showed Lacey and Ava to their rooms and introduced them to Miss Marie, the ladies' maid who'd be attending to their needs.

"Oh, that's okay. I'm sure I can look after myself." Lacey glanced around her temporary royal digs.

The palatial bedroom was decorated in various shades of creamy whites and ivories with heavy gold accents—as in, thick gold crown molding along the ceiling and framing the doorway, and a white velvet Queen Ann sofa and tufted wingback chairs propped up by carved gold legs.

An enormous bed sat off to the left of the sitting area, covered in a plush silk damask duvet—white, of course— and it stood just high enough off the ground that Lacey was sort of tempted to check and see if it'd been piled high with an extra mattress or two, Princess and the Pea style.

"It's no trouble," Miss Marie said, pulling back the tasseled curtains and securing each side behind a decorative gold curtain knob. A grove of lemon trees stood just outside the big bay window. "The castle is quite large. You'll need help finding your way around, and I'm here to assist with whatever you need."

Marie wore a short-sleeved, crisp white shirt with a simple dark skirt and matching vest. The vest had pockets lined with a red satin stripe, and her light brown hair was swept into a simple low ponytail. She looked like she might be in her mid to late thirties.

"Miss Marie is Rose's ladies' maid as well." Henry rested his hand on his daughter's small shoulder. "They're great friends, so Rose liked the idea of you two getting to know each other."

"In that case, how can I refuse?" Lacey smiled at Miss Marie. Still, she'd never had any sort of domestic help before. She wouldn't even know what to ask for assistance with.

"Would you like me to unpack your bags?" Miss Marie glanced toward the hanging bag containing Lacey's ballgown.

Lacey jumped in her path, blocking her way. "Thanks so much, but no. I'd rather do it myself."

Henry was *right there*. Lacey knew it might seem silly, but she didn't want him to see her pretty lilac gown until the night of the ball. Shouldn't it be a surprise?

You can take the girl out of the fairy tale, but you can't take the fairy tale out of the girl.

"As you wish." Miss Marie nodded.

Lacey placed the hanging bag inside an ornate, cream-colored wardrobe, tucking it away for safekeeping. Then their little group headed next door to get Ava situated in her suite.

Lacey had assumed they'd be sharing a room, which seemed silly now that she'd seen first-hand how spacious the palace was behind closed doors. She supposed it only made sense to make use of as many guest rooms as possible when you had a few dozen of them. The entirety of their small Fort Lauderdale apartment could've easily fit inside Lacey's bedroom at the palace, though. It was going to be strange staying in such an enormous space all by herself.

"Maybe you can pop over for a slumber party later," she whispered to Rose. "We can make a blanket fort."

"After my riding lesson?" Rose shot her a hopeful glance.

Lacey nodded. "Definitely."

"Ava, your room is right next door, but I'm afraid it's still a bit of a walk," Henry said, pulling Ava's wheelie suitcase behind them as they headed down the widest hallway Lacey had ever seen.

She wondered if Henry always gave palace guests such personal attention. Somehow, she doubted it.

"Thanks so much for this," she said, sidling up next to him. She could barely wrap her head around sharing a ladies' maid. Having a butler show them to their rooms would've been surreal.

Right, because having a prince do it is so much more relatable.

Why did she keep thinking of him as just plain Henry, the doting father who loved amusement park rides and food on a stick when reminders of his royal status were everywhere she turned?

For example—the proper-looking woman who was striding toward him from the opposite end of the hall. She was dressed in a sleek, dove-gray business suit and a tasteful string of pearls, and her gaze was trained on Henry in a way that said she meant business. Elite royal business, no doubt. Maybe Henry was late for christening a ship or getting fitted for a suit of armor...

And perhaps Lacey needed to expand her knowledge of princely duties beyond the realm of storybooks and theme parks.

"Henry, I've been looking all over for you." The woman in the pearls looked at the suitcase Henry pulled behind him as if she'd never seen such a contraption in her life. "What*ever* are you doing?"

"I'm helping my guests get settled," he said calmly. Apparently, that suit of armor could wait.

"Grandmère, look. Princess Sweet Pea is here." Rose clapped a hand over her mouth and then lowered her voice to a stage whisper. "I mean, Lacey. That's what we're supposed to call her now. It's her secret princess name."

Lacey's face went hot. Whoever this person was probably thought Lacey was some sort of compulsive liar with a weird royal fixation.

But then she turned Rose's words over in her mind and her attention snagged on one very important word—*Grandmère*. Lacey's high school French was a little rusty, but she used it every so often to speak with European guests at the park. She definitely knew what grandmère meant. Grandmother.

Panic seized her. This wasn't Henry's well-dressed assistant. She was his mother. The queen!

"Your Majesty," Lacey blurted.

And then years of muscle memory kicked in, and she lapsed into her royal fallback persona. Before she knew what she was doing, she dropped into a curtsey—not a sedate, tasteful curtsey, but an exaggerated theme park curtsey, complete with Cinderella hands.

Oh, good grief. What was she doing?

"Mother, this is Lacey Pope and her friend, Ava Rivera," Henry said, graciously ignoring Lacey's royal blunder.

"How do you do?" the queen said in a posh English accent with just a hint of French flair.

Was that a question? Was Lacey supposed to elaborate on how she felt at the moment? Ugh, why couldn't she remember how to have a basic conversation?

Because this is important. He's *important—not in a princely way, but in a I-might-be-falling-for-him way.*

Lacey opened her mouth to say something, anything, but before she could utter a word, Queen Elloise angled herself away from her to face Henry.

"I need to speak to you in my study, please." She arched a perfectly groomed eyebrow.

Henry nodded. "I'll be right there."

"At once." The queen's gaze flitted toward Lacey and darted right back to her son. "It's rather urgent."

"Go ahead." Lacey grabbed Ava's suitcase and waved him on. "We've got it from here. No problem. Rose can show us around, can't you, sweetheart?"

The little girl nodded, more than happy to oblige.

Henry apologized profusely and left with his mother to attend to whatever important matter required their attention, as a sinking feeling settled in the pit of Lacey's stomach.

So much for good first impressions.

"May I ask what's so urgent?" Henry crossed his arms and stood opposite his mother as she sat down at the vast French Provincial writing desk, where she conducted all of her official state business.

He much preferred talking to the queen over breakfast

than being summoned to her study. It made him feel like he was a school child who'd been called to the headmaster's office. In this particular instance, the insistence in his mother's sharp tone had also given him a headache.

She hadn't been particularly welcoming to Lacey. Granted, he'd sprung the visit on her out of nowhere, and the queen had made her feelings on the matter known. She clearly thought Henry wasn't exercising the best judgment.

What if I'm not? Henry gave a mental shrug. He hadn't stepped a foot wrong his entire life. He was tired of thinking with his head. Maybe it was time to start leading with his heart.

"We have a little problem." Queen Elloise folded her hands neatly on the surface of her desk and waited for Henry to take a seat.

Reluctantly, he lowered himself into a chair.

"Your friend Miss Pope seems sweet," she said.

"I'm surprised you've formed an opinion already. You haven't spent much time with her yet," he said, placing special, subtle emphasis on the word *yet*.

"Oh, I'm not referring to our meeting just now." The queen opened the top drawer of her desk, removed an oversized manilla envelope, and slid it toward him. "I meant this."

She tapped the thin parcel with a tastefully manicured fingernail.

Henry reached for it and undid the clasp, anxious to get this conversation over with, whatever it was about. And then he went still as an 8 x 10 photograph slid out of the envelope.

"That's you and Miss Pope, yes?" the queen said.

Henry stared down at the picture. It wasn't from the pirate ride, when he thought he'd seen a flash, but apparently had been taken while he and Lacey rode the Ferris wheel together. They were seated side by side, sharing that huge puff of cotton candy. Even though the photograph had been taken at twilight, Lacey was instantly recognizable in her voluminous, over-the-top theme park princess costume, and unfortunately, so was Henry.

"I lost my hat," he said quietly, unable to tear his gaze from the picture. "I was only without it for this one ride."

He'd felt so safe at Once Upon A Time. It was strange to think someone had recognized him and snapped a picture of what seemed like a private, intimate moment, and he was just now finding out about it.

Henry's jaw clenched. His annoyance flared, but he couldn't help feeling somewhat mesmerized by the picture. The photo would've been a lovely keepsake, if it hadn't felt like such an invasion of privacy. He and Lacey were looking intently into each other's eyes, perfectly framed by the shape of their little gondola. The picture had been snapped from behind, and their silhouettes were backlit by the neon colors and flashing lights of the park spread out before them. The effect was magical, almost as though sparks of electricity were bouncing back and forth between them. Despite his exposed, hatless head, Henry barely recognized himself. The expression on his face was one he'd never seen before—not in a single one of the pictures that had been taken of him throughout his many years of public life. By all appearances, he was completely smitten.

Had he really ever thought his feelings for Lacey were purely platonic?

Henry looked up and met his mother's gaze. "Where did you get this?"

"From the local press. They apparently bought it off a tourist who recognized you and subsequently sold the image to a news agency here in Bella-Moritz. They've been holding on to it until the Flower Festival in order to make the biggest splash." The queen sighed. "They sent a copy to the palace with a request for a comment."

"Fine. Just say no." Henry shrugged. "We decline to comment."

"I'm afraid it's not so easy, son. Lacey is the first woman you've been photographed with in years." His mother gave him an apologetic smile. "And now she's here. In our home."

Henry nodded. The queen didn't have to spell things out any further. Once the photo ran in the local paper, Lacey would be instantly recognized at the ball. Everyone on the Mediterranean coast—possibly even the world—would think they were an item.

Henry didn't even want to think about what they might have to say about her job.

"I have an idea, if you'd like to hear it," Queen Elloise said gently.

"I'm not sending her home." Henry shook his head. Lacey had only just arrived. If she left now, Rose would be heartbroken. Not to mention Henry himself...

He'd been restless since returning from Florida—unsettled in a way that made his chest ache. Seeing Lacey again, even for only a few minutes, had been a balm. He could breathe again.

"That's not what I was going to suggest at all. Why not simply release a statement to run alongside the image? You can say Miss Pope is simply a family friend." His mother tilted her head. "Even better, she's just a special acquaintance of Caitriona's. After all, that's the truth, isn't it?"

Was it? Henry wasn't quite so sure anymore.

He pinched the bridge of his nose and sighed. It should've been the easiest thing in the world for him to say that Lacey was simply a friend of the family. There was nothing romantic going on between them whatsoever.

Then why can't I bring myself say it?

CHAPTER FOURTEEN

Could We Get Beheaded For This?

"**D**ID YOU HAVE A PARTY in here and forget to invite me?" Ava stood in the center of Lacey's luxurious room at the palace and glanced around at the duvet and pillows piled on top of the sitting area. A tray holding a few stray remains of chocolate eclairs sat on the coffee table, along with empty glasses and a fine china pitcher that last night had held the creamiest, ice-cold milk Lacey had ever tasted. The floor was scattered with books—fairy tales, along with the hardback volume of *Black Beauty* Lacey had brought with her from the States, a gift for Rose. It was good thing Lacey had texted a picture of the elegant room to her dad and stepmom *before* she'd made such a mess.

"Sort of." Lacey laughed as she flipped through the clothes in her suitcase. "Rose spent the night. We made a blanket fort, read books, and right before we went to sleep, Miss Marie came and brought us a midnight snack."

Lacey still couldn't get used to the idea of having a ladies' maid, but she'd never been one to turn down chocolate. Especially, as it turned out, European chocolate.

"That little girl thinks you hung the moon." Ava plopped down on the settee and picked at a bite of eclair. "Oh my gosh, this is delicious."

"I know, right? But you do realize we're about to eat, don't you?" Lacey pulled out a floral linen dress with a flippy, ruffled hem. This might be the first time in the history of her adult life that she'd worn anything that required ironing to breakfast. Back home, she normally wore her pajamas.

"I do, but we don't know if there will be eclairs there, do we?" Ava licked a bit of dark chocolate from the tip of her finger.

"Point taken." Lacey slipped into the dress and frowned at her reflection in the mirror.

"What's wrong? You look really cute."

Lacey ran her fingertips over the dainty sprigs of daisies printed on the light blue linen. She'd chosen the dress because Henry had invited her for a walk through the Grand Flower Park this morning, but in the midst of all the splendor surrounding her, she thought it might be too unsophisticated.

What was a person supposed to wear on a date with a prince? Lacey thought she'd solved that problem with her borrowed ballgown, but nothing in her suitcase remotely resembled the elegant suit Queen Elloise had been wearing yesterday. And the invitation to the park had certainly seemed like a date. Henry had texted her the night before to ask if she'd like to see the flowers today, and he'd signed the message with more of those little x's that always made her head spin.

Then he'd written *I'm so glad you're here,* and Lacey hadn't been able to wipe the smile off of her face for two straight hours.

"Are you sure? I think I'm having an existential wardrobe crisis." Lacey bit her lip. "Also, I'm getting seriously bad vibes from Henry's mother."

Ava cocked her head. "How is that possible? You hardly even spoke to her."

"Exactly." Lacey swept her hair into a loose pony, then promptly undid it. "It was weird, don't you think?"

"She's a queen. She probably has a lot on her plate. I'm sure you have nothing to worry about. Parents adore you. Everyone does. You're one of the most popular characters at the park."

Lacey slipped her feet into her ballerina flats. "They adore Princess Sweet Pea, not me. There's a difference."

"Not really. I tell you that all the time. But if you're worried about making a good impression on the queen, we should probably get going. We might need a map to find the dining room in this place." Ava stood, and a pillow fell off the settee and onto the floor. "Oh, no."

"What? Did you change your mind about my dress? Should I change?"

"No, it's worse than that." Ava winced. "I think I just got chocolate on the sofa."

Spots floated before Lacey's eyes. She thought she might faint. "Please tell me you're kidding."

"I wish I was." Ava reached for a napkin and prepared to dab at a tiny smear of dark chocolate on the settee's tufted seat.

Lacey held up a hand. "Don't! That might make it worse."

"Oh, my gosh. What are we going to do? Could we get beheaded for this?"

Lacey took a deep breath. Panicking wouldn't help, but how could she not? "We need to do an internet search on the best way to get chocolate out of white silk damask."

Ava started pacing back and forth in front of the blanket fort. "But we're supposed to be in the dining room in less than ten minutes."

"Right. Okay." Lacey picked up the fallen pillow and placed it gently over the stain. "Let's go eat, and I'll deal with this later."

"Maybe Miss Marie can help?" Ava bit her lip.

"Maybe, but I hate to ask her to do that." Also, would she tell the queen? What if that settee was a family heirloom or something?

And to think, Lacey had been worried about first impressions when this second impression could end up being so, so much worse.

Lacey somehow survived breakfast—even the part where Rose recited all of Sweet Pea's rules of proper princessing. The queen had looked beyond baffled at the mention of bubble baths, and even though Henry had winked at Lacey and his eyes had sparkled with amusement, Lacey had simply jumped into the middle of the conversation and tried to steer it in a less embarrassing direction.

Flowers had seemed like a safe topic, or so she'd assumed. The queen was worried about the tour of the palace greenhouse. Something had apparently gone awry with the temperature controls, and the plants weren't blooming as much as they had in years past. The Flower Festival was the only time of the year the greenhouse was open to the public, and Henry's mother didn't want to let down the people of Bella-Moritz.

So maybe flowers hadn't been such a safe topic, after all. On the plus side, continually worrying about sticking her foot in her mouth kept Lacey from obsessing about her little chocolate problem.

After the minefield of the morning meal, Henry took Lacey for a walk through the Grand Flower Park, as promised. Overnight, breezy white tents had been set up all along the park's pebbled pathways. Lacey's favorite booth in the pop-up market had bushel baskets filled with hand-milled, fragrant soaps wrapped in flower petal paper. She chose a bar that smelled like rosewater and had been covered in handmade ecru paper, dotted with pink tea rose petals and tiny green fern leaves, to bring back to Fort Lauderdale for Madeline. Fairy godmothers never got enough credit for the fine work they did.

"So, no baseball cap today?" she asked, sliding her gaze toward Henry as he walked beside her along a winding sidewalk lined with day lilies and Shasta daisies.

He smiled. "No. A baseball cap won't quite do the trick here."

"I suppose not," Lacey said.

Everyone recognized Henry—not only did each person they came across seem to know instantly who he was, but they tried earnestly to please him. Children offered him small bouquets; vendors wanted to give him the best handmade flower products they had to offer. It was sweet how much the citizens seem to care about it him, but it also made Lacey wonder if people still thought of him as the grief-stricken prince from the viral photograph taken four years ago. She supposed they did—she'd even done so herself before she'd gotten to know him.

Carrying that sort of image around like a mantle must not be easy. It might even make it harder to move on.

"I can't get over how beautiful it is here." Lacey gazed into the distance, where a field of foxgloves danced in the slight summer breeze. "I get now why you call Bella-Moritz a 'quaint principality,' although I think you're underselling it a bit."

Henry's mouth curved into a boyish grin, reminding her

that even though a glamorous palace loomed behind him, he was still the same man who'd held a hummingbird in his hands for her and had run around after his daughter screaming *fee-fi-fo-fum*. "You're seeing us at our best. The rest of the year, we're not quite this impressive."

"Somehow I doubt that."

Their eyes met and held. Lacey couldn't believe how much she'd missed him over the past few days. Every time she'd swished into Ever After Castle for her tea party this week, her gaze had immediately darted toward the table where she'd first seen him sitting alongside Rose—just the two of them, all alone at that big table. And even though she'd known he wouldn't be there, her heart sank a little bit all the same. Henry was tangled up with all of her best memories of the park now. She still loved her job, obviously, but it just wasn't the same anymore. She'd simply been going through the motions, counting the days until she could see him again. Now that she was actually in Bella-Moritz, it was almost too good to be true.

Henry leaned toward her, and she felt warmth coming off him—so deep and lovely that it seemed to reach every part of her. And then a bumble bee rose up from a nearby Shasta daisy, causing them to spring apart.

Lacey let out a squeal, and they both laughed at their overreaction as the bee zipped over toward the foxgloves.

Henry raked a hand through his hair. "So much for bravery. I'd better make an effort to look less frightened next time that happens, or Ian's going to come over here and wrestle a flying insect to the ground."

He tipped his head toward Ian and Ava, following at a discreet distance. They'd browsed the pop-up market as a foursome, but as they'd made their way deeper into the park grounds and away from the crowds, Ian had hung back a bit to give Henry privacy. If the protection officer's broad smile was any indication, he was pleased to have

Ava along to keep him company. Every time Lacey looked over at them, they had their heads close together in quiet conversation. She'd never seen Ava so instantly besotted with anyone before.

"What would you like to do next?" Henry asked, glancing at his watch. "Rose has a riding lesson this afternoon, and I really need to check on her progress. But I'm all yours until then."

All mine.

Wasn't she supposed to be taking a break from dating? Why was that, again?

And weren't she and Henry supposed to be just friends?

Lacey didn't feel like an ordinary friend when he looked at her, though. Every time Henry's soulful blue eyes turned in her direction, she felt lit up inside, like Once Upon A Time's dazzling fireworks display. And when they walked side-by-side and his fingertips brushed against hers, she practically turned to mush.

"You know what I'd most like to do?" she said.

Henry peered at her as if trying to read her mind. "Go to the beach? Visit the harbor? There's a floating restaurant near the dock that serves fresh-steamed lobster with drawn butter and corn on the cob."

"All of those things sound amazing." And very, very public. As fond as she was of Ian, Lacey kind of liked the idea of getting to know Henry better without him having to worry about bringing a bodyguard along. "But I want to know more about your regular, everyday life."

"Really?"

"Really." She shrugged. "You know, the things you like to do at home or how you spend your time when you're not busy working."

Henry went quiet for a moment. "Actually, I work almost all the time. But lately I've been making an effort to change that."

"You mentioned that back at Once Upon A Time. How's it going so far?"

He blew out a breath. "I had a bit to catch up on after being away, but I managed to make it to Rose's room in time for bedtime stories every evening—with the notable exception of last night, when my daughter was busy with an important social engagement." He arched a brow.

"Blanket forts are serious business," Lacey said in her best mock-stern voice.

"So I've heard." His gaze met hers again, and a warm intimacy percolated between them.

It caught Lacey off-guard. Back at Once Upon A Time, she'd chalked up such moments as a combination of theme park magic and sitting close together in the dark. But here they were, just the two of them—no costumes, no special effects. And still, the air all around them felt different somehow.

Almost enchanted.

"Actually, if you'd like to explore the palace a bit—" Henry's smile went lopsided, just the way Lacey liked it, "—I might have an idea."

"That sounds like an offer I can't refuse."

Half an hour later, Lacey found herself on the palace balcony overlooking the dancing fountain on the royal square and the wide avenue that stretched through the heart of the town center, all the way to the Grand Flower Park, where they'd just been. The park was a splash of color on the horizon, and the cluster of white-peaked tents in the pop-up market looked almost like a castle itself.

To the left, the mountain struck a rugged pose against a clear sky, the exact shade of blue hydrangeas. To the right, the sea sparkled like a jewel. The cool breeze smelled like sea water and sun-kissed flowers.

Lacey took a deep inhale. "The view up here is incredible."

"It is, isn't it?" Henry's smile went bittersweet. "I guess I take it for granted sometimes. This is where the royal family gathers for big public appearances and national holidays. When my mother gives her Christmas Eve address, the square below is always packed with people carrying small white candles. It's a sight to behold."

"That sounds almost too beautiful to imagine," Lacey said, stopping herself before she went so far as to say she wished she could see it someday.

She had no clue if she'd ever set foot in Bella-Moritz after this trip was over. Doubtful, probably. But she couldn't bring herself to think about that right now. She just wanted to enjoy the moment before it was over. Ian and Ava were somewhere looking around the palace grounds, and Rose was preparing for her riding lesson. Lacey was getting to spend some rare alone time with Henry, and she definitely didn't want to spoil it by thinking about how soon it would end.

"I didn't bring you up here for the view, though." Henry's eyes twinkled with mischief. "I thought I'd teach you the proper royal wave."

Laughter bubbled up Lacey's throat. "What?"

"You schooled me on theme park royal behavior." He shrugged. "The way I look at it, turnabout is fair play."

Lacey had a sudden flashback to when he'd first invited her to the ball. It had been such a surprise, and the look on his face had been so ardent as fireworks had lit up the night sky.

"We've danced in your castle. It seems only fair that we should dance in mine."

The man was far too charming for his own good. She wanted to believe it was simply an occupational hazard, but it was getting harder and harder to pretend she wasn't developing feelings for Henry. Feelings that had nothing to do with being just friends.

She did her best imitation of a proper royal wave, keeping her fingers glued together and swiveling her hand at the wrist. Wasn't this how the queen of England always did it?

Henry shrugged. "Not too bad." But his mouth twisted into a telltale smirk.

"Okay, Prince Charming." She gave him a playful shove. "Give me the tutorial."

He spent the next twenty minutes teaching her to wave like a princess. From there, they moved on to the mews, where the royal stables were located. Lacey went giddy when Henry had one of the grooms arrange for her to ride in a real horse-drawn carriage. They made a few small passes though the courtyard, clip-clopping at a moderate pace. Afterward, he showed her how to wield a ceremonial sword and perform an accolade ceremony.

"I have to admit I've never heard of an 'accolade ceremony' before," Lacey said as she examined the sword's narrow silver blade. It felt like it weighed about ten times more than the fake ones the knights in shining armor at Once Upon A Time carried.

"It's more commonly known as a dubbing ceremony." Henry dropped to his knees in front of her. "It's how you make someone a knight or a dame."

Lacey felt her eyes go wide. "That sort of thing still happens? I thought it was just for medieval times."

"Still happens. Right here, in this very room." He lifted his arms, gesturing at the red silk brocade walls and heavy crimson curtains in the long, narrow receiving hall where he'd taken her. In its own way, the palace was like a fun house. There was something new and different around every corner.

"Wow," she said, and as gently as she could, she lifted the sword and tapped the blade against one of Henry's shoulders and then the other. "I dub thee Henry…"

Prince of my heart.

He smiled at her and rose to his feet, and suddenly he was so close. *Too* close. They'd been having such a fun, goofy time all afternoon, but underneath all the flirty banter, there was a new sense of tenderness between them. At times, Lacey wanted to close her eyes and just lean into it, but then she'd remember who they both were. She and Henry were like flip sides of a coin—so similar, so familiar, but different in a way that meant they'd never meet on the same side.

"You've gone quiet on me," he murmured, brushing a loose strand of hair from her eyes.

Longing wound its way around her heart.

"I was just thinking about how all of this is kind of like a mirror image of your trip to Florida—the castle, the ball, a colorful world steeped in so much history. Except everything at Once Upon A Time is pretend, obviously." Lacey blew out a breath. "And here, it's real."

Henry cupped her cheek with one of his warm, strong hands and tilted her face upward, prompting her to look him in the eye.

And there was nothing pretend about the affection she saw shining in the depths of his beautiful eyes. Forget-me-not blue.

Lacey's heart beat as fast as a hummingbird's wings.

I couldn't forget this man if I tried, and it has nothing at all to do with his royal status.

"Oh, princess," he said. "Don't you know by now? It's all been real to me."

CHAPTER FIFTEEN

Lemons to Lemonade

"Excuse me, Your Royal Highness."

A uniformed footman bustled into the room, and Lacey nearly dropped the heavy ceremonial sword right on Henry's foot.

"Yes?" Henry removed his hand from Lacey's cheek, but kept his feet planted right where he stood, within kissing distance—which was a perfectly valid unit of measurement, thank you very much.

"Princess Caitriona is waiting for you at the stables," the footman said.

Where had he come from, anyway? Did the palace have hidden passageways? It was like he'd materialized out of thin air.

"Right." Henry nodded. "Her riding lesson." He glanced at his watch and winced.

"Go." Lacey waved a hand, and again the sword wobbled in her grasp. Henry gently took it from her and placed it back on the special display shelf where he'd gotten it. "You two need to practice for the parade."

Henry angled his head toward her. "You'll be all right on your own for a while?"

"Of course. Don't be silly. There's plenty to do around here," Lacey said.

Henry turned his attention back to the footman, still standing by like a royal chaperone. "Could you please escort Miss Pope back to her suite?"

This was a relief, since Lacey's room was clear on the other side of the castle. She wasn't sure she could've found it on her own, and she was low-key terrified of bumping into the queen somewhere.

Although, maybe they could've bonded somehow. Had a nice little chat.

Yeah, because we have so much to talk about.

Henry reached and gave Lacey's hand a squeeze before heading off in one direction, while she and the footman exited from a door on the opposite end of the room.

"Are you enjoying your stay in Bella-Moritz?" he asked as they traversed their way through the maze of gilded hallways and narrow banquet halls, toward the palace living quarters.

"Very much," Lacey said.

They walked past a wide window that overlooked a large building made entirely of glass, shimmering beneath the Mediterranean sun.

Lacey's steps slowed. "Oh, is that the greenhouse?"

"Yes. Would you like to take a look?"

She nodded. "I'd love to."

The footman led her to a hidden doorway that blended in perfectly with the silk-covered walls of the hallway. They stepped outside, and the soft hush of the palace was replaced with the birdsong and roar of the ocean in the distance. A cobblestone path wound its way through lush greenery toward the greenhouse, sparkling like cut crystal beneath the late afternoon sun.

As soon as she walked inside the tall glass building, Lacey understood why Queen Elloise had been worried about the lack of blossoms. In any ordinary home or park, the greenhouse would've been spectacular, but after seeing how the rest of the principality was practically blanketed with flowers, the contents of Her Majesty's greenhouse did seem a little...underwhelming. It had obviously been lovingly tended to, with baskets of lush ferns and dripping ivy hanging from the ceiling and a little waterfall area in the center, surrounded by moss-covered stones.

Lacey especially liked how the plants weren't arranged in neat rows, but spaced throughout the area in little nooks, or staged in vignettes, decorated wheelbarrows, and wicker rocking chairs with floral chintz cushions. Her favorite part of the greenhouse was a pond, scattered with lily pads, that looked like something out of a Monet painting. Still, everything was so green, while everyplace else in Bella-Moritz was all dressed up in bright, blooming color.

Lacey was still thinking about it half an hour later when she was back in her room, trying to convince Miss Marie to leave Rose's blanket fort intact. First, Rose would be seriously bummed if she came back and found it gone. Second, Lacey hadn't had a chance to rectify the tiny chocolate problem, and she didn't want Miss Marie to find it and decide Lacey was a plague on the house of Chevalier and recommend the queen banish her from the kingdom until the end of time. A little dramatic, probably, but anything seemed possible in this place.

"As you wish," Miss Marie said, and ran a feather duster over the windowsill.

Lacey watched her quick-moving hands, and then her gaze snagged on the lemon grove beyond the glistening glass window. "Miss Marie." She moved closer and saw a family with two young children strolling among the lemon trees.

The kids each had a basket slung over an arm, filled to the brim with ripe, yellow fruit. "Can anyone pick lemons from the orchard?"

"Of course. The royal lemon grove is part of the public park space of Bella-Moritz," Marie said. Her feather duster stilled. "Would you like me to go gather some lemons for you?"

"No, thank you. I can do that, but is there any way you could get me a dozen or so nice, flat plates and a dish of sugar cubes? Maybe a few spools of wire, if it's not too much trouble?" Lacey pressed her palms together, like the prayer hands emoji.

"Yes, Miss Pope. If that's really what you want." Marie hugged her feather duster to her chest and tilted her head. "But can I ask what for? I don't believe I've ever had a guest in the palace ask me for wire before."

"Just a little craft project." Lacey took a deep breath. *Am I really going to do this?* "I have an idea for the greenhouse."

"Where's Caitriona?" Queen Elloise glanced around the table the following morning at breakfast, but her question was very obviously directed at Henry.

He could feel the queen's impatience in his bones, just as he could feel the pressing weight of the impending publication of the photograph from Once Upon A Time—a nagging detail he'd yet to deal with. There simply hadn't been time.

No, that wasn't quite true. Henry had yet to *make* time to draft a statement for the press office because he'd been too busy alternating between enjoying himself with Lacey and trying to prepare Rose for the royal procession, which was now a mere twenty-four hours away.

Yesterday, she'd managed to sit in the saddle while Daisy took a few tentative steps. It had hardly been the triumphant ride the queen, and everyone else in Bella-Moritz, expected. Henry was at a loss. If he didn't do something soon, he'd have virtually no ammunition in his arsenal to fight his mother's idea of hiring a governess and limiting what little life his daughter had outside the palace walls.

The fact that Rose was now late for breakfast certainly wasn't helping matters.

Beside him, Lacey blinked. "She spent the night in my room, but I haven't seen her since early this morning."

The queen looked up from her tea. "Caitriona spent the night in your room?"

Lacey nodded. "We've been reading *Black Beauty*. I brought the book with me from Florida. You know, because of the horse thing."

Henry turned toward her, a smile tugging at his lips. "Why is this the first I'm hearing of this?"

"We girls have to have our secrets." Lacey grinned at him, but her smile seemed to freeze in place when she glanced back toward the queen. "But like I said, she went right back to her room around six o'clock. She said she needed to get ready for breakfast."

"And yet, she's still not here," Queen Elloise said.

Henry stiffened. "Mother."

Before the queen could respond, Rose's ladies' maid came rushing into the dining room with her hands behind her back. Apparently, Henry's mother had sent a search party out for his tardy seven-year-old. "I've found her, Your Majesty. Princess Caitriona will be here in just a moment."

"Brilliant. Thank you, Marie. Now we can stop worrying and get back to our meal," Henry said, stabbing at his omelet with his fork. "Right, Mother?"

It was breakfast, not a state dinner.

"Yes, thank you, Marie," the queen said.

But when Marie turned to go, Henry spotted a flash of sparkle behind her back. Whatever it was didn't go unnoticed by the monarch.

Queen Elloise narrowed her gaze at Marie. "What do you have there?"

Ava, seated closest to the spot where Marie stopped in her tracks, went pale. "Uh-oh."

"It's nothing, really." Marie shook her head. The poor thing looked like a deer caught in the headlights. "Just doing a little light housekeeping, Your Majesty."

Henry's gut churned. Why did he feel like something was about to go terribly wrong?

"Show me." The queen held out her hand.

Then Marie winced as she produced a dripping-wet crown from behind her back—not a plastic crown like the one Rose had worn at Once Upon A Time before she'd given it away, but one of the heirloom tiaras from his mother's private collection. Henry had most recently seen it on his mother's head at a white tie dinner in the palace's grand dining room.

Marie's hand shook as she placed the glittering tiara in Queen Elloise's hand, along with a tiny puddle of soap suds.

A bubble on one of the crown's pointed, platinum prongs popped, and his mother blinked. Hard.

Marie's eyes went wide. "I'm so sorry, Your Majesty. Princess Caitriona must've gotten it from your suite and decided to play dress-up, but I take full responsibility."

"Why is it *wet*?" the queen asked.

Henry closed his eyes.

Oh, no.

"I found her wearing it in the bath just now," Marie said, her voice as small as Henry had ever heard it. "A bubble bath, I'm afraid."

"Please don't blame Marie. This is all my fault." Lacey flew to her feet.

"Lacey, don't," Henry said. "It's okay."

The tiara was a little wet, not ruined. And frankly, Rose so rarely acted her age that Henry couldn't help but feel proud she was finally behaving more like a child than a mini-adult.

His mother turned to study Lacey through narrowed eyes, and Lacey immediately dropped into a panicked theme park curtsey.

"Sorry," she said, straightening. "Again. It's a habit."

Ava looked as if she were trying not to laugh.

"Anyway, the tiara thing is definitely my fault. It's part of the royal rules at Once Upon A Time. 'Never take off your crown—not even in a bubble bath.'" Lacey mimed having a crown on her head, and then slowly sat back down.

An awkward silence fell over the table, and just as Henry was about to try to say something—anything—to diffuse the situation, a footman scurried into the dining room and stood beside Marie. His face was beet red and he panted a little, as if he'd just come from running circles around the castle.

Which he apparently had. Sort of, anyway.

"Your Majesty," he said, struggling to catch his breath.

The queen set her damp crown down on the table. "I'm almost afraid to ask, but what is it?"

"It's the greenhouse, ma'am." The footman's face cracked into a smile. "I apologize for interrupting, but I know you'll want to come see. It opens for visitors in less than an hour, and well..."

"And well...?" Queen Elloise prompted.

"I can't really describe it, ma'am. You must see it to believe it." The footman waved toward the dining room exit with a flourish.

"I love a field trip," Ava said.

Henry was up for anything that would take his mother's mind off the bubble bath incident. Lacey looked like she wanted to disappear under the table. He wanted to reach for her and give her hand a reassuring squeeze, but she was too far away.

"Let's go." He folded his napkin and stood.

"Breakfasts are majorly dramatic around here," Ava muttered as they made their way through the corridors toward the palace doors closest to the greenhouse.

Henry let out a little laugh. "You have no idea."

The sun was already high in the sky, promising a bright, clear day for the public's tour of the palace grounds. Sunlight glinted off the diamond-shaped panes of the greenhouse walls, and maypoles festooned with ribbons flanked its wide, open entryways on all four sides.

It was lovely. While sympathetic toward his mother's concerns about the greenhouse tour, having Lacey in Bella-Moritz had given him a new perspective on things. They lived in a seaside paradise, surrounded by beauty on every side. There was magic in the life they lived here in the palace. He'd just lost of sight of it for a while.

But what Henry saw when he walked into the greenhouse stopped him dead in his tracks. Butterflies—hundreds of them, maybe even thousands—fluttered through the air in delicate, graceful pirouettes. Tiny, colorful ballerinas.

There were so many of them they almost didn't seem real. He squinted, but he wasn't seeing things. They were there—bright tangerine-hued Monarch butterflies, as big as his hand, all the way down to small, vivid blue ones with lacy, ruffled wings.

"Oh, my." His mother gasped and pressed a hand to her heart. Then her lips curved into a smile the likes of which Henry hadn't seen light up her face in a long, long time. "It's beautiful."

"Where did they all come from?" Ian said.

"I don't know." The footman shrugged. "They just appeared overnight. It's the strangest thing."

"Butterfly feeders," Ava said.

Queen Elloise titled her head. "Pardon?"

Ava pointed to a plate, suspended by thin wire from a nearby tree branch. It was one of the china plates they sold in the palace gift shop, decorated with the royal family crest and ringed with gold. The plate was covered with sliced lemons, pink sugar cubes, and tiny piles of Shasta daisies, like the ones that had lined the path where Henry and Lacey had strolled through the flower park.

A butterfly floated down to feed on one of the lemon slices, moving its wings in dainty slow motion. Lacey's lovely mouth curved into a gentle smile as she stood quietly beside Henry.

"Look, they're everywhere." Ian pointed to another plate tucked beneath a nearby fern and two more, hanging by the waterfall.

"I don't think I've ever heard of a butterfly feeder before," the queen said.

"They're attracted to bright colors and anything sweet. Right, Lacey?" Ava's gaze flitted toward Lacey. "You've made these before at children's parties at Ever After Castle before, haven't you?"

"Maybe." Lacey shrugged. "But they're pretty common. Anyone could've done this."

No, not just anyone. It seemed so obvious to Henry. How could everyone else not see it?

Lacey met his gaze and gave him a tiny, almost unnoticeable shake of her head. So Henry kept quiet, even though every beat of his heart seemed to scream out loud.

This is the princess I've been waiting for.

Later that evening, just after Lacey had ended a call with

dad, her phone buzzed with an incoming text from Henry.

The birds and butterflies are taken care of. The tiara got its bubble bath. I think it's time we fulfill another of your princess rules.

Lacey peered at the message, smiling despite herself. The bubble bath incident still mortified her to her core. There simply weren't enough butterflies in the entire world to make her forget the look on the queen's face when she'd spied the crown in Miss Marie's hands, dripping with soap suds.

But she liked that Henry kept texting her, even though she was right there in his palace instead a completely different continent. It felt so normal, as if he was a regular person instead of a member of the nobility. He was still the same Henry who liked sausage on a stick and who'd called her late at night just to murmur sweet dreams, even amid the gilded trappings of his position.

She typed out a reply message. *What did you have in mind?*

No sooner did Lacey press send than a quiet knock sounded on the door to her suite. She practically floated across the expansive room, eager to see what Henry wanted to show her.

"Ready for a beastly adventure?" he asked with a wink when she swung the door open. He was dressed in another pair of his finely tailored pants, paired with a light blue dress shirt that brought out the color in his eyes.

Lacey gripped the doorknob as she went a little weak in the knees. "Beastly adventure?" She tilted her head. "Don't tell me this place has an actual zoo."

"No, but the palace in Monaco does." He shrugged one manly shoulder. "Wrong prince, sweetheart."

Lacey arched an eyebrow. *No, there's only one prince for me, and I'm looking right at him.* "Fine. Don't tell me where we're going. Unlike other people, I actually enjoy surprises."

"Yes, I know, and I aim to deliver," he said, reaching for

her hand and weaving his fingers through hers.

Lacey didn't care where they were headed. She was just glad to have time alone with him, especially before the big royal procession tomorrow. Her time in Bella-Moritz was already winding down to a close. She knew the royal ball was supposed to be the big, grand finale, and she was looking forward to it with all of her heart. But there was something extra special about these unexpected, stolen moments—something intimate and private, just between the two of them.

Henry squeezed her hand tight and led her through the maze of palace hallways until they ended up in a corridor she'd yet to set foot in before. Then he paused in front of a closed door with a massive gold doorknob and intricately carved wooden details in the smooth, dark mahogany. "Are you ready?" he asked, and a thrill coursed through her.

"As ready as I'll ever be. Unless it's a dragon. In that case, no. I'm not ready at all."

Henry grinned.

"It's not, is it?" Lacey said.

He seemed way too pleased himself all of a sudden. Coming face to face with a dragon didn't seem any more unlikely than dancing with a real prince in Ever After Castle. She just had to ask.

Henry flashed her a wink and opened the door.

Golden light spilled from the expansive room. There wasn't a scaly dragon in sight, just row upon row of glossy wooden bookshelves and more books than Lacey had ever seen in one place in her entire life.

She walked inside and turned a slow circle, inhaling the comforting scent of ink on paper. "What is this place?" she whispered.

"It's the palace library," Henry said, voice going soft. "Rule number two, remember? Read lots of books, as many as you possibly can."

How did he do it? How did he remember everything she'd said at Sweet Pea's tea party, word for word?

"Do you like it?" he asked.

Lacey's throat went tight. This was the best beastly surprise ever. She felt like Belle...except no, not really. She felt like herself, just the way Henry saw her. And that was infinitely better than playing pretend.

"I love it," she whispered. "More than I can possibly say."

CHAPTER SIXTEEN

Mirror, Mirror on the Wall

THE FOLLOWING MORNING, THE ENTIRE palace was abuzz with preparations for the royal procession and flower parade. Even though the queen's mood had improved considerably since the surprise butterfly migration, Lacey was still filled with relief when Miss Marie swished into her room carrying a tray of hot coffee, buttery croissants, and homemade rose petal jam.

After the wet tiara debacle, Lacey dreaded setting foot in the dining room again. No amount of butterflies could erase the memory of the queen's disapproving expression when she'd set eyes on the sudsy crown. She shot off a text to Ava. *Come have breakfast with me.*

Three little dots appeared, and then a return text popped up. *I'll be right there,* followed by a crown emoji, a bubble bath emoji, and a red circle with a line through it.

Lacey laughed, and bit into a warm croissant. The jam melted her on tongue. She wasn't sure she could go back to eating generic toaster pastries every morning before work.

She would, of course. This was a vacation, not real life—even though the line between fantasy and reality was becoming blurrier than ever.

Lacey closed her eyes and let her mind wander back to the tender expression on Henry's face when he'd almost kissed her in the sword room.

Oh, princess. Don't you know by now? It's all been real to me.

She could've happily lived the rest of her life right there in that one, stolen moment. Minus the footman's interruption, obviously.

A knock sounded on her door, so she shoved the rest of her croissant in her mouth and padded across the room to let Ava in.

When she swung the door open, Ava was nowhere to be seen. Instead, Henry's warm smile greeted her. He was wearing a dress military uniform, complete with gold epaulettes on his shoulders and so many medals pinned to his chest she was surprised she hadn't heard him rattling from all the way down the palace hall. He looked like every cartoon version of Prince Charming she'd ever seen.

Lacey coughed on her oversized bite of croissant. Crumbs sprayed Henry's medal collection.

He laughed and wiped them away with brush of his white gloved hand.

"Sorry. You caught me off guard with all the"—she waved a hand, indicating his overall princely appearance—"regalia."

"Apology accepted." Henry arched a brow. "May I come in?"

"Sure." She opened the door wider, feeling distinctly underdressed in her pajamas and bare feet.

"You've got a little jam." Henry's eyes twinkled and he brushed a fingertip across her cheek. "Right there."

Lacey swiped it away with the back of her hand. "Careful.

I wouldn't want you to mess up those white gloves of yours."

"I never take them off," he said. "It's in the palace hand-book."

"Sure it is," she said, but her heart gave a forbidden little pitter-patter.

Oh, no. Panic zinged through Lacey, like a tiny white ball in one of the pinball machines in a theme park arcade. *I think I love him.*

She couldn't, though. She wouldn't. The uniform and the medals and the gold cartoon epaulettes were just messing with her head, that was all.

Your head isn't the problem, Sweet Pea. It's your heart that's running wild.

"I..." she stuttered, unsure what to say. She didn't even know what he was doing there. Wasn't the parade supposed to start in just an hour or so?

"I wanted to talk to you for a minute before the procession," he said, and only then did Lacey notice his smile didn't quite reach his eyes.

"Is everything okay?" she asked. "Rose didn't steal any more of the Crown Jewels for bath time, did she?"

"Not that I'm aware of, but I wouldn't rule it out." The corner of Henry's mouth hitched into a half grin. "She's still not wild about riding in the procession. If she makes it from the park all the way to the palace in the saddle, I'll loan her my own crown for her bubble bath tonight."

He had a crown. Because of course he did.

"I wanted to let you know that someone took a picture of you and me together," he said quietly. "There's a chance it could appear in the newspaper."

"Oh." Lacey crossed her arms and promptly uncrossed them. Her picture? In the Bella-Moritz paper? "When?"

Her mouth went dry. Images of every royal girlfriend she'd ever heard about flashed through Lacey's head: Lady Diana, Kate Middleton, Meghan Markle. Every one of them had been picked apart by the press, simply because they'd been dating princes. The fairy tales always seemed to leave that part out, didn't they?

"I don't know. Maybe today, maybe tomorrow, but definitely before you go."

Before I go. A stupid, stupid lump formed in her throat. Of course she was leaving. She had the return plane ticket tucked into her handbag, along with her passport and her employee identification card from Once Upon A Time.

"I suppose someone took the photo at the flower park the other day," Lacey said. She hadn't seen anyone lurking in the flower beds when they'd walked off by themselves, but anything was possible. Maybe it was a picture of her and Henry with Ian and Ava, but the photographer had cropped the other couple out of the picture.

"Actually, no. It's from the theme park."

An icy chill ran down Lacey's spine. "The theme park?"

"The Ferris wheel, to be exact." He nodded. "I probably should've kept better track of my baseball cap."

Lacey shook her head. This couldn't be happening. Her picture was going to be on the front page, wasn't it? Not just in Bella-Moritz, but maybe the whole world. She might even go viral...and she'd be dressed in a theme park princess costume.

"Your mother is going kill me," Lacey said.

"No, she's not. And it doesn't matter what anyone else thinks. I just didn't want you to get caught off-guard." Henry reached for her hand and squeezed it tight. "We're in this together, okay? Just you and me. I can make a statement and say whatever we want it to say—we're just friends. It was Rose's birthday, and I was on holiday. Or..."

Or...

Henry took a step forward, closing the space between them, and every last piece of Lacey's battered heart seemed to hang on that one little word.

"Hi, sorry it took me so long. I—" Ava breezed into the room and came to stuttering halt when she saw Henry. "Oh my goodness, look at you." She waved a hand at his uniform. "You seriously look like you just climbed out of the Disney vault."

"Ava," Lacey said. *Not now. Please, not now.*

But Henry just laughed. "I should go check on Rose. She was a lot more enthusiastic about the carousel at Once Upon A Time than she is about riding in this parade."

"Wait a minute." Lacey drew in a sharp breath. "That's it!"

Henry's brow furrowed. "What?"

"The carousel." Lacey ran to her suitcase and yanked out a pair of jeans and a T-shirt, the first thing she could get her hands on. "We can dress Daisy in flowers and ribbons so she looks like a carousel horse. Rose will love it."

"You're a genius," Ava said.

Henry nodded, beaming at her. "I think it might work."

"We've got to hurry though, right?" Lacey ran to the bathroom to get dressed, grateful for a distraction from the question she'd yet to answer.

Or...?

Never in her life had she been ashamed of her job, but this was serious. She and Mark had broken up over that puffy pink dress. Sort of, anyway.

And now she was supposed to decide if she wanted to let the world at large gawk at a photo of her dressed as Princess Sweet Pea alongside Henry while speculation ran wild, or to ask him to explain the image away as a meaningless summer holiday. They'd started off in a fairy tale, but now they'd gone off book, and there was no magic mirror on the wall to tell her how to proceed.

She didn't have time to think about it right now, though. Nor did she have a chance to give the matter another thought for the rest of the day. Miss Marie managed to help them gather enough ribbon and cut flowers to transform Daisy into the most whimsical, romantic carousel horse anyone had ever seen. Ava braided ribbons through the pony's mane while Lacey made a daisy chain wreath to go around her neck. Henry helped tie tiny bows along the horse's forelock, and when Rose arrived at the stables, dressed in her finest princess attire, she broke down in happy tears when she saw Daisy.

Lacey and Ava barely had time to change and make it down to the palace gates to watch the parade. But when she saw Henry riding on his big stallion alongside his little girl, prancing toward her on top of a proud pony, Lacey realized she didn't need a magic mirror to tell her how she felt.

She knew.

Lacey had only been back in her pristine—well, except for the tiny hidden chocolate stain on the sofa—bedroom for a few minutes after the end of the parade when there was a soft knock at the door.

Henry.

Happiness sparkled through her as she padded barefoot across the lush carpeting toward the threshold. She'd just changed into her pajamas and was about to slip into bed with a book. Today had been a good day. She was finally beginning feel a bit more at home in the palace—although, come on, it was more like a museum than a cozy home. No wonder Rose had been so enamored with the sights and sounds at Once Upon A Time. The little girl was a real-life princess, but from what Lacey had seen so far, she didn't get much of a chance to be just a regular kid.

Rose had such a special dad, though. Why was he at her door? She didn't think he'd press her about the photograph again—not so soon. Dare she hope for a goodnight kiss?

The very idea of it made her breathless as she swung the door open. "Hey, you."

And then she froze, all thoughts of a goodnight kiss dissipating into a fog of alarm.

She gripped the doorknob so tight that her hand went numb. "Your Majesty."

Henry's mother stood in the gilded palace hallway with her spine as perfectly straight as it always was and not a hair out of place. Despite the late hour, she was still dressed in her usual pressed pastel suit, sheer pantyhose, and tasteful stilettos.

Lacey wondered if she even owned a bathrobe. Or sweatpants. She hoped so.

But it was difficult to worry about what the queen might wear if she ever decided to lounge about and binge-watch a Hallmark movie marathon when Lacey had no idea what the monarch was doing at her door.

"Lacey." Queen Elloise smiled and gave Lacey a polite, queenly nod.

Lacey swallowed and dropped into her Princess Sweet Pea curtsey. She even held up the ruffled trim of her pajama shorts with her fingertips arranged in Cinderella hands. Ugh, why did she keep doing that?

Old habits died hard. Or maybe Lacey just felt more comfortable taking on the role of someone else, someone who *everybody* seemed to like, instead of trying to fit in all on her own.

Now is the not the time for an existential crisis. There's a queen at your door. Invite her in.

Lacey straightened. "Come on in," she said as she held the door open wide, grateful that Queen Elloise seemed to be ignoring her slip into character.

"I apologize for intruding on you so late, but I wanted to have a little chat, if you don't mind," the queen said in her perfect, clipped accent.

"Oh, there's no need to say you're sorry. After all, it's your house." Lacey waved a hand at the luxurious decor. "Um. I mean, castle."

Seriously?

She needed to stop talking. Right now.

"Would you like to sit down?" Lacey tried to lead her toward the sitting area, but her footsteps faltered when she spotted her fancy silk duvet strewn over the top of the white velvet Queen Ann sofa and both tufted wingback side chairs. "Oops. I made a blanket fort earlier." Lacey scrambled to gather the duvet into her arms.

She thought it best not to mention the blanket fort had been for Rose, even if it would be very odd to make one for herself. The little girl had been so spectacular at the royal procession earlier. Lacey didn't want to risk getting her into trouble. The queen might not like the idea of Rose visiting Lacey in her room every day.

"No need to put yourself out." The queen tucked an invisible wayward strand of hair behind her ear. "This won't take long."

Lacey kept bunching the duvet into a manageable heap, but it seemed to go on forever in an endless trail of silk damask. She finally gave up and tossed it onto the bed. In the flurry of activity, the throw pillow on the settee fell over, exposing Ava's chocolate stain. Lacey had been so busy making butterfly feeders and decorating Rose's pony that she still hadn't had a chance to deal with it. With the queen in the room, the smudge of chocolate no longer seemed so tiny. It seemed about as obvious as a footman with bunny ears.

Lacey wished the grand palace floor would open up and swallow her whole.

"It's really all right," the queen said. "I'll stand."

She didn't utter a word about the mess. Lacey wished

she would. Somehow, the monarch's gracious silence only made her feel worse.

Lacey wrapped her arms around herself, wishing fervently she wasn't dressed in ruffled pajamas for an impromptu tête-a-tête with Henry's mother. Why was she always so underdressed for these surprise royal visits? "Okay. Well, what can I do for you, Your Majesty?"

She resisted another irrational urge to curtsey. It seemed to happen every time she called the queen by her royal title. Instead, she wiggled her toes in the carpet, wondering if her lavender toenail polish broke some sort of royal protocol.

Queen Elloise's gaze darted to Lacey's feet before meeting her gaze again. "I wanted to speak to you about Rose's performance today in the procession."

Lacey relaxed a little, despite how nervous speaking to the queen one-on-one made her feel—particularly since only one of them was dressed for a pajama party. "She was amazing, wasn't she? I'll bet Henry was so proud of her."

The queen nodded. "Yes, we all were."

"I took a bunch of pictures. Would you like to see some of them?" She glanced around in search of her phone.

It was on the nightstand beside the book she'd started reading on the plane from Florida, a cozy mystery novel about a dog walker who solved crimes with the help of her Cavalier King Charles Spaniel.

The queen's gaze snagged on the book. "You read mysteries?"

Lacey clutched her phone to her chest. "Yes. I spent a lot of time alone as a kid, so I've always been a big reader. Henry showed me the palace library. It's one of the most beautiful things I've ever seen. It would take a lifetime to read all of those books."

Henry's mother smiled. "The library has always been my favorite room of the house. I spent many, many hours there when I was a young girl."

Lacey felt herself smile. So they actually had something in common—one tiny thing—even though the queen was the sort of person who referred to a grand, gilded palace as a house. She tried to imagine Queen Elloise tucked away as a lonely little girl in that big library with her head buried in a book. The queen was so regal, though. So confident. Her mannerisms and just the way she walked was so elegant that it *always* seemed as though she were wearing an invisible crown. Lacey couldn't imagine her looking any different than she did right this moment.

She took a deep breath and refocused on the phone, tapping the photo album icon on the small screen and flipping through the pictures as she searched for the start of the ones she'd taken of Rose at the parade.

"Tell me more. I'm interested in knowing why, if you don't mind," Queen Elloise said.

Lacey glanced up from her phone. "Why I like mysteries or why I spent a lot of time alone as a kid?"

Her mouth went dry. *Please let it be the former.*

The queen tilted her head. "Both, actually."

Okay, then. She was going to have to bare her soul to Henry's mother...while standing barefoot among the ruins of a blanket fort. Good times.

Lacey took a deep breath. "My mom got sick when I was five or so. She passed away when I was seven. Mysteries were her favorite type of book, so I guess reading them has always made me feel closer to her."

Queen Elloise's gaze softened in a way Lacey hadn't seen before. The tender look in the monarch's eyes almost made her feel like she could breathe a full breath again. "That must've been very difficult for you."

"It was." Lacey nodded. Behind her breastbone, she felt a dull ache in her chest, like she always did when she talked about her mom's passing. "But it was a long time ago, and I like to think it made me into the person I am today."

"I think I'm beginning to see why Rose feels such a kinship with you."

"Perhaps." Lacey smiled. "I know we come from vastly different backgrounds, but I think I understand her a bit."

The tightness in her chest intensified. Should she really be talking to the queen this way? Lacey doubted Henry's mother seriously thought she had much in common with her grandchild. They came from vastly different worlds—far different than Lacey could've ever imagined.

"Here we go." Lacey scrolled to her favorite picture of Rose from the parade—a close-up, cropped just to show her beaming face alongside Daisy's striking gray head and the colorful flowers and ribbons that had been woven through the mane along her crest and forelock. "I really like this one."

The queen studied the photograph until her customary stoic expression melted a bit around the edges. "It's lovely. She looks so happy. I couldn't have imagined her smiling so broadly in the saddle just a few days ago."

Lacey thought back to their ride on the carousel at Once Upon A Time, and her heart gave a little squeeze. So much had happened since then. Sometimes she felt like she'd stepped onto an amusement park ride the moment she'd landed in Bella-Moritz and was still spinning round and round in dizzying circles, unable to get off.

Did she *want* to get off?

Lacey wasn't altogether sure anymore.

"You did this, didn't you?" Queen Elloise said, handing the phone back to Lacey.

Lacey blinked. "Pardon?"

"The ribbons and the flowers. Dressing Daisy up to look like a carousel horse. All of it was your idea, wasn't it?" The queen's mouth curved into a rare smile. "We have you to thank for Rose riding so beautifully in the procession."

A lightness came over Lacey and she forgot all about the chocolate stain and the blanket fort and her common lavender toenails. She'd done something right, and the queen had noticed. After feeling so out of place for the past few days, she might actually have a chance to get in Henry's mother's good graces.

But taking credit for Rose's success didn't feel right. Flowers and ribbons were just window dressing. Henry was the one who'd whisked his daughter halfway across the world so she could see the magic in her everyday existence. It had taken a theme park castle and dressing as a storybook princess for his little girl to realize that a life of royal duty could be filled with joy, not just responsibility. And taking Rose there, giving her the gift of that insight, had been Henry's idea. Not Lacey's.

"It was all Henry," she said softly.

The queen's eyes narrowed, unconvinced.

"He loves Rose, and he's a wonderful father," Lacey continued. "Seeing her happy and thriving means more to him than anything else in the world. That's all every parent wants for their child, right?" She cleared her throat. Why, oh why, did she want to curtsey again? "But I'm sure you know that already."

Queen Elloise nodded, but her eyes had gone steely again. Lacey had either said something wrong or overstepped.

Shocker.

"Good night, Lacey," she said.

"Good night." Lacey gave her a little wave, but the queen didn't look back.

She just let the door click shut behind her, echoing off the impossibly tall palace walls.

CHAPTER SEVENTEEN

I'm Guessing She Doesn't Show Up to Your Dates in Princess Clothes

HENRY STRODE INTO HIS MOTHER'S office the day after the parade, even though he'd had to practically wrestle a footman to get inside.

With preparations under way for the royal ball, the palace had been turned upside down. He'd seen Lacey for a grand total of forty-five minutes, and that had been at breakfast, where they'd been unable to have a single word in private. Henry had been inundated all day with last-minute details, so they still hadn't had chance to finish talking about the photograph.

But that was fine, because Henry had made a decision.

"I can't do it," he said, muscles going tense, prepared to argue his case if necessary.

The queen looked up from the papers on her desk. Even today, the most important date on the royal calendar, she was busy reviewing the stack of daily briefings from her palace advisors, dealing with the necessary details of keeping Bella-Moritz strong and thriving.

She regarded him over the top of her reading glasses, and then carefully removed them. "Henry, you're going to have to give me more information than that. Can't do what, exactly?"

"I can't issue a statement saying Lacey is just a family friend." The moment the words left his mouth, he felt as though he could exhale for the first time in a week. "She's more than that, and I can't say otherwise."

Queen Elloise sat back in her chair.

"Do you even know why she does what she does at Once Upon A Time?" Henry asked. "Her mother died when she was just a small girl, about the same age as Rose is now, and princesses from a theme park would come keep children company at the hospital where her mom was getting treatment."

The queen nodded. "I know about Lacey's mom."

This came as a surprise to Henry, but he kept talking. Now that he'd decided he couldn't deny his feelings a minute longer, he couldn't stop. "I'm in love with her."

"And is Lacey aware of your feelings?"

"Not yet." He swallowed.

"Don't you think she should have a say in whether the palace releases a statement?" His mother leaned forward with her hands loosely interwoven on her desk. "Your feelings aren't the ones we should be concerned about, are they?"

For a moment, Henry was stunned into silence. He didn't know which surprised him more—the fact that his mother didn't seem surprised by his announcement or the fact that she was worried about Lacey's feelings. Perhaps the queen was fonder of Lacey than she'd let on.

Fond enough to accept her as part of his life for good, though? For forever?

Henry nodded. "I agree, but the papers won't go to press until after the ball. I want to tell how I feel tonight, and if she feels the same way, then that will be that. No statement."

Henry met his mother's gaze and held it, daring her to blink first. He had a duty to the Crown and he'd pledged his entire life to uphold it, but he shouldn't have to do it without the person he loved at his side.

No one should.

Lacey and Ava spent the day exploring the town center beyond the palace gates. They bought macarons in floral varieties, like lavender honey and raspberry rose, with hand-painted flowers brushed on their delicate meringue surfaces and dusted in edible glitter. Lacey picked up a postcard for her dad. They stopped at a sidewalk café and ordered *citron pressé*, a French version of homemade lemonade, served with fresh-squeezed lemon juice in individual glasses, along with a pitcher of ice-cold water and frosted sugar. Lacey sipped hers and didn't utter a word to Ava about the strange late-night visit she'd received from the queen.

She still wasn't sure what to make of it, but she'd decided that, in light of the picture Henry had warned her about, it couldn't have been good.

Lacey felt paralyzed every time she thought about the photograph. She didn't know what to do about it anymore. It might break her heart to read a statement from the palace implying she and Henry were simple acquaintances, that she was just someone who'd crossed paths with a prince— theme-park royalty who Henry would likely never see again once this week was over. But the conversation with Queen Elloise had left her more than a little rattled.

"Are you excited about tonight?" Ava asked as they made their way back to the palace with their small, pastel-colored shopping bags swinging from their arms.

Lacey grinned. "Yes."

A royal ball was a royal ball, regardless of how Henry's mother felt about her. She couldn't wait to dance with Henry again. Their waltz at Ever After Castle seemed like it had taken place ages ago. Whatever happened tomorrow, they would still have this. They'd had cotton candy and fireworks. Butterflies and balconies. And tonight, they'd have music and dancing and a night she would've never even dreamed about before this summer.

"Text me if you need any help with your dress, but I'm going down to the ballroom early," Ava said. "Ian wants to give me a private tour of the decorations before the guests start arriving."

"Does he, now?" Lacey grinned. "You two are getting awfully chummy, aren't you?"

Ava's eyes danced. "He's so sweet, Lace. He's already invited me to come back to Bella-Moritz in two months for my birthday."

Lacey blinked. "Wow, that's amazing. I'm so happy for you."

Could dating someone long-distance really be that easy? Lacey supposed it could, unless the person you were dating was royal. The crown, and all that went with it, definitely seemed to complicate things.

"I'll be fine. You enjoy your time with Ian. I got into the gown with no problem at Madeline's." Lacey dropped her bags in front of the door to her room, and she wrapped her arms around Ava. "I'm so happy you came with me on this trip. Thank you."

"Are you kidding?" Ava laughed and tried to her hug back without dropping her shopping bags. "I'm having the time of my life."

"See you at the ball?" Lacey said.

"See you at the ball."

Once inside her room, Lacey wrote out the postcard to her dad and stepmom while she nibbled one of her macarons. Then she took her time with her makeup, sweeping her eyeliner into a cat's-eye shape like she'd seen on a YouTube tutorial. All she had left to do was slip into her pretty lilac gown, and her transformation into Cinderella would be complete.

She reached into the antique wardrobe for the garment bag and hung it on the outside door. Then, just as she reached to unzip it, her phone rang.

Lacey darted to her nightstand to answer the call, figuring it must be Ava, needing help with her gown instead of the other way around. But when she glanced at the name on the screen, she nearly dropped her phone.

It was Mark. Why on earth could he be calling her?

She stared at the ringing phone for a beat, tempted to let it roll straight to voicemail. But if she ignored the call, she'd wonder about it all night. Mark had never been a big fan of voicemail. The last thing she wanted to be low-key worried about at the ball was why her ex-boyfriend had tried to call her out of the blue.

She tapped the green button. "Hello," she said flatly.

"Lace? It's Mark."

She cleared her throat. "Mark, hi."

He sounded perfectly normal. Cheery, even—as if they hadn't parted on such painful terms. Surely he didn't want to get back together. Goodness, she really hoped not. That was a conversation Lacey did *not* want to have while she was standing in a palace half a world away.

"Now really isn't a good time," she said, hoping to put him off. "I'm out of town."

Understatement of the century.

"Oh, okay. This won't take long, actually. It's just there's going to be an announcement in the paper tomorrow, and I didn't want you to get caught off-guard," Mark said.

Lacey was confused for a second. Was he talking about the picture of her and Henry on the Ferris wheel? How could he possibly know about that? "What kind of announcement?"

"Um." Mark breathed out a loud breath like he always did when he was nervous. "An engagement announcement. I'm getting married."

"*Oh.* Wow."

She couldn't have been more shocked if a fire-breathing dragon jumped down from the top of the palace and came stomping into her room. As surprised as she was, though, she didn't experience even a twinge of jealousy. In fact, she felt genuinely happy for him.

"Congratulations," she said. "Who's the lucky girl?"

"She's a corporate attorney. We dated back in college but broke up when she went off to law school. We were engaged back then, actually, and I don't know...seeing her again just felt right. We've sort of picked up where we left off."

Lacey understood. She truly did. Falling for Henry was the last thing she'd ever expected. But sometimes the heart was much better at this sort of thing than the head.

Also...an attorney? No surprise there. Mark had found his proper woman with a proper job who'd make a proper wife. "I'm guessing she doesn't show up to your dates in princess clothes?"

"About that," Mark said. "No hard feelings, okay? I was out of line. I'm glad you love your job. You're great at it, and I had no right to press you about what you're going to do when it's over. I care about you, Lace. And I always will. Things work out for the best, right?"

Henry's face flashed in Lacey's mind. "Of course they do. I'm happy for you, Mark. Truly."

"Thanks. And Lace?"

"Yes?"

"I hope you have a great vacation."

Lacey smiled into her phone. "I already am."

They ended the call, and Lacey took a deep breath. *That was unexpected.* She was excited for Mark, though. She really was. And now...

Now she was going to be late if she didn't get dressed right away. Anticipation sparked through her as she reached for the zipper on the garment bag again. She slid it down, slowly and carefully, so as not to snag the delicate chiffon fabric.

A pop of pink tulle spilled from the bag, followed by a glittery ruffle. Lacey blinked. It took a minute or two to make sense of what she was seeing.

No. *It can't be.* She felt like she was going to be sick. Why was her Princess Sweet Pea costume hanging inside this bag instead of her borrowed ball gown?

Lacey dug through the tulle, hoping against hope that the elegant chiffon gown was buried somewhere beneath the garish pink dress she wore every day on roller coasters, sleigh rides, and spinning teacups. But it wasn't there.

She must've mixed up her garment bags and dropped off the lilac gown at the dry cleaners instead of her costume before she'd left town. It was the only explanation. Without the enormous petticoat she wore beneath the princess dress, it wasn't quite as voluminous as usual. Also, Madeline had tucked tissue paper all around the lilac gown to keep it from wrinkling. Tucked away inside their garment bags, the dresses had seemed almost identical in weight. Lacey had been so careful. How could she have made such a terrible mistake?

Did it really matter what had happened? The bottom line was she had nothing to wear to the ball.

I can't go.

Tears pricked her eyes. There was no way she could show up in the ballroom in this dress. It was bad enough that she might be pictured on the front page of the paper dressed as Princess Sweet Pea. She couldn't walk around the palace dressed as a theme park princess.

Lacey slumped onto the bed and dropped her head in her hands. How had she not seen this coming? She didn't belong here. Could it have been any more obvious? The queen clearly hadn't been thrilled to meet her. Then there'd been the chocolate stain and tiara-gate and the uncomfortable conversation with Henry's mother last night after the parade. Her old boyfriend had just called, and while she was thrilled he'd found happiness, his engagement now seemed to underscore the reasons for their breakup.

I'm unsuitable. I was improper to Mark, and I'm improper for Henry too.

The dress hanging on the door to the wardrobe was like a giant, pink exclamation point, hammering the message home. She'd let herself get caught up in a royal fantasy, and now the coach was turning back into a pumpkin. It was time to pack her bags and go home.

Lacey pulled her nightstand drawer open and pulled out a thick sheet of palace stationery. Then she wrote Henry a note, thanking him for his family's hospitality and for the best week she'd ever had, but telling him she'd given it a lot of thought and she couldn't go to the ball. He should issue the statement they'd talked about. It would be best for everyone.

She managed not to cry until she wrote the final sentence, asking him to kiss Rose goodbye for her. Then a fat teardrop fell onto the page.

The door to her suite opened just as she placed the letter into an envelope, and Miss Marie walked inside the room. "I'm so sorry to interrupt. I thought you'd be headed to the ballroom by now." Marie took in Lacey's tear-stained face and pressed a hand to her heart. "Oh, Miss Pope. What's wrong? Is there anything I can do to help?"

"I'm fine. Really." She placed the envelope into Marie's hand. "But could you give this to Henry, please?"

Miss Marie shook her head. "Oh, no. That can't be what you want."

"It is," Lacey lied.

And just like that, her fairy tale was over.

CHAPTER EIGHTEEN

I'm fine. It's fine. Everything is Fine.

LACEY FLEW OUT OF HER room and pounded on Ava's door. "Ava, let me in." Her voice cracked.

Do not cry. You can cry all you want once you find Ava, but you cannot weep in the middle of a gilded hallway.

No amount of mental lecturing could keep her voice from breaking, though. "Please."

How could this be happening? Of all the things she could've left behind in Florida, why did it have to be the pretty lilac gown she was supposed to wear to the ball?

Lacey's eyes stung with the effort to hold back her tears. She felt her lower lip begin to wobble, so she bit down hard on it while she waited for Ava to open the door and let her inside.

She wasn't sure what her friend could possibly do to help the situation. What was done was done. She'd already written the letter to Henry explaining she wouldn't be at the ball. Miss Marie was probably handing it to him right this very second. Lacey knew if she'd waited to write it until after she'd seen Ava, she wouldn't have had the courage to pick up the pen.

Besides, knowing Ava, she would've insisted Lacey wear her flowy red dress with the dainty bow at the waist. She would've gladly traded places with Lacey and sat this one out. Well, maybe not gladly...but she would've done it. And once Ava got an idea into her head, she never took no for an answer.

Lacey couldn't let Ava do that, though. Bringing the wrong dress had been her screw-up, and there was no way Lacey was going to let Ava miss out on her one and only chance to attend a royal ball. Plus there was definitely something more than just friendship going on between Ava and Ian. Ava was probably looking forward to tonight as much as Lacey had been.

A rebellious tear slid down Lacey's cheek as she rested her forehead against the closed door to Ava's room. Maybe it was best that her friend wasn't in her suite. Lacey didn't want to bring her down and ruin her evening. But right at that moment, she could've definitely used a hug.

She squeezed her eyes shut tight. What was it Ross from *Friends* had so deliriously said when everything around him was falling apart?

I'm fine. It's fine. Everything is fine.

For once, quotes from her favorite television show didn't make Lacey feel the slightest bit better. Had she really been foolish enough to think she and Henry belonged together?

After another futile tap on the door, she gave up, wiped her face, and headed back to her room. Maybe she could throw her things into a suitcase, summon an Uber, and catch a late-night flight back to the States. She'd simply text Ava from the airport and tell her not to worry. They'd see each other soon, back at home. Or maybe she'd hunker down at the airport in Nice and wait for Ava to show up for her flight in the morning. Lacey didn't know. Her thoughts were spiraling. She just wasn't sure she could face Henry after tonight. Saying goodbye to him seemed almost impossible, even if she knew in her heart that it was the right—the *proper*—thing to do.

Did Bella-Moritz even have Ubers? Or did everyone in the kingdom travel via golden, horse-drawn carriage?

Goodness, she was losing her mind. She needed to get back to her pretend life in her pretend castle, where she knew her place.

Tears spilled over, blurring Lacey's vision as she flung her door open and returned to her room. She choked on a sob, but all her breath seemed to bottle up tight in her throat when she realized she wasn't alone.

"Ava, thank goodness." Lacey blinked back her tears and threw herself toward the blurry figure dressed in a deep red, floor-length gown and standing in front of the antique wardrobe, where Lacey's Princess Sweet Pea costume was bursting from the garment bag in all of its fluffy, theme-park glory. "I was just looking for you. I—"

Her words died on her tongue. Now that Lacey was closer and she'd wiped a fresh wave of tears from her eyes, she saw the woman dressed in the beautiful red gown with her hands clasped behind her back wasn't Ava at all.

It was the queen.

"You." Lacey attempted to swallow around the hard lump in her throat and instead made a humiliating, anguished noise that barely sounded human. She was certain weeping was probably against the royal rules. She'd never once seen Queen Elizabeth break down in tears.

Yet another reason Lacey was way out of her element. Life was messy sometimes. *She* was messy. It didn't seem right to have to hold everything inside.

Still, crying in front of Henry's mother made her feel ill—spinning-teacup-ride-after-swallowing-three-mermaid-tail-ice-cream-bars-in-rapid-succession sick to her stomach.

She sniffed in a horribly un-regal manner, one last desperate attempt to get ahold of herself. "I mean, Your Majesty. Um, what are you doing here?"

It wasn't the politest greeting in the world, but Lacey was too heartbroken for niceties. She was doing the right thing—she was leaving before she accidentally spilled the beans and told Prince Charming she'd fallen head over heels in love with him. She'd worry about her manners later.

Queen Elloise didn't seem fazed by the abrupt question, though. As always, she seemed as cool as a cucumber—if cucumbers wore crowns, that is. A dazzling tiara was perched on top of her dark hair, which had been fashioned into a sleek French twist. Every stone in the crown's platinum, filigree setting glittered like sunlight on a cool, clear ocean. It was so beautiful that Lacey's head spun for a second. Never had she been so aware of the difference between the real deal and the plastic crown she anchored to her head with thirty-five bobby pins every day for work.

No wonder Mark had always gotten so irritated when she forgot to take it off.

"It seems there's been a misunderstanding," the queen said, and then she unclasped her hands from behind her back and held up a familiar sheet of paper.

My letter.

Lacey let out a shaky sigh. Could this situation get any more terrible?

"I know you're wondering, so I'll just come out and tell you. Yes, I've read it," the queen said. Then her voice went bittersweet. "And no, my son has not."

Lacey's entire body seemed to exhale. Henry hadn't read her letter? She'd poured her soul into those words. That letter had been the most difficult and humbling thing she'd ever had to write. As much as she'd loved her time in Bella-Moritz, there'd been moments where it had seemed like a boulder had been sitting square on top of her chest. She hadn't wanted to let anyone down—not Rose, and especially not Henry. When she'd unzipped her garment bag and found her Sweet Pea costume instead of the lovely organza gown she was supposed to wear to the ball, the boulder had seemed to double in size. Then, as she'd thought more about Mark's phone call and about how she hadn't even been proper enough for him, let alone a prince...she'd been crushed beyond repair. As heartbreaking as it had been, writing the letter to Henry had allowed her to finally breathe.

And now here was the queen, telling her he hadn't even seen it.

Lacey should be crushed all over again. The last thing in the world she should be feeling right now was relief, and yet...

A tiny spark of it glittered inside her, along with something she'd hadn't let herself feel since she'd landed in Henry's kingdom...something she'd foolishly let herself lose sight of the night she'd broken up with Mark. *Hope.*

Lacey glanced down at her handwriting on the thick ivory paper in the queen's hands. The monarch may as well have been holding Lacey's heart in her palm.

"Marie came to me because she wanted me to know there was a problem with your ballgown. She said you'd asked her to deliver a note to Henry and she was worried you were going to miss tonight's festivities. As I said, there seems to have been a misunderstanding," Henry mother said, folding the paper into a neat square, banishing Lacey's words from sight.

"A misunderstanding?" Lacey shook her head. "I'm not following."

"I had my doubts when Henry told me he'd invited you to come visit during the Flower Festival, and I'll admit I was a bit...confused...by your chosen profession. But please know that was only out of concern for Henry and Rose. Rose suffered a terrible loss when her mother died, as I'm sure you understand." Queen Elloise reached for Lacey's hand and gave it a tender squeeze.

The display of affection was so unexpected that a dam broke inside Lacey, and another tear slipped down her cheek. She wiped it away and gave Henry's mother a wobbly smile.

"But children are sometimes far more resilient than adults. Rose has always been an open book, just waiting for the right person—the right mother figure—to take notice of her and lovingly tend to her story. Henry, on the other hand..." Queen Elloise took a deep breath, and to Lacey's complete and total astonishment, she saw the hard glitter of tears in the monarch's eyes. "He closed himself up. I didn't think he'd risk losing his heart to anyone ever again, and believe me, I've done my share of prodding. What was it you said last night?"

Lacey was at a loss. She'd said a lot of things the night before, but all she could seem to remember was rambling on about cozy mystery novels and other things Queen Elloise probably had zero interest in. She'd also asked the queen to scroll through the picture roll on her phone, as if they were BFFs chatting over whipped frappuccinos at the corner Starbucks. Super-royal behavior.

"You said that seeing their children happy and thriving meant more to a parent than anything else in the world. I think I'd given up on that for Henry." The queen squeezed Lacey's hand even harder—so hard that the knuckles of her elegant fingers turned white. "Until you came along."

Wait. *What?*

"But Henry is royal," Lacey said. "He's going to be a king someday." She glanced at the queen's sparkling crown for emphasis. It was a wonder she wasn't blinded by the luster of so many diamonds. "I'm just a commoner."

"Lacey, dear. Anyone who's been paying attention over the past few days can see you're anything but common."

Lacey's mouth dropped open. Ava had told her the very

same thing back at their apartment in Fort Lauderdale, but of course her best friend would think so. Things were different here in Bella-Moritz.

Were they, though? Henry and Rose and Queen Elloise were indeed royal, but they were also a family. Perhaps behind the palace doors, family came first too, even before the bonds of king and country.

"I know it was you who helped Rose overcome her fear of riding in the procession, yet you refused to take credit for it. And I know the butterfly feeders at the flower festival were your idea," the queen said.

Lacey lowered her gaze. *Busted.*

"'Always make friends with birds and butterflies.' How could I forget?" The queen dipped her head to look Lacey in the eye. "Those rules of yours aren't quite as simple as they appear at first. They come from someplace deep inside you, and take my word for it, dear. Nothing is more royal or proper than authenticity."

It took every ounce of self-control Lacey possessed to not throw her arms around the queen and hug her. Protocol or not, she probably would have, if she hadn't been worried about ruining the queen's gorgeous red gown with her runny mascara and tear-stained cheeks.

"So, it's all settled, then." Henry's mother released Lacey's hand and gave her one of the commanding looks she was exceptionally adept at wielding about. "You'll go to the ball as planned."

Lacey glanced at her Princess Sweet Pea dress hanging beside them and winced. "I can't. I brought the wrong garment bag by mistake, and the only gown I have is my costume from the theme park."

"Ah, that's right. I'd almost forgotten." The queen's lip twitched as if she were trying not to laugh.

Authenticity might be regal and all, but that didn't mean it was always fashionable.

"Come with me. I'm sure we can find you something else to wear. In fact, I have a tiara decorated with tiny seed pearls that would be lovely on you." The queen winked.

Lacey was so overcome that she couldn't stop herself anymore. She wrapped her arms around the monarch and gave her the biggest, most effusive bear hug she could muster. Queen Elloise gasped in surprise, but quickly recovered and hugged Lacey back.

The last thing Lacey saw before she squeezed her eyes closed and melted into the hug was her puffy pink princess gown, and she realized she was kind of glad she'd brought it with her by mistake. She wouldn't have wanted to miss this special moment with Queen Elloise. It was the stuff of fairy tales—pure storybook magic.

In all honesty, it was better. Because Lacey had years of experience with fairy godmothers, but it had been a long, long time since she'd been wrapped up in the warm embrace of motherly love.

CHAPTER NINETEEN

How All Good Fairy Tales End

Henry paced the upper level of the marble ceremonial staircase that overlooked the palace's Grand Ballroom as a growing sense of panic gnawed at his insides.

Lacey had been due to meet him at the top of the stairs, just behind the red velvet curtain at the stairway's entrance, ten minutes before the ball had been set to start. His gaze bore into the gilded clock with its deep blue lapis face. It hung above the spot where two divergent flights of stairs joined and became one wide staircase that led to the dance floor. According to its gold hands, he'd been waiting for well over an hour. Henry couldn't keep postponing his arrival. The herald had already announced every guest and member of the royal family. He kept shooting worried glances at Henry, wondering why the Crown Prince hadn't joined the festivities and was instead hovering around the edge of the ballroom like a teenager who'd been stood up for a school dance.

Henry nodded in the herald's direction and held up a finger. *One more minute.*

He should've gone to Lacey's room before the ball and escorted her to the ballroom, as if they'd been on a proper date. Because that was what this was supposed to be, wasn't it? A real date—their first official one.

So much had happened since he'd first seen her at that nutty tea party. So much had changed. *He'd* changed. Henry was ready to tell Lacey exactly how he felt, and he'd foolishly thought the ball would be the best place to do so. He'd even arranged a little surprise for Lacey—a nod to the first time they'd danced together back in Ever After Castle. But now he was beginning to second-guess everything.

Where *was* she? Had she gotten lost on her way to the ballroom? The palace was a like a maze. Sometimes even Rose had trouble navigating the trickier sections of the castle, and she'd lived here all her life. Lacey had insisted she'd be able to find her way, though. And she'd charmed so many of the palace staff members by now that if she'd been wandering aimlessly through the royal residence's halls, there would've been no shortage of people to help her find her way.

Traditionally, the royal family liked to greet their guests in a receiving line as they approached the grand marble staircase, which was why Lacey had planned on meeting Henry just outside the red velvet curtain. Tonight, though, everything had gone topsy-turvy. Up was down, down was up, and Henry felt rather like he'd been tossed about by one of the rides at Lacey's amusement park. Even the queen had missed the receiving line, with no warning at all to Henry, the herald, or the royal courtiers who'd been buzzing about, trying to act as if they hadn't been shocked by her late arrival. When his mother had finally deigned to make an appearance, she'd floated down the stairs with her head held high, as if nothing had been amiss.

But Henry was too concerned about his date's where-
abouts to think too hard on what had caused the queen to
change her plans. He glanced at the clock again. If Lacey
didn't get here soon, she'd miss his surprise.

He strode to the end of the balustrade, checking once
again to make sure she wasn't waiting for him on the other
side of the divergent staircases. His heart sank even lower
when he saw no one was there.

Something was wrong. He could feel it.

Henry stepped in front of the curtain and scanned the
ballroom floor with his gaze, searching for a glimpse of
Lacey's honey-blond hair. Again, nothing. But he did manage
to spot Ian and Ava, laughing and dancing together on the
left outer edge of the ballroom's black-and-white marble
floor. He managed to catch Ian's gaze and beckon him up-
stairs with what he hoped was a subtle jerk of his head.

It seemed to take an eternity for the two of them to reach
him. And when they finally did, the first words out of Ava's
mouth were, "Where's Lacey?"

Henry's temples throbbed. The back of his throat burned.
He shook his head. "She's not here. I was hoping you might
have an idea where she was."

A line appeared between Ava's eyebrows and she shook
her head. "I don't. Ian offered to give me a tour of the decorated ballroom before all the guests arrived, so I left my
room early. I haven't seen her for hours."

Ian held out his hands. "Let's calm down. She's got to
be around here somewhere."

But where?

The lapis-and-gold clock hanging overhead chimed,
marking the passing of another half hour. Henry had a
sudden, vivid memory of the big grandfather clock in the
ballroom of Ever After Castle at Once Upon A Time and how
untethered he'd felt when Lacey had pulled away from him,
ready to flee and leave her glass slipper behind.

He blinked hard, vaguely aware of Ava offering to go to Lacey's room to look for her, but then a strange sense of calm came over him as the smile he knew and loved lit up their little vestibule at the top of the stairs.

"Oh my gosh, Lacey." Ava's hand flew to her throat. "Look at you."

Henry clutched his heart beneath the smooth silk lapels of his white-tie and tails. "I was beginning to think you'd pulled another Cinderella on me." He barely managed to get the words out. His breath hitched in his throat at the sight of her, dressed in an airy, pale blue ballgown, spun from delicate netting and dotted with tiny crystals and sequins so luminous, the fabric seemed to shimmer as if it'd been dipped in fairy dust. Her hair was wound into the same sort of updo she always wore at the park, swept gently around a delicate tiara.

He took a closer look at the crown, and tenderness wrapped its way around his heart. So that was where the queen had been earlier. Instead of greeting their guests, his mother had been with Lacey, loaning her a tiara for the evening—a symbol of her acceptance of the woman who'd claimed Henry's heart.

"Nope. No more dashing away at midnight." Lacey shook her head. "In fact, I think I might stick around for good this time. I've never made it all the way to the end of a ball before. It'll be nice to see how it turns out."

Henry offered her his elbow and as they paused at the top of the grand staircase so the herald could announce their arrival, he dipped his head and whispered low in Lacey's ear, "It ends how all good fairy tales end—happily ever after."

"Presenting His Royal Highness, Prince Henry Frederick Augustus Ranier Chevalier, and Miss Lacey Pope," the herald called out, and everything in the elegant ballroom seemed to go still.

The room itself was a sight to behold. Its painted ceilings, gilded molding, and massive gold chandeliers, casting a kaleidoscope of light and color across the sweeping floor, took Lacey's breath away. There was opulence on every side, too much to take in all at once—columns covered in shimmering mosaic tiles, towering torchères topped with frosted bulbs, massive candelabras holding slender white candles. And flowers! Flowers were everywhere, covering every available surface in huge, overflowing arrangements, dotting the ballroom with explosions of color in a lush display honoring Bella-Moritz's most esteemed summer tradition—the Flower Festival.

Lacey breathed in the heady fragrance of sweet peonies, dahlia petals, and roses of every conceivable color and variety. Their rich, floral perfumes made her head spin. Or maybe it was only the simple fact that she was here, by Henry's side, when just a short time ago, she'd been ready to give it all up and run away as if an invisible clock had struck midnight, marking an end to her time with the prince who'd captured her heart.

She'd never been so aware that she was no longer in a theme park. The assembled crowd was far larger than her quaint little tea party in Ever After Castle, and every set of eyes was trained on her and Henry. He looked so handsome in his white-tie and tails. She really couldn't blame anyone for staring. But somehow she got the sense the guests at the palace weren't merely looking at him. They were smiling at both of them, gazing at Bella-Moritz's beloved Crown Prince and the woman on his arm.

Happily ever after...
Could it be?

As pretty as the lilac dress she'd planned on wearing had been, Lacey couldn't have been more grateful for the queen's intervention. The pale blue confection she'd chosen for Lacey to wear was the most beautiful gown she'd ever seen—fit for a princess. If she'd been wearing anything else or if she'd had anyone other than Henry escorting her down the enormous marble staircase, she might've been intimidated by all the curious stares and whispers. Which was really saying something, considering Lacey greeted thousands of people from all over the world every day at Once Upon A Time.

When she'd arrived in Bella-Moritz and had gotten her first real glimpse at Henry and Rose's royal life, she'd been so struck by the stark differences between her theme park castle and their palace home. Lacey had always been proud to play the part of Princess Sweet Pea, but the idea of a real-life prince and a theme park princess falling for one another seemed almost laughable. That was exactly what she'd done, though. She'd fallen in love with Henry, despite every effort not to. She wasn't sure if he felt the same way or not, and she was trying her best just to live in the moment and soak everything up—the beautiful surroundings, the music, the way the air seemed perfumed with every kind of flower imaginable. But more than any of those things, she wanted to cherish the warmth of Henry's touch and the light in his eyes when he looked at her. He made her feel like she was the special one. He always had.

Lacey knew all those days of pinning a plastic crown to her head, waltzing with a succession of novice Prince Charmings, and doing her best to make the park guests forget their troubles and find the magic in everyday life had uniquely prepared her for this moment. If the palace where they were standing had been on the pages of a storybook, and if the prince standing beside her had been the lonely royal from "The Princess and the Pea," Lacey would've passed his family's princess test with flying colors.

Thank goodness she hadn't needed to sleep on top of twenty mattresses piled with twenty feather beds to get here. That seemed liked overkill.

But when she and Henry reached the bottom of the staircase and he bowed and held his hand out to her in a silent invitation to dance, she knew there'd never been a test. Henry had never treated her as inferior. And he was more than a prince—he was a father, a son, and a friend. He was a real flesh-and-blood man, not a one-dimensional character or just a royal title. Lacey had fallen in love with him for who he was, not what he was. She could only hope he felt the same way about her.

Lacey placed her fingertips gently in his waiting hand, and in a gesture that reminded her so much of their first encounter at Sweet Pea's Royal Tea Party, Henry pulled her into a dance hold. A shiver coursed through her at the feel of his warm hand on the small of her back, and he flashed her a knowing smile.

Lacey tilted her head. She felt like he was trying to tell her something, but she wasn't sure what. Then the music in ballroom wound down to a close before changing to a different tune.

Together, they took their first step, then another and another, until they were waltzing and twirling across the glossy black-and-white floor. The music grew louder and louder, until Lacey gasped.

"This song." A smile rose up from the deepest part of her heart. "This is the same song we danced to at Once Upon A Time."

Henry's mouth curved into a smile. "It is, isn't it? What a fitting coincidence."

He led her in a sweeping curve as he held her closer, so close that she could've rested her head on his broad shoulder if she wanted to.

She couldn't, obviously. Not here, but that was okay, because even though the Flower Festival was drawing to a close, she had a feeling the future was still up for grabs. And the way Henry was holding her left no doubt in her mind that no matter what her crown was made of, she was the princess of his heart. His noble heart beat wildly against her own, telling its own story, but she still wanted to hear him say the words. She *needed* it. They'd been dancing around the truth long enough.

"You're not fooling me for a second. This song is no coincidence," she said, pulse pounding in time with the music.

Henry's eyes danced. "Surprised?"

Lacey laughed. "Yes, and you know how I feel about surprises."

"Good, because I've got one more."

Then he dipped her low, just as he'd done in a faraway, candy-colored castle in the land where fairy tales came true. A cheer rose up from the crowd, and just over Henry's shoulder, Lacey saw Rose, smiling as brightly as she'd ever seen the little girl smile before. She flashed Henry's daughter a wink, and then her gaze found Henry's again.

His eyes were impossibly bright. Ever blue, ever true. "I love you, princess."

Joy sparkled inside Lacey. This was it, but instead of feeling like the end of a fairy tale, it felt the beginning. The beginning of something bright and beautiful, a life she and Henry would build together.

"I love you too," she said, marveling at how easy the words came, as if she'd been waiting a lifetime to say them to just the right person.

"Will you marry me?"

"Yes!" She might've even forgotten where she was for a moment and screamed her answer as if she were trying to make herself heard over a roller coaster rattling its way up the Snow Queen's Mountain and through Hansel and

Gretel's Haunted Forest.

Then Henry kissed her, right there in the middle of the ballroom. His lips came down on hers, soft and sweet. Somewhere in the distance, Lacey heard the striking of a clock.

Was it midnight already?

She wrapped her arms around Henry's strong neck and kissed him back, feet firmly planted in the here and now. In real life—just as magical, just as sweet as the fairest of fairy tales. What difference did the number of chimes from the clock make?

Lacey and her prince had all the time in the world.

The End

CUCUMBER DILL TEA SANDWICHES

Prep Time: 15 minutes
Serves: 6

Ingredients

- 1 package (4 ounces) cream cheese, softened
- 1 tablespoon fresh dill, chopped
- 1 teaspoon fresh lemon juice
- Kosher salt and fresh ground black pepper, to taste
- 12 slices good quality thin sliced white bread, crusts removed with serrated knife, for best results
- 1/2 English (hothouse) seedless cucumber, thin-sliced into 48 slices

Preparation

- In a small bowl, combine cream cheese and dill, lemon juice and stir to blend; season to taste with kosher salt and pepper.

- Spread the cream cheese mixture evenly on 12 slices of bread; arrange 6 of the cream cheese covered bread slices on flat work surface.
- Top each with 6 cucumber slices; close with top halves of tea sandwiches and press lightly to close. Using a serrated knife carefully cut off crusts.
- Diagonal slice each sandwich in half and arrange on a serving plate. Garnish with additional fresh dill sprigs, if desired.
- Serve immediately or cover and refrigerate to hold.

Thanks so much for reading
Once Upon a Royal Summer. We hope you enjoyed it!

You might like these other books
from Hallmark Publishing:

Wedding in the Pines
The Secret Ingredient
A Dash of Love
Beach Wedding Weekend
Sailing at Sunset

For information about our new releases and
exclusive offers, sign up for our free newsletter at
hallmarkchannel.com/hallmarkpublishing-newsletter

You can also connect with us here:

Facebook.com/HallmarkPublishing

Twitter.com/HallmarkPublish

ABOUT THE AUTHOR

Teri Wilson is the Publishers Weekly bestselling author/ creator of the Hallmark Channel Original Movies Unleashing Mr. Darcy, Marrying Mr. Darcy, The Art of Us, and Northern Lights of Christmas, based on her book Sleigh Bell Sweethearts. She is also the author of Christmas Charms and a recipient of the prestigious RITA Award for excellence in romantic fiction. Teri has a major weakness for pretty dresses, Audrey Hepburn films, and cute animals. Visit her at www.teriwilson.net or on Twitter @TeriWilsonauthr.

You might also enjoy

NEW YORK TIMES BESTSELLING AUTHOR
CARIDAD PIÑEIRO

CHAPTER 1

NEW YORK CITY

THE CITY BUS HIT A pothole and sent a tsunami of dirty rainwater rushing toward the pedestrians at the curb.

Tony Sanchez dodged and jumped to try to evade the wave but failed miserably. He stared down at the splotches of nasty brown and black on his freshly laundered jeans and hoped the rest of his day wouldn't be as horrible.

Shrugging deeper into the shearling collar of his leather jacket to battle the damp bite of the late spring day, Tony hurried down Park Avenue toward his Chelsea restaurant. He had been up at the Hunts Point Produce Terminal Market at the crack of dawn to select only the finest fruits and vegetables so he could plan the menus for the next few days.

As he walked, his sneakers squished noisily, soaked by the heavy rain that not even an umbrella could keep at bay. His wet jeans clung to his legs and chilled him to the bone. A stinging breeze rushed eastward on 23rd Street from Waterside Park and hit his face like tiny ice needles.

He shivered with the wet cold and yearned for the warm summer days that still seemed so far away.

It had been a difficult winter and spring both personally and professionally. His longtime girlfriend, a fellow chef, had walked out on him, claiming that he spent more time at work than he did with her. He couldn't argue with her. Work *had* dominated his life lately because he'd suffered an assortment of setbacks at his restaurant. But even if work hadn't commanded so much of his time, it had been rough being involved with another chef. There had been too much professional rivalry between them, and both of their long hours had made the relationship difficult. It made him wonder if he could ever find a woman who would be able to deal with the life he led. A woman who would be strong enough to be at his side and help build a family.

He shook off the gloomy thoughts and rushed the last few steps to his place. The wintry wind chased him into the restaurant, but he shoved the door closed and shook the rain off his coat and umbrella. The musical clang of pots and pans and animated chatter coming from the kitchen announced that his crew was already hard at work. It pulled a broad smile from him and dispelled any lingering negativity from his earlier thoughts.

He pushed through the swinging door into the kitchen where his sous and station chefs and the rest of his staff were busy prepping all that they'd need for that day's meals including the stocks and sauces that were essentials for the various dishes they prepared. When he entered, heads shot up and several people shouted out greetings to him, but others just grimaced and buried their heads in their work. He understood. He'd been tough on them lately. Maybe tougher than he should have been.

He smiled and waved a greeting, but then grew serious once more when he entered his office and eyed the foot-high pile of paperwork stacked in the center of his desk.

"Why does it seem that the stack grew from last night?" he murmured to himself and hurried to the small closet at one side of the room where he kept an extra set of street clothes and his chef's garb. He always kept a change of clothes handy, because you never knew what might happen in the kitchen.

Tony peeled off his wet clothes and slipped into his chef's duds, hoping that he'd be able to get into the kitchen today—something that hadn't happened a lot lately, with all the administrative obligations of running the restaurant. Changes in minimum wages, an increase in his rent, and the fact that he was no longer that week's celebrity chef had all contributed to lower profits at the restaurant and more work for him to keep things running smoothly.

He waded through the papers in the pile to triage what needed immediate attention and what could wait until to-morrow. Just below the first few bills lay a thick envelope with his name elegantly lettered in hand-scripted calligraphy. The return address was his sister's and he wondered what was inside.

A faux wax seal on the other side bore an ornate R for his sister's married surname and he opened the envelope to reveal a liner in pale peach dusted with glitter that spilled out and anointed his desk with sparkle. Not his conservative lawyer sister's usual tastes, but as he removed the invitation he realized why.

"What's with the glitter, *jefe*?" his sous chef Amanda asked as she entered his office.

"It came in an invitation to my niece Angelica's *quinceañera*." Tony held the card out so Amanda could read it.

"Whoa, very fancy. This is one of those high-end hotels in South Beach, isn't it?"

"It is. My sister does everything big." He also knew that Sylvia, a perfectionist, would put on quite an amazing event.

"You'll have a nice time then." Amanda handed him

back the invite.

Tony drew in a long breath and nodded. "Thanks. How can I help you?"

Amanda smiled. "Just wanted to confirm we got the meat shipment you ordered, and everything is good. No issues, like last time."

"Awesome. Thank you," he said. When Amanda left, he set the invitation aside and got to work, although he was distracted with thoughts on how he'd take the time off.

By late afternoon and well past the lunch rush, Tony had dealt with the most urgent matters on his plate. He was about to head into the kitchen to see how lunch clean-up and dinner prep were going when his cell phone blared out conga beats to trumpet: his sister's ringtone. Since he hadn't spoken to her in close to two weeks and he was sure she was calling about the invitation, he swiped and answered. "Sylvita, *como estas?*"

A heavy sigh escaped her as she said, "I could be doing better, *hermanito.*"

Hermanito. "Little bro," only he wasn't so little anymore—not that Sylvia got that. To him, she would always be the little brother she bossed around. Before he could reply, Sylvia barged right on. "You know it's Angelica's *quinceañera* in a little over two months, right? You did open the invite, didn't you? Or is it still sitting in a pile of papers on your desk?"

Guilt the likes of which only family could rouse swamped him. "Of course, I got it and opened it, *hermanita.* Hard to believe she's growing up so fast," he said. His niece Angelica was a good kid who, as he recalled, played a mean game of dominos. He had always loved spending time with her.

"She is growing up way too fast. You'd know that if you and Javi visited. What's it been? Three years since you came down?" she said, piling on more guilt. At least this load wasn't his alone. She'd do the same to their older brother Javier who had spent even less time with the family in recent years thanks to the obligations of his tech start-up on the West Coast.

"I know I haven't been good about visiting—"

"And *mami* and *papi* miss you so much. Our parents aren't getting any younger, you know," Sylvia said. In his mind's eye he pictured them and his siblings. They'd always been so close, but for the past few years....

"I'll try, Sylvita. I'd like to see everyone."

His words were followed by a long silence before his sister blurted out, "I need your help, Tony. This event is really, really, important to Angelica and to the family."

There was a tone in his sister's voice he rarely heard. Desperation.

"Is everything okay, *hermanita*?" he asked, worry replacing guilt.

He could picture her shrug as she said, "This *quince* is a big deal, and it's not just about celebrating Angelica becoming a woman. Esteban's real estate business could use a boost and a lot of Miami's elite are coming to the party. We need to make the meal something really special and I know you can do that," Sylvia said. His heart warmed a little at the confidence in her tone, her faith in his cooking.

"You want me to help? Like plan the menu? Cook?" Tony asked, wanting to be absolutely certain about what his sister was asking.

"*Sí*. I know you're the only one who can do it right. And handling the food would mean you'd have to come in early. You could take some time off and visit—maybe stay for the month. See *mami* and *papi*. Get to know your nieces and nephews better. Before you know it, they'll be all grown up and gone."

His sister was laying on the guilt in layers as thick as frosting on a cake, and he couldn't deny that it had him wanting to give in. But he had so much to do at the restaurant that he wasn't sure he could swing it. *So much to do, like the paperwork I hate?*

"*Por favor, Antonio,*" his sister pleaded which surprised him. She wasn't normally the type to beg.

"I'm not sure I can take that much time off," he said, thinking about all the work he'd have to do before he left and all that would be waiting for him once he returned.

With an exasperated sigh, Sylvia said, "You and Javi. It's like herding cats to get both of you to come home."

"Is Javi going to the *quince*?" He couldn't remember the last time that Javi had visited Miami or for that matter, come East.

"It sounded like he was, but you know Javi. Absent-minded genius."

"Workaholic," he added.

"Just like the two of us, *hermanito*. We're all overachievers," Sylvia said and they both laughed. He missed how they could laugh together. Fight together. He just plain missed her. His parents. His old friends.

"I can't make any promises, but let me think about it, okay? Regardless of whether I come in early to handle the menu, I'll be there for the party." It was the least he could do. The *very* least—which again roused guilt. Sylvia wasn't the kind to ask for help and that she was doing so was quite telling.

"I'll take that...for now. *Hasta luego.*"

Knowing Sylvia, she'd be calling again tomorrow for a more definitive answer, but by then he hoped he'd be able to figure out whether he could take the time off to help her out. And if he couldn't, how to say "No" without starting a family war.

Sara's brother handed her the last of that week's meat order along with a receipt for the purchase. "I think that's it for now."

She peered at the sealed tray holding the lollipop lamb chops and smiled. "Tell Manny he's the best. These chops are gorgeous. Perfectly butchered."

Matt grinned and chuckled. "That's why he loves you, Sara. Which reminds me—I forgot something for you. Be back in a little bit."

As Matt hurried from the room, Sara placed the lamb on a shelf in the walk-in refrigerator at the back of her restaurant's kitchen and slipped the receipt into her apron pocket. Hands on her hips, she glanced around at the fully-stocked shelves and an immense grin erupted on her face. When she and her partner had first opened their restaurant two years ago, they'd barely been able to afford enough product to put together a menu every day, but with the restaurant's quickly growing clientele that had all changed. In fact, the business was going so well that she hoped to either expand the space or find a bigger one. They had even talked about the possibility of opening a second location.

"Don't you look pleased with yourself?" Matt teased and handed her a package wrapped in butcher's paper and tied with twine.

"I most certainly am. Just look at all this," she said as she accepted the bundle from her brother. From the familiar shape beneath the wrapping, she immediately knew what it was. "A tomahawk steak? For me?" she said and at her brother's nod, added, "That's a lot of meat for just one person to eat."

Matt wrapped an arm around his sister's shoulder. "If you want, I know a few guys who'd love to share it with you."

Sara rolled her eyes. "Always matchmaking, but no thanks, bro. I'm just way too busy lately." The restaurant demanded most of her attention, so she barely had time for a personal life. She had friends and family, but still... once in a while, she was lonely.

"All work and no play, Sara," Matt warned and hugged her hard.

"I'll survive. Anything new with you?"

"Since three days ago? Same ol' same ol'." As they walked out of the refrigerator and headed to Sara's office, Matt added, "But I may have found a place for that party that Dolores is insisting on."

"The *quinceañera*? Is that what it's called?" Her sister-in-law Dolores had mentioned it when she'd gone to her brother's for Sunday dinner.

"That's it. The *quinceañera*. Sweet fifteen to me."

Sara could tell her brother wasn't quite buying into the whole idea, but she could understand why it was such a big deal for her sister-in-law.

"Dolores's family lost so much when they came here from Cuba," she reminded him. "It's important to her to keep her traditions alive—and this sounds to me like a fun one."

She sat behind her desk and Matt plopped into the chair across from her. "You mean an expensive one, don't you? And Samantha is inviting a lot of kids from that fancy prep school she's going to—"

"On a scholarship since she's so smart, just like her aunt," she teased.

Her brother laughed and shook his head. "Stubborn like you, also. I'm not sure Samantha's as into this idea as Dolores, but she'd do anything for her mom."

"And you would too. You said you may have found a place?"

Matt quickly bobbed his head. "There's a fancy yacht club up on the Miami River that I deliver to. Someone cancelled their wedding—which means they forfeited the deposit. Since they've already made some money on it, the owner is being nice enough to let me have it that day for a reduced price."

"I've been to that place for an event. It's a gorgeous location," Sara said, picturing the stunning views of the Miami River and surrounding luxury homes along the banks near the yacht club.

"I may need help with the catering and stuff. Can I count on you to assist?" Matt arched one eyebrow.

Sara hesitated and disappointment bloomed on her brother's face. Before he could say another word, she jumped in with, "Things are crazy here, but I'll find a way. Besides, I'm sure you're inviting lots of big shot types—"

"There's a ton of them that are parents at that fancy school," he half-groused.

"All the better to help both of us grow our businesses, right?" she said, warming to the idea as she gave them both a pep talk. "You'll feed them the best meat and fish available and my food will be irresistible. Before you know it, they'll be knocking down our doors for more," she said. In truth, if there were a lot of high-powered people at the party it would be good for both of them.

"Thanks, Sara. You're the best," he said and hopped out of the chair to come around and give her another big bear hug.

"Anything for family, Matt. You know that." She returned the embrace before shooing him away good-naturedly. "Now go. I've got a lot of work to do if I'm going to take time off to help you."

"Yes, chef," he teased, echoing the response he'd heard coming from her kitchen staff so many times.

"Get out of here," she said with a dismissive wave, keeping her smile firmly in place.

Only when he was gone did she sag back into her chair as she thought about the promise she'd just made. She'd do anything for her brothers and sister, but a big event like her niece's party was going to take a lot of time. Time that was already in short supply, thanks to the restaurant's success.

But as she'd told her brother, this would not only be a wonderful opportunity to help Dolores keep her traditions, it might be a good way to grow their businesses and impress some of the local elites.

I can do this. She braced her hands on the arms of her desk chair and hopped up to return to the kitchen. She had to get to work because she didn't have any time to waste. The restaurant would open for lunch in a few hours and stay open into the night long past when many others closed. The post-clubbing late night crowd was the perfect clientele for her restaurant's small plate eclectic menu. Even the name of the place—*Munch*—told people exactly what they would get: tasty bites to satisfy their cravings.

But unlike most late-night munchies, she was proud to serve food that would be suitable in any high-end starred restaurant. It was what had made her place a favorite spot in the South Beach area, and why she'd often thought that they should open another location. But despite the restaurant's success, she still didn't think they could swing a new storefront without additional financing—and securing that financing was a dicey proposition in the restaurant business, especially if you were young and female. There was a decided bias in favor of male chefs. No one expected a woman to be able to succeed at all, much less grow and expand.

And if she did expand the business, she could kiss her personal life goodbye.

With a heavy sigh, Sara set aside those thoughts and started prepping the menus for the next few days. She'd have to have all her ducks in a row if she was going to keep her promise to her brother and that meant being uber organized and talking to her partner to see what could be done to free her and some of her staff for Samantha's party.

It was going to turn out perfectly, with zero hiccups if she could help it. The best *quinceañera* ever...one that the guests would remember for some time to come.

CHAPTER 2

ANGELICA RODRIGUEZ RUSHED TOWARD THE cafeteria, her heels tapping out a staccato beat on the marble of the hallway floors. Her friends would already be waiting for her at their usual lunch table. Located next to the windows that faced a stand of palm trees and the bay, it was a prime place to eat and only the coolest kids shared those prized tables.

The room was packed and as Angelica rushed in, heads turned and whispers chased her. Her confusion only increased as she caught sight of her two best friends huddled over papers they guiltily tucked away into their notebooks as she reached the table.

"*Que pasa?*" she asked, eyes narrowed as she examined the apprehensive looks on Maya and Daisy's faces.

"Nothing."

"*Nada,*" they responded, almost in unison, but Angelica knew something was definitely up.

She jammed her hands on her hips and cocked her head at a defiant angle. "You know you *chicas* can't keep a secret from me."

Maya, the more pliable of her friends, reluctantly opened her notebook and pulled out a pale pink envelope. She placed it on the table and slowly slid it across to Angelica.

Angelica peered at Maya's name in flowery script and then gingerly picked up the envelope. A sudden hush in the cafeteria made her pause and look around. Like meerkats coming out of their burrows, her classmates had perked up and focused their attention on her.

So not good. Angelica sucked in a breath to brace herself. She withdrew the notecard in a pale pink that matched the envelope. The embossed gold lettering in the center simply said, "You're invited..."

She flipped open the card and couldn't believe what she was reading. Another *quinceañera*—from her biggest rival, Samantha Kelly, no less—and just a day before her *quinceañera*. It wasn't even close to Samantha's birthday. She was almost certain that Samantha had a summer birthday when school was out of session.

Whirling, the invite fisted in her hand, she marched toward Samantha's table where her nemesis sat with her friends. A tight smile graced her rival's lips as Angelica approached and slapped the invitation down on the table.

She crossed her arms, cocked a hip and said, "Really? The day before mine? It's not even close to your birthday!"

"Sorry, but it was the only day we could get. By the way, here's your invite," Samantha said, whipping an envelope out of her knapsack, and handing it to Angelica.

Anger clouded her vision for a millisecond before she reined it in and plastered a smile on her face. She couldn't let everyone see how upset she truly was. "*Gracias*, Samantha. *No sabía que eres Latina.*" She'd said the words in Spanish as a subtle jab, but they were true all the same. She genuinely hadn't known the other girl had a Latino background—the name "Samantha Kelly" wasn't exactly typical.

Samantha's smile tightened even more, and she tilted her chin up in challenge. "*Mi mama es de Cuba.*" A Cuban mother explained it. Well, explained the choice to have a *quinceañera,* anyway. Nothing could explain her terrible timing.

"Great. Wonderful. Thanks," Angelica bit out, spun, and stomped to where her friends sat, expectant looks on their faces.

When she neared the table, she snapped her hand up like a cop directing traffic. "Not one word. Not one," she warned, still flummoxed by Samantha's actions. To keep the discussion from going there, she said, "Are you guys going to soccer tryouts this afternoon?"

Maya grimaced and shrugged negligently. "Probably even though I'm sure I won't make the team."

"Way to be positive," said Daisy as she stuffed a potato chip into her mouth.

Maya chuckled and said, "I *am* being positive. I'm positive I won't make it."

Angelica likewise laughed and wagged her head. "At least you're trying. You never know what will happen."

"I know that you and Samantha will make the team," Maya said.

Daisy jumped in with, "And you'll have to kick her butt to be the team captain again."

"Again and again," Angelica murmured. It seemed as if she and Samantha were always battling for the top spot at everything. Soccer team captain. Which Angelica had won last year. Student class president which Samantha had won earlier that semester. Class valedictorian which was most definitely up for grabs.

Best quinceañera ever? she wondered. *For sure it would be* her *quinceañera!*

Tony peered past the crowds lining the sidewalk in the airport's pick-up area, ignoring the bright plumage of the tourists in their tropical-colored shirts, the locals in their everyday T-shirts and shorts, and the fashionistas who paraded along the curb in designer clothing as if the area was a Milanese runway. He worried that he'd be hard-pressed to find his petite sister, but then a tricked-out lime green Jeep whipped up to the curb and stopped with the squeal of chrome-rimmed tires.

The driver honked and waved. He did a doubletake, wondering if he was seeing things, until his sister hopped down from the Jeep and emerged through the crowd like Moses parting the Red Sea. She launched herself into his arms, nearly knocking him over with the force of the embrace.

"*¡Hermanito!* I can't believe you're really here," she said, then stepped back and examined him as she settled onto four-inch-high heels that still only brought her up to his chin. A stylish romper in a bright floral pattern – a shocking deviation from her usual power suit - complimented her Cuban curves; bare, toned arms; and the heavy gold chain and medallion around her neck. Her thick dark hair was in messy knot on top of her head, and she had the barest hint of laugh lines around her mouth and eyes.

He raised his brows in disbelief at her statement. "*¿De verdad?* Even though you called every day until I finally said 'Yes'? And don't you roll your eyes at me," he said as he circled his index finger around her expressive face.

Sylvia laughed, grabbed hold of his hand, and hauled him toward the Jeep. *She might be tiny, but she is mighty*, he thought as they wove through the crowd to her car.

"Admit it, Tony. You wanted to come home. You missed

us. You missed Miami. You missed *me* most of all," she teased and pinched his cheek in that annoying way she always had since they were kids.

At the curb, she jerked open the tailgate of the Wrangler with one powerful pull.

"You got three of the four right, *hermanita*," he kidded as he hoisted his suitcase to load it into the cargo area of the Jeep.

"When did you get this?" he asked as he walked to the passenger side, thinking that despite the bright color, a sure Sylvia trademark if there ever was one, it just wasn't what he would have guessed to be his sister's kind of ride. He couldn't imagine her pulling up to an important business lunch in this beast.

"A few weeks ago, after someone totaled my sedan," she said as she climbed into the driver's side. "I told myself no one is going to mess with me in this," she added with a definitive bop of her head that shook loose some strands of hair from her top knot.

"No one with half a brain would mess with you anyway, Sylvita."

She expertly pulled away from the curb, gold bangles dancing on her wrists as she threaded into a narrow opening in the traffic. Her very feminine hands, sporting multiple rings and bright pink nail polish, looked incongruous on the masculine leather of the steering wheel.

His sister shot him a look her eyes wide. "If that's the case, why did it take you so long to agree to come and visit?"

He shrugged. "I had things to get in order. It's not easy to just up and leave the restaurant for a month."

"And I appreciate that you did. Hopefully you'll also get to relax a little while you're here," she said, navigating through traffic like a Formula One race car driver. Even though his seat belt held him securely, Tony braced one hand on the dash and gripped the console with the other to steady himself in the seat. He sucked in a breath as they barely avoided the bumper of one car. His heartbeat jumped in his chest as Sylvia accelerated past a lumbering bus, pressing him back into the seat with almost G force strength.

"I could start relaxing right now if you'd just slow down," he said and muttered a prayer after a near miss with another of the airport buses.

With wave of her hand that had the bangles musically dancing, she said, "*¡Calmate!* You'll be home before you know it."

"I'll be dead before I know it," he mumbled to himself. He finally relaxed as they left the congestion of the airport behind on the highway to Miami's Little Havana. Their parents had refused to leave the area even though all the kids had moved out to the suburbs along with a good number of their friends.

"*Mami* and *papi* are so excited that you're staying with them, but if they get to be too much you can always come stay with me," Sylvia said as she shot him a quick look.

It was all Tony could do to hold back his laughter. If anyone was going to be too much it was Sylvia. She had likely planned every day of his stay in the same way she would prepare for a courtroom trial.

"Angelica is excited also!" she forged on without giving him a chance to speak. "We can hardly wait to see what ideas you have for the menu. It's so important for Angelica, Tony."

"And not for you?" he asked, peering at his sister. More than him and Javi, Sylvia had always needed attention and affirmation.

With a delay that roused worry again, she said, "I'm done trying to please everyone, Tony. Now I want to please myself, without worrying about what everyone else thinks. But Angelica is in that difficult teen mode. You know, All Drama All the Time."

"And it's drama because...?" he asked, emphasizing the question with a lift of his brow.

"She lost the election for Class President to another girl who is suddenly having a *quinceañera* the day before Angelica's. Plus, they're battling to be captain of the soccer team and class valedictorian." She sighed. "You know how it is."

Tony chuckled and shook his head. "Sorry, but it's been a long time since I was a hormonal fourteen-year-old girl."

Sylvia bopped him on the arm and shot daggers at him with dark brown eyes like his own. "Be serious, Tony. She just wants things to go well. We all do. There will be lots of important people there, so it'll help Esteban with his real estate business. Mine, too."

A social event like this would be a big help in building his reputation and getting some clientele if he decided to relocate to Miami, not that he was *really* thinking about it. At least not that much. But he had to admit he preferred the warm Miami spring over the chilly one in New York City.

As they drove the last few miles to Little Havana and his parents' small cinder block home just off *Calle Ocho*, he fisted his hands to keep from reaching for his smartphone to check on his employees yet again. Instead, he listened as his sister started listing all they'd have to get done in the short time left before the big event. Luckily his one and only expected contribution was the menu.

"The theme is Miami Spice. We're hoping you can do what you do best. Upscale nouvelle Cuban food."

"So what I usually do," he said and wondered why doing the same recipes suddenly didn't seem so appetizing.

His sister side-eyed him. "Is everything okay with you?"

He hesitated for a heartbeat, but this was his sister. The one who, despite her need for attention, always seemed to know what was right for her loved ones. Who would fight tooth and nail to *make* things right for them, no matter what?

"Things have been rough lately," he reluctantly admitted.

"Financially? Esteban and I could help you out, *sabes*," she offered without any reluctance.

He smiled at her generosity. "*Gracias*, but no. I'm okay that way for now. I broke up with Dina –"

"*Gracias a Dios*. She wasn't the right woman for you," Sylvia said and made a face. Tony thought that thanking God for the breakup was a little extreme—but his sister tended to be all or nothing when it came to her personal relationships. She loved you or she couldn't stand you. And Dina...well, Sylvia certainly hadn't loved her.

"According to Dina I wasn't the right man for *her*. Besides, we were both always working crazy hours on different shifts. It's hard being involved with another chef. As for the restaurant, lately I'm always getting pulled out of the kitchen for paperwork. That's just not my thing."

"And now I've pulled you away for a whole month," she said, clear regret filling her voice.

They had just reached their family home and as Sylvia parked and killed the engine, he reached over and hugged her. "I'm glad you did. I think I need the time away even if it's making me antsy. Now I know how new parents feel the first time they leave their baby with someone else."

"It's not easy, *hermanito*, but you'll survive," she said and returned his embrace.

Tony had no doubt he would, but would his restaurant?

Read the rest!
South Beach Love is available now!